THE COLLECTED WORKS OF
HENRIK IBSEN

VOLUME VI

THE LEAGUE OF YOUTH
PILLARS OF SOCIETY

THE COLLECTED WORKS OF
HENRIK IBSEN

Copyright Edition. Complete in 11 Volumes
12mo. Price $1.00 each

ENTIRELY REVISED AND EDITED BY
WILLIAM ARCHER

CHARLES SCRIBNER'S SONS

THE COLLECTED WORKS OF
HENRIK IBSEN

COPYRIGHT EDITION

VOLUME VI

THE LEAGUE OF YOUTH
PILLARS OF SOCIETY

WITH INTRODUCTIONS BY

WILLIAM ARCHER

NEW YORK
CHARLES SCRIBNER'S SONS
1906

CONTENTS

THE LEAGUE OF YOUTH

INTRODUCTION*

AFTER the momentous four years of his first visit to Italy, to which we owe *Brand* and *Peer Gynt*, Ibsen left Rome in May, 1868, visited Florence, and then spent the summer at Berchtesgaden in southern Bavaria. There he was busy "mentally wrestling" with the new play which was to take shape as *De Unges Forbund* (*The League of Youth*); but he did not begin to put it on paper until, after a short stay at Munich, he settled down in Dresden, in the early autumn. Thence he wrote to his publisher, Hegel, on October 31: "My new work is making rapid progress. . . . The whole outline is finished and written down. The first act is completed, the second will be in the course of a week, and by the end of the year I hope to have the play ready. It will be in prose, and in every way adapted for the stage. The title is *The League of Youth; or, The Almighty & Co.*, a comedy, in five acts." At Hegel's suggestion he omitted the second title, "though," he wrote, "it could have given offence to no one *who had read the play*."

Apparently the polishing of the dialogue took longer than Ibsen anticipated. It was his first

* Copyright, 1906, by Charles Scribner's Sons.

play in modern prose, and the medium did not come easy to him. Six or seven years earlier, he wrote the opening scenes of *Love's Comedy* in prose, but was dissatisfied with the effect, and recast the dialogue in rhymed verse. Having now outgrown his youthful romanticism, and laid down, in *Brand* and *Peer Gynt*, the fundamental positions of his criticism of life, he felt that to carry that criticism into detail he must come to close quarters with reality; and to that end he required a suppler instrument than verse. He must cultivate, as he afterwards* put it, " the very much more difficult art of writing the genuine, plain language spoken in real life." Probably the mastery of this new art cost him more effort than he anticipated, for, instead of having the play finished by the end of 1868, he did not despatch the manuscript to Copenhagen until March, 1869. It was published on September 30 of that year.

While the comedy was still in process of conception, Ibsen had written to his publisher: " This new, *peaceable* work is giving me great pleasure." It thus appears that he considered it less polemical in its character than the poems which had immediately preceded it. If his intentions were pacific, they were entirely frustrated. The play was regarded as a violent and wanton attack on the Norwegian Liberal party, while Stensgård was taken for a personal lampoon on Björnson. Its first performance at the Christiania Theatre (October 18, 1869) passed quietly enough; but at the second and third per-

* Letter to Lucie Wolf, May, 1883. *Correspondence*, Letter 171.

formances an organised opposition took the field,
and disturbances amounting almost to a riot occurred. Public feeling soon calmed down, and
the play (the first prose comedy of any importance in Norwegian literature) became one of
the most popular pieces in the repertory of the
theatre. But it led to an estrangement from
Björnson and the Liberal party which was not
healed for many a day—not, indeed, until *Ghosts*
had shown the Norwegian public the folly of at-
tempting to make party capital out of the works
of a poet who stood far above party.

The estrangement from Björnson had begun
some time before the play appeared. A certain
misunderstanding had followed the appearance of
Peer Gynt,* and had been deepened by political
differences. Björnson had become an ardent National Liberal, with leanings towards Republi-
canism; Ibsen was not at all a Republican (he
deeply offended Björnson by accepting orders and
decorations), and his political sympathies, while
not of a partisan nature, were mainly " Scandinavian "—that is to say, directed towards a closer
union of the three Scandinavian kingdoms. Dis-
tance, and the evil offices of gossiping friends,
played their part in begetting dissension. Ibsen's
last friendly letter to Björnson (of these years)
was written in the last days of 1867; in the first
days of 1869, while he was actually busied with
The League of Youth, we find him declining to
contribute to a Danish magazine for the reason
(among others) that Björnson was to be one of
its joint editors.

* See *Correspondence*, Letters 44 and 45.

The news of the stormy reception of his comedy reached Ibsen in Egypt, where, as the guest of the Khedive, he was attending the opening of the Suez Canal. He has recorded the incident in a poem, *At Port Said*. On his return to Dresden he wrote to Hegel (December 14, 1869): "The reception of *The League of Youth* pleases me very much; for the disapprobation I was prepared, and it would have been a disappointment to me if there had been none. But what I was not prepared for was that Björnson should feel himself attacked by the play, as rumour says he does. Is this really the case? He must surely see that it is not himself I have had in mind, but his pernicious and 'lie-steeped' clique who have served me as models. However, I will write to him to-day or to-morrow, and I hope that the affair, in spite of all differences, will end in a reconciliation." The intended letter does not appear to have been written; nor would it, probably, have produced the desired effect, for Björnson's resentment was very deep. He had already (in November) written a poem to Johan Sverdrup, the leader of the Liberal party, in which he deplored the fact that "the sacred grove of poetry no longer afforded sanctuary against assassination," or as the Norwegian word vigorously expresses it, "sneak-murder." Long afterwards, in 1881, he explained what he meant by this term: "It was not the portrayal of contemporary life and known personages that I called assassination. It was the fact that *The League of Youth* sought to represent our young Liberal party as a gang of ambitious speculators, whose patriotism was as empty as their phraseology; and particularly that prominent men were first made clearly recognisable, and then had false hearts and shady characters foisted upon them." It is difficult to see, indeed, how Ibsen can have expected Björnson to distinguish very clearly between an attack on his "lie-steeped clique" and a lampoon on himself. Even Stensgård's religious phraseology, the confidence with which he claims God as a member of his party, was at that time characteristic of Björnson. The case, in fact, seems to have been very iike that of the portraiture of Leigh Hunt in Harold Skimpole. Both Dickens and Ibsen had unconsciously taken more from their respective models than they intended. They imagined, perhaps, that the features which did not belong to the original would conceal the likeness, whereas their actual effect was only to render the portraits libellous.

Eleven years passed before Björnson and Ibsen were reconciled. In 1880 (after the appearance of *A Doll's House* and before that of *Ghosts*), Björnson wrote in an American magazine: "I think I have a pretty thorough acquaintance with the dramatic literature of the world, and I have not the slightest hesitation in saying that Henrik Ibsen possesses more dramatic power than any other play-writer of our day. The fact that I am not always partial to the style of his work makes me all the more certain that I am right in my judgment of him."

The League of Youth soon became very popular in Norway, and it had considerable success in Sweden and Denmark. It was acted with notable excellence at the Royal Theatre in Copenhagen. Outside of Scandinavia it has never taken any hold of the stage. At the date of its appearance Ibsen was still quite unknown, even in Germany; and when he became known, its technique was already antiquated. It has been acted once or twice both in Germany and England, and has proved very amusing on the stage; but it is essentially an experimental, transitional work. The poet is trying his tools.

The technical influence of Scribe and his school is apparent in every scene. Ibsen's determination not to rest content with the conventions of that school may already be discerned, indeed, in his disuse of the soliloquy and the aside; but, apart from these flagrant absurdities, he permits himself to employ almost all the devices of the Scribe method. Note, for example, how much of the action arises from sheer misunderstanding. The whole second act turns upon the Chamberlain's misunderstanding of the bent of Stensgård's diatribe in the first act. As the Chamberlain is deliberately misled by his daughter and Fieldbo, the misunderstanding is not, perhaps, technically inadmissible. Yet it has to be maintained by very artificial means. Why, one may ask, does not Fieldbo, in his long conversation with Stensgård, in the second act, warn him of the thin ice on which he is skating? There is no sufficient reason, except that the great situation at the end of the act would thus be rendered impossible. It is in the fourth act, however, that the methods of the vaudevillist are most apparent. It is one string of blunders of the particular type which the French significantly call "quiproquos." Some arise through the quite diabolical genius for malicious wire-pulling developed by old Lundestad; but most of them are based upon that deliberate and elaborate vagueness of expression on the part of the characters which is the favourite artifice of the professor of theatrical sleight-of-hand. We are not even spared the classic quiproquo of the proposal by proxy mistaken for a proposal direct—Stensgård's overtures to Madam Rundholmen on behalf of Bastian being accepted by her as an offer on his own behalf. We are irresistibly reminded of Mrs. Bardell's fatal misunderstanding of Mr. Pickwick's intentions. All this, to be sure, is excellent farce, but there is no originality in the expedients by which it is carried on. Equally conventional, and equally redolent of Scribe, is the conduct of the fifth act. The last drop of effect is wrung out of the quiproquos with an almost mathematical accuracy. We are reminded of a game at puss-in-the-four-corners, in which Stensgård tries every corner in turn, only to find himself at last left out in the cold. Then, as the time approaches to ring down the curtain, every one is seized with a fever of amiability, the Chamberlain abandons all his principles and prejudices, even to the point of subscribing for twenty copies of Aslaksen's newspaper, and the whole thing becomes scarcely less unreal than one of the old-comedy endings in which the characters stand in a semicircle while each delivers a couplet of the epilogue. It is difficult to believe that the facile optimism of this conclusion could at any time have satisfied the mind which, only twelve years later, conceived the picture of Oswald Alving shrinking together in his chair and babbling, " Mother—give me the sun."

But, while we realise with what extraordinary rapidity and completeness Ibsen outgrew this phase of his art, we must not overlook the genuine merits of this brilliant comedy. With all its faults, it was an advance on the technique of its day, and was hailed as such by a critic so penetrating as George Brandes. Placing ourselves at the point of view of the time, we may perhaps say that its chief defect is its marked inequality of style. The first act is purely preparatory; the fifth act, as we have noted, is a rather perfunctory winding-up. The real play lies in the intervening acts; and each of these belongs to a different order of art. The second act is a piece of high comedy, quite admirable in its kind; the third act, both in tone and substance, verges upon melodrama; while the fourth act is nothing but rattling farce. Even from the Scribe point of view, this jumping from key to key is a fault. Another objection which Scribe would probably have urged is that several of Fieldbo's speeches, and the attitude of the Chamberlain towards him, are, on the face of them, incomprehensible, and are only retrospectively explained. The poetics of that school forbid all reliance on retrospect, perhaps because they do not contemplate the production of any play about which any human being would care to think twice.

The third act, though superficially a rather tame interlude between the vigorous second act and the bustling fourth, is in reality the most characteristic of the five. The second act might be signed Augier, and the fourth Labiche; but in the third the coming Ibsen is manifest. The scene between the Chamberlain and Monsen is,

in its disentangling of the past, a preliminary
study for much of his later work—a premonition,
in fact, of his characteristic method. Here, too,
in the character of Selma and her outburst of
revolt, we have by far the most original feature
of the play. In Selma there is no trace of French
influence, spiritual or technical. With admirable
perspicacity, Dr. Brandes realised from the outset the significance of this figure. " Selma," he
wrote, " is a new creation, and her relation to the
family might form the subject of a whole drama.
But in the play as it stands she has scarcely room
to move." The drama which Brandes here fore-
saw, Ibsen wrote ten years later in *A Doll's
House.*

With reference to the phrase " De lokale forhold," here lamely represented by " the local
situation," Ibsen has a curious remark in a letter
to Markus Grönvold, dated Stockholm, September 3, 1877. His German translator, he says, has
rendered the phrase literally " lokale Verhältnisse "—" which is wrong, because no suggestion
of comicality or narrow-mindedness is conveyed
by this German expression. The rendering ought
to be ' unsere berechtigten Eigenthümlichkeiten,'
an expression which conveys the same meaning
to Germans as the Norwegian one does to us
Scandinavians." This suggestion is, unfortunately, of no help to the English translator, especially when it is remembered in what context
Aslaksen uses the phrase " de lokale forhold " in
the fifth act of *An Enemy of the People.*

PILLARS OF SOCIETY

INTRODUCTION*

In the eight years that intervened between *The League of Youth* and *Pillars of Society*—his second prose play of modern life—Ibsen published a small collection of his poems (1871), and his " World-Historic Drama," *Emperor and Galilean* (1873). After he had thus dismissed from his mind the figure of Julian the Apostate, which had haunted it ever since his earliest days in Rome, he deliberately abandoned, once for all, what may be called masquerade romanticism— that external stimulus to the imagination which lies in remoteness of time and unfamiliarity of scene and costume. It may be that, for the moment, he also intended to abandon, not merely romanticism, but romance—to deal solely with the literal and commonplace facts of life, studied in the dry light of everyday experience. If that was his purpose, it was very soon to break down; but in *Pillars of Society* he more nearly achieved it than in any other work.

Many causes contributed to the unusually long pause between *Emperor and Galilean* and *Pillars of Society*. The summer of 1874 was occupied with a visit to Norway—the first he had paid since the Hegira of ten years earlier. A good deal of time was devoted to the revision of some of his earlier works, which were republished in Copenhagen; while the increasing vogue of his plays on the stage involved a considerable amount of business correspondence. *The Vikings* and *The Pretenders* were acted in these years, not only throughout Scandinavia, but at many of the leading theatres of Germany; and in 1876, after much discussion and negotiation, *Peer Gynt* was for the first time placed on the stage, in Christiania.

The first mention of *Pillars of Society* occurs in a letter from Ibsen to his publisher, Hegel, of October 23, 1875, in which he mentions that the first act, "always to me the most difficult part of a play," is ready, and states that it will be "a drama in five acts." Unless this be a mere slip of the pen, it is curious as showing that, even when the first act was finished, Ibsen did not foresee in detail the remainder of the action. In the course of further development an act dropped out of his scheme. On November 25, 1875, he reports to Hegel: "The first act of my new drama is ready—the fair copy written; I am now working at Act Second"; but it was not until the summer of 1877 that the completed manuscript was sent to Copenhagen. The book was published in the early autumn.

The theatrical success of *Pillars of Society* was immediate and striking. First performed in Copenhagen, November 18, 1877, it soon found its way to all the leading stages of Scandinavia. In Berlin, in the early spring of 1878, it was produced at five different theatres within a single

fortnight; and it has ever since maintained its
hold on the German stage. Before the end of the
century it had been acted more than twelve hundred times in Germany and Austria. An adapta-
tion of the play, by the present writer, was produced at the old Gaiety Theatre, London, for a
single performance, on the afternoon of December
15, 1880—this being the first time that Ibsen's
name had appeared on an English playbill. Again,
in 1889, a single performance of it was given at
the Opera Comique Theatre; and yet again in
May, 1901, the Stage Society gave two perform-
ances of it at the Strand Theatre. In the United
States it has been acted frequently in German,
but very rarely in English. The first performance
took place in New York in 1891. The play did
not reach the French stage until 1896, when it
was performed by M. Lugné-Poë's organisation,
L'Œuvre. In other countries one hears of a
single performance of it, here and there; but,
except in Scandinavia and Germany, it has nowhere taken a permanent hold upon the theatre.
Nor is the reason far to seek. By the time the
English, American, and French public had fully
awakened to the existence of Ibsen, he himself
had so far outgrown the phase of his development marked by *Pillars of Society* that the
play already seemed commonplace and old-fash-
ioned. It exactly suited the German public of
the 'eighties; it was exactly on a level with their
theatrical intelligence. But it was above the
theatrical intelligence of the Anglo-American
public, and—I had almost said—below that of
the French public. This is, of course, an exaggeration. What I mean is that there was no

possible reason why the countrymen of Augier
and Dumas should take any special interest in
Pillars of Society. It was not obviously in advance of these masters in technical skill, and the
vein of Teutonic sentiment running through it
could not greatly appeal to the Parisian public
of that period. Thus it is not in the least sur-
prising that, outside of Germany and Scandinavia, *Pillars of Society* had everywhere to follow
in the wake of *A Doll's House* and *Ghosts*, and
was everywhere found something of an anti-
climax. Possibly its time may be yet to come
in England and America. A thoroughly well-
mounted and well-acted revival might now appeal
to that large class of play-goers which stands on
very much the same intellectual level on which
the German public stood in the eighteen-eighties.

But it is of all Ibsen's works the least characteristic, because, acting on a transitory phase of
theory, he has been almost successful in divesting
it of poetic charm. There is not even a Selma
in it. Of his later plays, only *An Enemy of the
People* is equally prosaic in substance; and it is
raised far above the level of the commonplace by
the genial humour, the magnificent creative energy, displayed in the character of Stockmann.
In *Pillars of Society* there is nothing that rises
above the commonplace. Compared with Stockmann, Bernick seems almost a lay-figure, and
even Lona Hessel is an intellectual construction
—formed of a blend of new theory with old sentiment—rather than an absolute creation, a living
and breathing woman, like Nora, or Mrs. Alving,
or Rebecca, or Hedda. This is, in brief, the only
play of Ibsen's in which plot can be said to pre-

ponderate over character. The plot is extraordi-
narily ingenious and deftly pieced together. Several of the scenes are extremely effective from the
theatrical point of view, and in a good many
individual touches we may recognise the incom-
parable master-hand. One of these touches is the
scene between Bernick and Rörlund in the third
act, in which Bernick's craving for casuistical
consolation meets with so painful a rebuff. Only
a great dramatist could have devised this scene;
but to compare it with a somewhat similar passage in *The Pretenders*—the scene in the fourth
act between King Skulë and Jatgeir Skald—is
to realise what is meant by the difference between
dramatic poetry and dramatic prose.

I have called Lona Hessel a composite character because she embodies in a concentrated form
the two different strains of feeling that run
through the whole play. Beyond the general attack on social pharisaism announced in the very
title, we have a clear assertion of the claim of
women to moral and economical individuality
and independence. Dina, with her insistence on
" becoming something for herself " before she will
marry Johan, unmistakably foreshadows Nora
and Petra. But at the same time the poet is far
from having cleared his mind of the old ideal
of the infinitely self-sacrificing, dumbly devoted
woman whose life has no meaning save in relation to some more or less unworthy male—the
Ingeborg-Agnes-Solveig ideal, we may call it. In
the original edition of *The Pretenders*, Ingeborg
said to Skulë: " To love, to sacrifice all, and be
forgotten, that is woman's saga "; and out of that
conception arose the very tenderly-touched figure

of Martha in this play. If Martha, then, stands
for the old ideal—the ideal of the older generation—and Dina for the ideal of the younger generation, Lona Hessel hovers between the two. At
first sight she seems like an embodiment of the
" strong-minded female," the champion of Woman's Rights, and despiser of all feminine graces
and foibles. But in the end it appears that her
devotion to Bernick has been no less deep and
enduring than Martha's devotion to Johan. Her
" old friendship does not rust " is a delightful
speech; but it points back to the Ibsen of the
past, not forward to the Ibsen of the future. Yet
this is not wholly true; for the strain of sentiment which inspired it never became extinct in
the poet. He believed to the end in the possi-
bility and the beauty of great self-forgetful human emotions; and there his philosophy went
very much deeper than that of some of his
disciples.

In consistency of style, and in architectural
symmetry of construction, the play marks a great
advance upon *The League of Youth*. From the
end of the first act to the middle of the last, it
is a model of skilful plot-development. The exposition, which occupies so much of the first act,
is carried out by means of a somewhat cumbrous
mechanism. No doubt the "Kaffee-Klatsch" is in
great measure justified as a picture of the tattling society of the little town. It does not altogether ignore the principle of economy. But it
is curious to note the rapid shrinkage in the
poet's expositions. Here we have the necessary
information conveyed by a whole party of subsidi-
ary characters. In the next play, *A Doll's House*,

we have still a set exposition, but two characters suffice for it, and one the heroine. In the next play again—that is to say, in *Ghosts*—the poet has arrived at his own peculiar formula, and the exposition is indistinguishably merged in the action. Still greater is the contrast between the conclusion of *Pillars of Society* and that of *A Doll's House*. It would be too much to call Bernick's conversion and promise to turn over a new leaf as conventional as the Chamberlain's right-about-face in *The League of Youth*. Bernick has passed through a terrible period of mental agony which may well have brought home to him a conviction of sin. Still, the way in which everything suddenly comes right, Olaf is recovered, the *Indian Girl* is stopped, Aune is reconciled to the use of the new machines, and even the weather improves, so as to promise Johan and Dina a prosperous voyage to America—all this is a manifest concession to popular optimism. We are not to conceive, of course, that the poet deliberately compromised with an artistic ideal for the sake of popularity, but rather that he had not yet arrived at the ideal of logical and moral consistency which he was soon afterwards to attain. To use his own metaphor, the ghost of the excellent Eugène Scribe still walked in him. He still instinctively thought of a play as a storm in a tea-cup, which must naturally blow over in the allotted two hours and a half. Even in his next play—so gradual is the process of evolution—he still makes the external storm, so to speak, blow over at the appointed time. But, instead of the general reconciliation and serenity upon which the curtain falls in *The League of Youth* and

Pillars of Society—instead of the "happy end-
ing" which Helmer so confidently expects—he
gives us that famous scene of Nora's revolt and
departure, in which he himself may be said to
have made his exit from the school of Scribe,
banging the door behind him.

The Norwegian title, *Samfundets Stötter*,
means literally *Society's Pillars*. In the text, the
word "Samfund" has sometimes been translated
"society," sometimes "community." The noun
"stötte," a pillar, has for its correlative the verb,
"at stötte," to support; so that where the English phrase "to support society" occurs, there is,
in the original, a direct allusion to the title of
the play. The leading merchants in Norwegian
seaports often serve as consuls for one or other
foreign Power—whence the title by which Bernick is addressed. Rörlund, in the original, is
called "Adjunkt"—that is to say, he is an as-
sistant master in a school, subordinate to the
head-master or rector.

W. A.

THE LEAGUE OF YOUTH
(1869)

CHARACTERS.

CHAMBERLAIN BRATSBERG,[1] *owner of iron-works.*
ERIK BRATSBERG, *his son, a merchant.*
THORA, *his daughter.*
SELMA, *Erik's wife.*
DOCTOR FIELDBO, *physician at the Chamberlain's works.*
STENSGÅRD,[2] *a lawyer.*
MONS MONSEN, *of Stonelee.*[3]
BASTIAN MONSEN, *his son.*
RAGNA, *his daughter.*
HELLE,[4] *student of theology, tutor at Stonelee.*
RINGDAL, *manager of the iron-works.*
ANDERS LUNDESTAD, *landowner.*
DANIEL HEIRE.[5]
MADAM[6] RUNDHOLMEN, *widow of a storekeeper and publican.*
ASLAKSEN, *a printer.*
A MAID-SERVANT AT THE CHAMBERLAIN'S.
A WAITER.
A WAITRESS AT MADAM RUNDHOLMEN'S.
Townspeople, Guests at the Chamberlain's, etc. etc.

The action takes place in the neighbourhood of the iron-works, not far from a market town in Southern Norway.

[1] "Chamberlain" (Kammerherre) is a title conferred by the King of Norway upon men of wealth and position. Hereditary nobility was abolished in 1821.
[2] Pronounce *Staynsgore.*   [3] In the original "Storli."
[4] Pronounce *Hellë.*   [5] Heire (pronounce *Heirë*)＝Heron.
[6] Married women and widows of the lower middle-class are addressed as Madam in Norway.

THE LEAGUE OF YOUTH.

ACT FIRST.

The Seventeenth of May.[1] *A popular fête in the Chamberlain's grounds. Music and dancing in the background. Coloured lights among the trees. In the middle, somewhat towards the back, a rostrum. To the right, the entrance to a large refreshment-tent ; before it, a table with benches. In the foreground, on the left, another table, decorated with flowers and surrounded with lounging-chairs.*

A Crowd of People. LUNDESTAD, *with a committee-badge at his button-hole, stands on the rostrum.* RINGDAL, *also with a committee-badge, at the table on the left.*

LUNDESTAD.

. . . Therefore, friends and fellow citizens, I drink to our freedom ! As we have inherited it from our fathers, so will we preserve it for ourselves and for our children ! Three cheers for the day ! Three cheers for the Seventeenth of May !

THE CROWD.

Hurrah ! hurrah ! hurrah !

[1] The Norwegian " Independence Day."

RINGDAL.

[*As* LUNDESTAD *descends from the rostrum.*] And one cheer more for old Lundestad!

SOME OF THE CROWD.

[*Hissing.*]   Ss! Ss!

MANY VOICES.

[*Drowning the others.*]   Hurrah for Lundestad! Long live old Lundestad!   Hurrah!

> [*The* CROWD *gradually disperses.* MONSEN, *his son* BASTIAN, STENSGÅRD, *and* ASLAK- SEN *make their way forward through the throng.*

MONSEN.

'Pon my soul, it's time he was laid on the shelf!

ASLAKSEN.

It was the local situation [1] he was talking about! Ho-ho!

MONSEN.

He has made the same speech year after year as long as I can remember.   Come over here.

STENSGÅRD.

No, no, not that way, Mr. Monsen.   We are quite deserting your daughter.

MONSEN.

Oh, Ragna will find us again.

---

[1] "Local situation" is a very ineffectual rendering of Aslaksen's phrase, "lokale forholde"—German, *Verhältnisse*—but there seems to be no other which will fit into all the different con- texts in which it occurs.   It reappears in *An Enemy of the People*, Act v.

BASTIAN.

She's all right; young Helle is with her.

STENSGÅRD.

Helle?

MONSEN.

Yes, Helle. But [*Nudging* STENSGÅRD *familiarly*] you have me here, you see, and the rest of us. Come on! Here we shall be out of the crowd, and can discuss more fully what——
        [*Has meanwhile taken a seat beside the table on the left.*

RINGDAL.

[*Approaching.*]   Excuse me, Mr. Monsen—that table is reserved——

STENSGÅRD.

Reserved?   For whom?

RINGDAL.

For the Chamberlain's party.

STENSGÅRD.

Oh, confound the Chamberlain's party! There's none of them here.

RINGDAL.

No, but we expect them every minute.

STENSGÅRD.

Then let them sit somewhere else.
        [*Takes a chair.*

LUNDESTAD.

[*Laying his hand on the chair.*]   No, the table is reserved, and there's an end of it.

MONSEN.

[*Rising.*]   Come, Mr. Stensgård ; there are just as good seats over there.   [*Crosses to the right.*] Waiter !   Ha, no waiters either.   The Committee should have seen to that in time.   Oh, Aslaksen, just go in and get us four bottles of champagne. Order the dearest; tell them to put it down to Monsen !

> [ASLAKSEN *goes into the tent; the three others seat themselves.*

LUNDESTAD.

[*Goes quietly over to them and addresses* STENS-GÅRD.]   I hope you won't take it ill——

MONSEN.

Take it ill !   Good gracious, no !   Not in the least.

LUNDESTAD.

[*Still to* STENSGÅRD.]   It's not my doing; it's the Committee that decided——

MONSEN.

Of course.   The Committee orders, and we must obey.

LUNDESTAD.

[*As before.*]   You see, we are on the Chamberlain's own ground here.   He has been so kind as to throw open his park and garden for this evening ; so we thought——

STENSGÅRD.

We're extremely comfortable here, Mr. Lundestad—if only people would leave us in peace—
the crowd, I mean.

LUNDESTAD.

[*Unruffled.*]   Very well ; then it's all right.
[*Goes towards the back.*

ASLAKSEN.

[*Entering from the tent.*]   The waiter is just coming with the wine.   [*Sits.*

MONSEN.

A table apart, under special care of the Committee !   And on our Independence Day of all
others !   There you have a specimen of the way
things go.

STENSGÅRD.

But why on earth do you put up with all this,
you good people ?

MONSEN.

The habit of generations, you see.

ASLAKSEN.

You're new to the district, Mr. Stensgård.   If
only you knew a little of the local situation——

A WAITER.

[*Brings champagne.*]   Was it you that ordered—?

ASLAKSEN.

Yes, certainly ; open the bottle.

THE WAITER.

[*Pouring out the wine.*]   It goes to your account, Mr. Monsen ?

MONSEN.

The whole thing; don't be afraid.

[*The* WAITER *goes.*

MONSEN.

[*Clinks glasses with* STENSGÅRD.]   Here's welcome among us, Mr. Stensgård ! It gives me great pleasure to have made your acquaintance ; I cannot but call it an honour to the district that such a man should settle here.   The newspapers have made us familiar with your name, on all sorts of public occasions.   You have great gifts of oratory, Mr. Stensgård, and a warm heart for the public weal.   I trust you will enter with life and vigour into the—h'm, into the——

ASLAKSEN.

The local situation.

MONSEN.

Oh yes, the local situation.   I drink to that.

[*They drink.*

STENSGÅRD.

Whatever I do, I shall certainly put life and vigour into it.

MONSEN.

Bravo ! Hear, hear ! Another glass in honour of that promise.

STENSGÅRD.

No, stop ; I've already——

MONSEN.

Oh, nonsense! Another glass, I say—to seal the bond!

[*They clink glasses and drink. During what follows* BASTIAN *keeps on filling the glasses as soon as they are empty.*

MONSEN.

However—since we have got upon the subject —I must tell you that it's not the Chamberlain himself that keeps everything under his thumb. No, sir— old Lundestad is the man that stands behind and drives the sledge.

STENSGÅRD.

So I am told, in many quarters. I can't understand how a Liberal like him——

MONSEN.

Lundestad? Do you call Anders Lundestad a Liberal? To be sure, he professed Liberalism in his young days, when he was still at the foot of the ladder. And then he inherited his seat in Parliament from his father. Good Lord! everything runs in families here.

STENSGÅRD.

But there must be some means of putting a stop to all these abuses.

ASLAKSEN.

Yes, damn it all, Mr. Stensgård—see if you can't put a stop to them!

STENSGÅRD.

I don't say that I——

ASLAKSEN.

Yes, you! You are just the man. You have the gift of the gab, as the saying goes; and what's more: you have the pen of a ready writer. My paper's at your disposal, you know.

MONSEN.

If anything is to be done, it must be done quickly. The preliminary election [1] comes on in three days now.

STENSGÅRD.

And if you were elected, your private affairs would not prevent your accepting the charge?

MONSEN.

My private affairs would suffer, of course; but if it appeared that the good of the community demanded the sacrifice, I should have to put aside all personal considerations.

STENSGÅRD.

Good; that's good. And you have a party already: that I can see clearly.

MONSEN.

I flatter myself the majority of the younger, go-ahead generation——

ASLAKSEN.

H'm, h'm! 'ware spies!

[1] The system of indirect election obtains in Norway. The constituencies choose a College of Electors, who, in turn, choose the Members of the Storthing or Parliament. It is the preliminary "Election of Electors" to which Monsen refers.

DANIEL HEIRE *enters from the tent ; he peers about*
  shortsightedly, and approaches.

HEIRE.

May I beg for the loan of a spare seat; I want
to sit over there.

MONSEN.

The benches are fastened here, you see ; but
won't you take a place at this table ?

HEIRE.

Here ?   At this table ?   Oh yes, with pleasure
[*Sits.*]   Dear, dear !   Champagne, I believe.

MONSEN.

Yes ; won't you join us in a glass ?

HEIRE.

No, thank you !   Madam Rundholmen's champagne—— Well, well, just half a glass to keep
you company.   If only one had a glass, now.

MONSEN.

Bastian, go and get one.

BASTIAN.

Oh, Aslaksen, just go and fetch a glass.
        [ASLAKSEN *goes into the tent.   A pause.*

HEIRE.

Don't let me interrupt you, gentlemen.   I
wouldn't for the world——!   Thanks, Aslaksen.
[*Bows to* STENSGÅRD.]   A strange face—a recent
arrival !   Have I the pleasure of addressing our
new legal luminary, Mr. Stensgård ?

MONSEN.

Quite right. [*Introducing them.*] Mr. Stensgård,
Mr. Daniel Heire——

BASTIAN.

Capitalist.

HEIRE.

Ex-capitalist, you should rather say. It's all
gone now: slipped through my fingers, so to speak.
Not that I'm bankrupt—for goodness' sake don't
think that.

MONSEN.

Drink, drink, while the froth is on it.

HEIRE.

But rascality, you understand—sharp practice
and so forth——   I say no more. Well, well, I
am confident it is only temporary. When I get my
outstanding law-suits and some other little matters
off my hands, I shall soon be on the track of our
aristocratic old Reynard the Fox. Let us drink to
that   You won't, eh ?

STENSGÅRD.

I should like to know first who your aristocratic old Reynard the Fox may be.

HEIRE.

Hee-hee ; you needn't look so uncomfortable,
man. You don't suppose I'm alluding to Mr.
Monsen. No one can accuse Mr. Monsen of
being aristocratic. No ; it's Chamberlain Bratsberg, my dear young friend.

STENSGÅRD.

What ! In money matters the Chamberlain is surely above reproach.

HEIRE.

You think so, young man ? H'm ; I say no more. [*Draws nearer.*] Twenty years ago I was worth no end of money. My father left me a great fortune. You've heard of my father, I daresay ? No ? Old Hans Heire ? They called him Gold Hans. He was a shipowner : made heaps of money in the blockade time ; had his window-frames and door-posts gilded ; he could afford it—— I say no more ; so they called him Gold Hans.

ASLAKSEN.

Didn't he gild his chimney-pots too ?

HEIRE.

No ; that was only a penny-a-liner's lie ; invented long before your time, however. But he made the money fly ; and so did I in my time. My visit to London, for instance—haven't you heard of my visit to London ? I took a prince's retinue with me. Have you really not heard of it, eh ? And the sums I have lavished on art and science ! And on bringing rising talent to the front !

ASLAKSEN.

[*Rises.*] Well, good-bye, gentlemen.

MONSEN.

What ? Are you leaving us ?

ASLAKSEN.

Yes ; I want to stretch my legs a bit.   [*Goes.*

HEIRE.

[*Speaking low.*]   He was one of them—just as grateful as the rest, hee-hee ! Do you know, I kept him a whole year at college ?

STENSGÅRD.

Indeed ?   Has Aslaksen been to college ?

HEIRE.

Like young Monsen.   He made nothing of it ; also like—— I say no more.   Had to give him up, you see ; he had already developed his unhappy taste for spirits——

MONSEN.

But you've forgotten what you were going to tell Mr. Stensgård about the Chamberlain.

HEIRE.

Oh, it's a complicated business.   When my father was in his glory, things were going down-hill with the old Chamberlain—this one's father, you understand ; he was a Chamberlain too.

BASTIAN.

Of course ; everything runs in families here.

HEIRE.

Including the social graces—— I say no more. The conversion of the currency, rash speculations, extravagances he launched out into, in the year

1816 or thereabouts, forced him to sell some of
his land.

STENSGÅRD.

And your father bought it?

HEIRE.

Bought and paid for it. Well, what then? I
come into my property; I make improvements
by the thousand——

BASTIAN.

Of course.

HEIRE.

Your health, my young friend!—Improvements
by the thousand, I say—thinning the woods,
and so forth. Years pass; and then comes
Master Reynard—the present one, I mean—and
repudiates the bargain!

STENSGÅRD.

But, my dear Mr. Heire, you could surely have
snapped your fingers at him.

HEIRE.

Not so easily! Some small formalities had
been overlooked, he declared. Besides, I happened then to be in temporary difficulties, which
afterwards became permanent. And what can a
man do nowadays without capital?

MONSEN.

You're right there, by God! And in many
ways you can't do very much with capital either.
That I know to my cost. Why, even my innocent
children——

BASTIAN.

[*Thumps the table.*]   Ugh, father ' if I only had certain people here !

STENSGÅRD.

Your children, you say ?

MONSEN.

Yes ; take Bastian, for example. Perhaps I haven't given him a good education ?

HEIRE.

A threefold education ! First for the University ; then for painting ; and then for—what is it ?—it's a civil engineer he is now, isn't it ?

BASTIAN.

Yes, that I am, by the Lord !

MONSEN.

Yes, that he is ; I can produce his bills and his certificates to prove it ! But who gets the town business ? Who has got the local road-making— especially these last two years ? Foreigners, or at any rate strangers—in short, people no one knows anything about !

HEIRE.

Yes; it's shameful the way things go on. Only last New Year, when the managership of the Savings Bank fell vacant. what must they do but give Monsen the go-by, and choose an individual that knew—[*Coughs*] – that knew how to keep his purse-strings drawn—which our princely

host obviously does not. Whenever there's a
post of confidence going, it's always the same!
Never Monsen—always some one that enjoys the
confidence—of the people in power.   Well, well;
commune suffragium, as the Roman Law puts it;
that means shipwreck in the Common Council,
sir.[1]   It's a shame!   Your health!

MONSEN.

Thanks!   But, to change the subject—how are
all your law-suits getting on?

HEIRE.

They are still pending; I can say no more for
the present.   What endless annoyance they do
give me!   Next week I shall have to summon
the whole Town Council before the Arbitration
Commission.[2]

BASTIAN.

Is it true that you once summoned yourself
before the Arbitration Commission?

HEIRE.

Myself?   Yes; but I didn't put in an appearance.

MONSEN.

Ha, ha!   You didn't, eh?

[1] In this untranslatable passage Daniel Heire seems to be
making a sort of pun on *suffragium* and *naufragium.*
[2] In Norway, before an action comes into Court, the parties are
bound to appear in person before a Commission of Arbitration
or Conciliation.   If the Commission can suggest an arrangement acceptable to both sides, this arrangement has the validity
of a judgment, and the case goes no further.   Counsel are not
allowed to appear before the Commission.

HEIRE.

I had a sufficient excuse : had to cross the river, and it was unfortunately the very year of Bastian's bridge—plump! down it went, you know——

BASTIAN.

Why, confound it all—— !

HEIRE.

Take it coolly, young man! You are not the first that has bent the bow till it breaks. Everything runs in families, you know—— I say no more.

MONSEN.

Ho ho ho! You say no more, eh? Well, drink, then, and say no more! [*To* STENSGÅRD.] You see, Mr. Heire's tongue is licensed to wag as it pleases.

HEIRE.

Yes, freedom of speech is the only civic right I really value.

STENSGÅRD.

What a pity the law should restrict it.

HEIRE.

Hee-hee! Our legal friend's mouth is watering or a nice action for slander, eh? Make your mind easy, my dear sir! I'm an old hand, let me tell you!

STENSGÅRD.

Especially at slander?

HEIRE.

Your pardon, young man! That outburst of
indignation does honour to your heart. I beg you
to forget an old man's untimely frankness about
your absent friends.

STENSGÅRD.

Absent friends?

HEIRE.

I have nothing to say against the son, of course
—nor against the daughter. And if I happened
to cast a passing slur upon the Chamberlain's
character——

STENSGÅRD.

The Chamberlain's? Is it the Chamberlain's
family you call my friends?

HEIRE.

Well, you don't pay visits to your enemies, I
presume?

BASTIAN.

Visits?

MONSEN.

What?

HEIRE.

Ow, ow, ow! Here am I letting cats out of
bags——!

MONSEN.

Have you been paying visits at the Chamberlain's?

STENSGÅRD.

Nonsense! A misunderstanding——

HEIRE.

A most unhappy slip on my part. But how was
I to know it was a secret? [*To* MONSEN.] Besides,
you musn't take my expressions too literally.
When I say a visit, I mean only a sort of formal
call ; a frock-coat and yellow gloves affair——

STENSGÅRD.

I tell you I haven't exchanged a single word
with any of that family !

HEIRE.

Is it possible? Were you not received the
second time either? I know they were "not at
home" the first time.

STENSGÅRD.

[*To* MONSEN.]   I had a letter to deliver from a
friend in Christiania—that was all.

HEIRE.

[*Rising.*]   I'll be hanged if it isn't positively
revolting !   Here is a young man at the outset of
his career ; full of simple-minded confidence, he
seeks out the experienced man-of-the-world and
knocks at his door ; turns to him, who has brought
his ship to port, to beg for——   I say no more !
The man-of-the-world shuts the door in his face ;
is not at home ; never is at home when it's his
duty to be——   I say no more ! [*With indignation.*]
Was there ever such shameful insolence !

STENSGÅRD.

Oh, never mind that stupid business.

HEIRE.

Not at home ! He, who goes about professing that he is always at home to reputable people !

STENSGÅRD.

Does he say that ?

HEIRE.

A mere empty phrase. He's not at home to Mr. Monsen either. But I can't think what has made him hate you so much. Yes, hate you, I say ; for what do you think I heard yesterday ?

STANSGÅRD.

I don't want to know what you heard yesterday.

HEIRE.

Then I say no more. Besides, the expressions didn't surprise me—coming from the Chamberlain, I mean. Only I can't understand why he should have added "demagogue."

STENSGÅRD.

Demagogue !

HEIRE.

Well, since you insist upon it, I must confess that the Chamberlain called you an adventurer and demagogue.

STENSGÅRD.

[*Jumps up.*]   What !

HEIRE.

Adventurer and damagogue—or demagogue and adventurer ; I won't answer for the order.

STENSGÅRD.

And you heard that?

HEIRE.

I? If I had been present, Mr. Stensgård, you
may be sure I should have stood up for you as you
deserve.

MONSEN.

There, you see what comes of——

STENSGÅRD.

How dare the old scoundrel——?

HEIRE.

Come, come, come! Keep your temper. Very
likely it was a mere figure of speech—a harmless
little joke, I have no doubt. You can demand an
explanation to-morrow; for I suppose you are
going to the great dinner-party, eh?

STENSGÅRD.

I am not going to any dinner-party.

HEIRE.

Two calls and no invitation——!

STENSGÅRD.

Demagogue and adventurer! What can he be
thinking of?

MONSEN.

Look there! Talk of the devil——! Come,
Bastian.   [*Goes off with* BASTIAN.

STENSGÅRD.

What did he mean by it, Mr. Heire?

HEIRE.

Haven't the ghost of an idea.—It pains you? Your hand, young man! Pardon me if my frankness has wounded you. Believe me, you have yet many bitter lessons to learn in this life. You are young; you are confiding; you are trustful. It is beautiful; it is even touching; but—but—trustfulness is silver, experience is gold : that's a proverb of my own invention, sir! God bless you! [*Goes.*

CHAMBERLAIN BRATSBERG, *his daughter* THORA, *and* DOCTOR FIELDBO *enter from the left.*

LUNDESTAD.

[*Strikes the bell on the rostrum.*] Silence for Mr. Ringdal's speech !

STENSGÅRD.

[*Shouts.*] Mr. Lundestad, I demand to be heard

LUNDESTAD.

Afterwards.

STENSGÅRD.

No, now ! at once !

LUNDESTAD.

You can't speak just now. Silence for Mr. Ringdal !

RINGDAL.

[*On the rostrum.*] Ladies and gentlemen ! We have at this moment the honour of seeing in our midst the man with the warm heart and the open hand—the man we have all looked up to for many a year, as to a father—the man who is always ready to help us, both in word and deed—the man whose door is never closed to any reputable citizen—

the man who—who—ladies and gentlemen, our honoured guest is no lover of long speeches ; so, without more words, I call for three cheers for Chamberlain Bratsberg and his family ! Long life to them ! Hurrah !

THE CROWD.

Hurrah ! hurrah ! hurrah !

[*Great enthusiasm ; people press around the* CHAMBERLAIN, *who thanks them and shakes hands with those nearest him.*

STENSGÅRD.

Now may I speak ?

LUNDESTAD.

By all means. The platform is at your service.

STENSGÅRD.

[*Jumps upon the table.*] I shall choose my own platform !

THE YOUNG MEN.

[*Crowding around him.*] Hurrah !

THE CHAMBERLAIN.

[*To the* DOCTOR.] Who is this obstreperous personage ?

FIELDBO.

Mr. Stensgård.

THE CHAMBERLAIN.

Oh, it's he, is it ?

STENSGÅRD.

Listen to me, my glad-hearted brothers and
sisters! Hear me, all you who have in your
souls—though it may not reach your lips—the
exultant song of the day, the day of our freedom!
I am a stranger among you——

ASLAKSEN.

No!

STENSGÅRD.

Thanks for that "No!" I take it as the
utterance of a longing, an aspiration. A stranger
I am, however; but this I swear, that I come
among you with a great and open-hearted sym-
pathy for your sorrows and your joys, your
victories and defeats. If it lay in my power——

ASLAKSEN.

It does, it does!

LUNDESTAD.

No interruptions! You have no right to speak.

STENSGÅRD.

You still less! I abolish the Committee! Freedom on the day of freedom, boys!

THE YOUNG MEN.

Hurrah for freedom!

STENSGÅRD.

They deny you the right of speech! You hear
it—they want to gag you! Away with this
tyranny! I won't stand here declaiming to a
flock of dumb animals. I will talk; but you
shall talk too. We will talk to each other, from
the heart!

THE CROWD.
[*With growing enthusiasm.*]   Hurrah !

STENSGÅRD.

We will have no more of these barren, white-
chokered festivities !   A golden harvest of deeds
shall hereafter shoot up from each Seventeenth of
May.   May !   Is it not the season of bud and
blossom, the blushing maiden-month of the year ?
On the first of June I shall have been just two
months among you ; and in that time what great-
ness and littleness, what beauty and deformity,
have I not seen ?

THE CHAMBERLAIN.

What on earth is he talking about, Doctor ?

FIELDBO.

Aslaksen says it's the local situation.

STENSGÅRD.

I have seen great and brilliant possibilities
among the masses ; but I have seen, too, a spirit
of corruption brooding over the germs of promise
and bringing them to nought.   I have seen ardent
and trustful youth rush yearning forth—and I
have seen the door shut in its face.

THORA.

Oh, Heaven !

THE CHAMBERLAIN.

What does he mean by that ?

STENSGÅRD.

Yes, my brothers and sisters in rejoicing !
There hovers in the air an Influence, a Spectre

from the dead and rotten past, which spreads darkness and oppression where there should be nothing but buoyancy and light. We must lay that Spectre; down with it!

THE CROWD.

Hurrah! Hurrah for the Seventeenth of May!

THORA.

Come away, father—— !

THE CHAMBERLAIN.

What the deuce does he mean by a spectre? Who is he talking about, Doctor?

FIELDBO.

[*Quickly.*]   Oh, it's about——
[*Whispers a word or two.*

THE CHAMBERLAIN.

Aha! So that's it!

THORA.

[*Softly to* FIELDBO.]   Thanks!

STENSGÅRD.

If no one else will crush the **dragon, I will!** But we must hold together, boys!

MANY VOICES.

Yes! yes!

STENSGÅRD.

We are young! The time belongs to us; but we also belong to the time. Our right is our duty! Elbow-room for faculty, for will, for power! Listen to me! We must form a League. The money-bag has ceased to rule among us!

THE CHAMBERLAIN.

Bravo! [*To the* DOCTOR.] He said the
money-bag; so no doubt you're right——

STENSGÅRD.

Yes, boys; we, we are the wealth of the
country, if only there's metal in us. Our will
is the ringing gold that shall pass from man to
man. War to the knife against whoever shall deny
its currency!

THE CROWD.

Hurrah!

STENSGÅRD.

A scornful "bravo" has been flung in my
teeth——

THE CHAMBERLAIN.

No, no!

STENSGÅRD.

What care I! Thanks and threats alike are
powerless over the perfect will. And now, God
be with us! For we are going about His work,
with youth and faith to help us Come, then,
into the refreshment-tent—our League shall be
baptized this very hour.

THE CROWD.

Hurrah! Carry him! Shoulder high with him!
[*He is lifted shoulder high.*

VOICES.

Speak on! More! More!

STENSGÅRD.

Let us hold together, I say! Providence is on the side of the League of Youth. It lies with us to rule the world—here in the district!

[*He is carried into the tent amid wild enthusiasm.*

MADAM RUNDHOLMEN.

[*Wiping her eyes.*] Oh, Lord, how beautifully he does speak! Don't you feel as if you could kiss him, Mr. Heire?

HEIRE.

Thank you, I'd rather not.

MADAM RUNDHOLMEN.

Oh, you! I daresay not.

HEIRE.

Perhaps you would like to kiss him, **Madam Rundholmen.**

MADAM RUNDHOLMEN.

Ugh, how horrid you are!

[*She goes into the tent;* HEIRE *follows her.*

THE CHAMBERLAIN.

Spectre—and dragon—and money-bag! It was horribly rude—but well deserved!

LUNDESTAD.

[*Approaching.*] I'm heartily sorry, Chamberlain——

THE CHAMBERLAIN.

Yes, where was your knowledge of character, Lundestad? Well, well; we are none of us

infallible.   Good-night, and thanks for a pleasant
evening.   [*Turns to* THORA *and the* DOCTOR.]   But
bless me, I've been positively rude to that fine
young fellow !

FIELDBO.

How so ?

THORA.

His call, you mean——— ?

THE CHAMBERLAIN.

He called twice.   It's really Lundestad's fault.
He told me he was an adventurer and—and I
forget what else.   Fortunately I can make up for
it.

THORA.

How ?

THE CHAMBERLAIN.

Come, Thora ; let us see to it at once———

FIELDBO.

Oh, do you think it's worth while, Chamberlain——— ?

THORA.

[*Softly.*]   Hush !

THE CHAMBERLAIN.

When one has done an injustice one should lose
no time in undoing it ; that's a plain matter of
duty.   Good-night, Doctor.   After all, I've spent
an amusing hour ; and that's more than I have to
thank you for to-day.

FIELDBO.

Me, Chamberlain ?

THE CHAMBERLAIN.

Yes, yes, yes—you and others.

FIELDBO.

May I ask what I—— ?

THE CHAMBERLAIN.

Don't be curious, Doctor. I am never curious.
Come, come—no offence—good-night!

> [THE CHAMBERLAIN *and* THORA *go out to
> the left;* FIELDBO *gazes thoughtfully
> after them.*

ASLAKSEN.

[*From the tent.*] Hei, waiter! Pen and ink!
Things are getting lively, Doctor!

FIELDBO.

What things?

ASLAKSEN.

He's founding the League. It's nearly
founded.

LUNDESTAD.

[*Who has quietly drawn near.*] Are many putting down their names?

ASLAKSEN.

We've enrolled about seven-and-thirty, not
counting widows and so forth. Pen and ink, I
say! No waiters to be found!—that's the fault
of the local situation.

> [*Goes off behind the tent.*

LUNDESTAD.

Puh! It has been hot to-day.

FIELDBO.

I'm afraid we have hotter days to come.

LUNDESTAD.

Do you think the Chamberlain was very angry ?

FIELDBO.

Oh, not in the least; you could see that,
couldn't you ?   But what do you say to the new
League ?

LUNDESTAD.

H'm ; I say nothing. What is there to be said ?

FIELDBO.

It's the beginning of a struggle for power here
in the district.

LUNDESTAD.

Well, well ; no harm in a fight.   He has great
gifts, that Stensgård.

FIELDBO.

He is determined to make his way.

LUNDESTAD.

Youth is always determined to make its way.
I was, when I was young ; no one can object to
that. But mightn't we look in and see——

HEIRE.

[*From the tent.*] Well, Mr. Lundestad, are you
going to move the previous question, eh ? To
head the opposition ? Hee-hee ! You must
make haste !

LUNDESTAD.

Oh, I daresay I shall be in time.

HEIRE.

Too late, sir !   Unless you want to stand god-
father.   [*Cheering from the tent.*]   There, they're
chanting Amen ; the baptism is over.

LUNDESTAD.

I suppose one may be permitted to listen; I
shall keep quiet.   [*Enters the tent.*

HEIRE.

There goes one of the falling trees !   There
will be a rare uprooting, I can tell you !   The
place will soon look like a wood after a tornado.
Won't I chuckle over it !

FIELDBO.

Tell me, Mr. Heire, what interest have you in
the matter ?

HEIRE.

Interest ?   I am entirely disinterested, Doctor !
If I chuckle, it is on behalf of my fellow citizens.
There will be life, spirit, go, in things.   For my
own part—good Lord, it's all the same to me ; I
say, as the Grand Turk said of the Emperor of
Austria and the King of France—I don't care
whether the pig eats the dog or the dog the pig.
            [*Goes out towards the back on the right.*

THE CROWD.

[*In the tent.*]   Long live Stensgård !   Hurrah !
Hurrah for the League of Youth !   Wine !
Punch !   Hei, hei !   Beer !   Hurrah !

BASTIAN.

[*Comes from the tent.*]   God bless you and every
one !   [*With tears in his voice.*]   Oh, Doctor, I
feel so strong this evening ; I must do something.

FIELDBO.

Don't mind me.   What would you like to do?

BASTIAN.

I think I'll go down to the dancing-room and
fight one or two fellows.

[*Goes out behind the tent.*

STENSGÅRD.

[*Comes from the tent without his hat, and greatly
excited.*]   My dear Fieldbo, is that you?

FIELDBO.

At your service, Tribune of the People!   For I
suppose you've been elected——?

STENSGÅRD.

Of course; but——

FIELDBO.

And what is to come of it all?   What nice little
post are you to have?   The management of the
Bank?   Or perhaps——

STENSGÅRD.

Oh, don't talk to me like that!   I know you
don't mean it.   You are not so empty and wooden
as you like to appear.

FIELDBO.

Empty and wooden, eh?

STENSGÅRD.

Fieldbo!   Be my friend as you used to be!
We have not understood each other of late.   You
have wounded and repelled me with your ridicule
and irony.   Believe me, it was wrong of you.
[*Embraces him.*]   Oh, my great God! how happy
I am!

FIELDBO.

You too?   So am I, so am I !

STENSGÅRD.

Yes, I should be the meanest hound on earth if all heaven's bounty didn't make me good and true.   How have I deserved it, Fieldbo?   What have I, sinner that I am, done to be so richly blessed?

FIELDBO.

There is my hand!   This evening I am your friend indeed!

STENSGÅRD.

Thanks!   Be faithful and true, as I shall be !— Oh, isn't it an unspeakable joy to carry all that multitude away and along with you?   How can you help becoming good from mere thankfulness? And how it makes you love all your fellow creatures !   I feel as if I could clasp them all in one embrace, and weep, and beg their forgiveness because God has been so partial as to give me more than them.

FIELDBO.

[*Quietly.*] Yes, treasures without price may fall to one man's lot.   This evening I would not crush an insect, not a green leaf upon my path.

STENSGÅRD.

You ?

FIELDBO.

Never mind.   That's apart from the question. I only mean that I understand you.

STENSGÅRD.

What a lovely night!   Listen to the music and merriment floating out over the meadows.   And

how still it is in the valley! I tell you the man
whose life is not reconsecrated in such an hour,
does not deserve to live on God's earth!

FIELDBO.

Yes; but tell me now: what do you mean to
build up out of it—to-morrow, and through the
working-days to come?

STENSGÅRD.

To build up? We have to tear down first.—
Fieldbo, I had once a dream—or did I see it?
No; it was a dream, but such a vivid one! I
thought the Day of Judgment was come upon
the world. I could see the whole curve of the
hemisphere. There was no sun, only a livid
storm-light. A tempest arose; it came rushing
from the west and swept everything before it:
first withered leaves, then men; but they kept
on their feet all the time, and their garments
clung fast to them, so that they seemed to be
hurried along sitting. At first they looked like
townspeople running after their hats in a wind;
but when they came nearer they were emperors
and kings; and it was their crowns and orbs they
were chasing and catching at, and seemed always
on the point of grasping, but never grasped. Oh,
there were hundreds and hundreds of them, and
none of them understood in the least what was
happening; but many bewailed themselves, and
asked: "Whence can it come, this terrible
storm? Then there came the answer: "One
Voice spoke, and the storm is the echo of that
one Voice."

FIELDBO

When did you dream that?

STENSGÅRD.

Oh, I don't remember when ; several years ago

FIELDBO.

There were probably disturbances somewhere
in Europe, and you had been reading the newspapers after a heavy supper.

STENSGÅRD.

The same shiver, the same thrill, that then ran
down my back, I felt again to-night.   Yes, I will
give my whole soul utterance.   I will be the
Voice——

FIELDBO.

Come, my dear Stensgård, pause and reflect.
You will be the Voice, you say. Good! But
where will you be the Voice? Here in the parish?
Or at most here in the county!   And who will
echo you and raise the storm?   Why, people like
Monsen and Aslaksen, and that fat-headed genius,
Mr. Bastian.   And instead of the flying emperors
and kings, we shall see old Lundestad rushing
about after his lost seat in Parliament.   Then
what will it all amount to?   Just what you at
first saw in your dream—townsfolk in a wind.

STENSGÅRD.

In the beginning, yes.   But who knows how
far the storm may sweep?

FIELDBO.

Fiddlesticks with you and your storm!   And
the first thing you go and do, hoodwinked and
blinded and gulled as you are, is to turn your
weapons precisely against all that is worthy and
capable among us——

STENSGÅRD.

That is not true.

FIELDBO.

It is true! Monsen and the Stonelee gang got hold of you the moment you came here; and if you don't shake him off it will be your ruin. Chamberlain Bratsberg is a man of honour; that you may rely on. Do you know why the great Monsen hates him? Why, because——

STENSGÅRD.

Not a word more! I won't hear a word against my friends!

FIELDBO.

Look into yourself, Stensgård! Is Mr. Mons Monsen really your friend?

STENSGÅRD.

Mr. Monsen has most kindly opened his doors to me——

FIELDBO.

To people of the better sort he opens his doors in vain.

STENSGÅRD.

Oh, whom do you call the better sort? A few stuck-up officials! I know all about it. As for me, I have been received at Stonelee with so much cordiality and appreciation——

FIELDBO.

Appreciation? Yes, unfortunately—there we are at the root of the matter.

STENSGÅRD.

Not at all! I can see with unprejudiced eyes.
Mr. Monsen has abilities, he has reading, he has a
keen sense for public affairs

FIELDBO.

Abilities? Oh, yes, in a way. Reading too :
he takes in the papers, and has read your speeches
and articles. And his sense for public affairs he
has of course proved by applauding the said
articles and speeches.

STENSGÅRD.

Now, Fieldbo, up come the dregs of your nature
again. Can you never shake off that polluting
habit of thought? Why must you always assume
mean or ridiculous motives for everything? Oh,
you are not serious! Now you look good and
true again. I'll tell you the real root of the
matter. Do you know Ragna?

FIELDBO.

Ragna Monsen? Oh, after a fashion—at second
hand.

STENSGÅRD.

Yes, I know she is sometimes at the Chamberlain's.

FIELDBO.

In a quiet way, yes. She and Miss Bratsberg
are old schoolfellows.

STENSGÅRD.

And what do you think of her?

FIELDBO.

Why, from all I have heard she seems to be a
very good girl.

STENSGÅRD.

Oh, you should see her in her home! She
thinks of nothing but her two little sisters. And
how devotedly she must have nursed her mother!
You know the mother was out of her mind for
some years before she died.

FIELDBO.

Yes; I was their doctor at one time. But
surely, my dear fellow, you don't mean that——

STENSGÅRD.

Yes, Fieldbo, I love her truly; to you I can
confess it. Oh, I know what you are surprised at.
You think it strange that so soon after—of course
you know that I was engaged in Christiania?

FIELDBO.

Yes, so I was told.

STENSGÅRD.

The whole thing was a disappointment. I had
to break it off; it was best for all parties. Oh,
how I suffered in that affair! The torture, the
sense of oppression I endured——! Now, thank
heaven, I am out of it all. That was my reason for
leaving town.

FIELDRO.

And with regard to Ragna Monsen, are you
quite sure of yourself?

STENSGÅRD.

Yes, I am indeed. There's no mistake possible
in this case.

FIELDBO.

Well, then, in heaven's name, go in and win!
It means your life's happiness! Oh, there's so
much I could say to you ——

STENSGÅRD.

Really?   Has she said anything?   Has she confided in Miss Bratsberg?

FIELDBO.

No; that's not what I mean.   But how can you,
in the midst of your happiness, go and fuddle
yourself in these political orgies?   How can town
tattle take any hold upon a mind that is——

STENSGÅRD.

Why not?   Man is a complex machine—I am,
at any rate.   Besides, my way to her lies through
these very party turmoils.

FIELDBO.

A terribly prosaic way.

STENSGÅRD.

Fieldbo, I am ambitious; you know I am.   I
must make my way in the world.   When I remember that I'm thirty, and am still on the first
round of the ladder, I feel my conscience gnaw-
ing at me.

FIELDBO.

Not with its wisdom teeth.

STENSGÅRD.

It's of no use talking to you.   You have never
felt the spur of ambition.   You have dawdled and
drifted all your days—first at college, then abroad,
now here.

FIELDBO.

Perhaps; but at least it has been delightful.
And no reaction follows, like what you feel when
you get down from the table after——

STENSGÅRD.

Stop that! I can bear anything but that.
You are doing a bad action—you are damping my
ardour.

FIELDBO.

Oh, come! If your ardour is so easily
damped——

STENSGÅRD

Stop, I say! What right have you to break in
upon my happiness? Do you think I am not
sincere?

FIELDBO.

Yes, I am sure you are.

STENSGÅRD.

Well, then, why go and make me feel empty,
and disgusted, and suspicious of myself? [*Shouts
and cheers from the tent.*] There—listen! They
are drinking my health. An idea that can take
such hold upon people—by God, it must have
truth in it!

THORA BRATSBERG, RAGNA MONSEN, *and* MR. HELLE
enter from the left and cross, half-way back.

HELLE.

Look, Miss Bratsberg; there is Mr. Stensgård.

THORA.

Then I won't go any further. Good-night,
Ragna dear.

HELLE AND MISS MONSEN.

Good-night, good-night.

[*They go out to the right.*

THORA.

[*Advancing.*] I am Miss Bratsberg. I have a
letter for you, from my father.

STENSGÅRD.

For me ?

THORA.

Yes; here it is.   [*Going.*

FIELDBO.

May I not see you home ?

THORA.

No, thank you. I can go alone. Good-night.
                              [*Goes out to the left.*

STENSGÅRD.

[*Reading the letter by a Chinese lantern.*]   What
is this !

FIELDBO.

Well—what has the Chamberlain to say to you ?

STENSGÅRD.

[*Bursts into loud laughter.*]   I must say I didn't
expect this !

FIELDBO.

Tell me—— ?

STENSGÅRD.

Chamberlain Bratsberg is a pitiful creature.

FIELDBO.

You dare to——

STENSGÅRD.

Pitiful ! Pitiful . Tell any one you please that
I said so. Or rather, say nothing about it——
[*Puts the letter in his pocket.*] Don't mention this
to any one !

[*The* COMPANY *come out from the tent.*

MONSEN.

Mr. President ! Where is Mr. Stensgård ?

THE CROWD.

There he is ! Hurrah !

LUNDESTAD.

Mr. President has forgotten his hat.

[*Hands it to him.*

ASLAKSEN.

Here; have some punch ! Here's a whole
bowlful !

STENSGÅRD.

Thanks, no more.

MONSEN.

And the members of the League will recollect
that we meet to-morrow at Stonelee——

STENSGÅRD.

To-morrow ? It wasn't to-morrow, was it—— ?

MONSEN.

Yes, certainly ; to draw up the manifesto——

STENSGÅRD.

No, I really can't to-morrow—I shall see about
it the day after to-morrow, or the day after that.

Well, good-night, gentlemen ; hearty thanks all round, and hurrah for the future !

THE CROWD.

Hurrah !   Let's take him home in triumph !

STENSGÅRD.

Thanks, thanks !   But you really mustn't——

ASLAKSEN.

We'll all go with you.

STENSGÅRD.

Very well, come along.   Good-night, Fieldbo; you're not coming with us ?

FIELDBO.

No ; but let me tell you, what you said about Chamberlain Bratsberg——

STENSGÅRD.

Hush, hush !   It was an exaggeration—I withdraw it !   Well, my friends, if you're coming, come ; I'll take the lead.

MONSEN.

Your arm, Stensgård !

BASTIAN.

A song !   Strike up !   Something thoroughly patriotic !

THE CROWD.

A song !   A song !   Music !

> [*A popular air is played and sung. The procession marches out by the back to the right.*

FIELDBO.

[*To* LUNDESTAD, *who remains behind.*]   A gallant procession.

LUNDESTAD.

Yes—and with a gallant leader.

FIELDBO.

And where are you going, Mr. Lundestad?

LUNDESTAD.

I?   I'm going home to bed.
       [*He nods and goes off.*   DOCTOR FIELDBO
          remains behind alone.

ACT SECOND.

A garden-room at the Chamberlain's, elegantly furnished, with a piano, flowers, and rare plants. Entrance door at the back. On the left, a door leading to the dining-room ; on the right, several glass doors lead out to the garden.

ASLAKSEN *stands at the entrance door.* A MAID-SERVANT *is carrying some dishes of fruit into the dining-room.*

THE MAID.

Yes, but I tell you they're still at table; you must call again.

ASLAKSEN.

I'd rather wait, if I may.

THE MAID.

Oh yes, if you like. You can sit there for the present.

> [*She goes into the dining-room.* ASLAKSEN *takes a seat near the door. Pause.* DR. FIELDBO *enters from the back.*

FIELDBO.

Ah, good evening, Aslaksen : are you here ?

THE MAID.

[*Returning.*] You're late this evening, sir.

FIELDBO.

I was called to see a patient.

THE MAID.

The Chamberlain and Miss Bratsberg have both
been inquiring about you.

FIELDBO.

Indeed ?

THE MAID.

Yes.   Won't you go in at once, sir ; or shall I
say that—— ?

FIELDBO.

No, no ; never mind.   I can have a snack afterwards ; I shall wait here in the meantime.

THE MAID.

Dinner will soon be over.

[*She goes out by the back.*

ASLAKSEN.

[*After a pause.*]   How can you resist such a
dinner, Doctor—with dessert, and fine wines, and
all sorts of good things ?

FIELDBO.

Why, man, it seems to me we get too many
good things hereabouts, rather than too few.

ASLAKSEN.

There I can't agree with you.

FIELDBO.

H'm.   I suppose you are waiting for some one.

ASLAKSEN.

Yes, I am

FIELDBO.

And are things going tolerably at home ? Your wife—— ?

ASLAKSEN.

In bed, as usual; coughing and wasting away.

FIELDBO.

And your second child ?

ASLAKSEN.

Oh, he's a cripple for the rest of his days; you know that. That's our luck, you see; what the devil's the use of talking about it ?

FIELDBO.

Let me look at you, Aslaksen !

ASLAKSEN.

Well; what do you want to see ?

FIELDBO.

You've been drinking to-day.

ASLAKSEN.

Yes, and yesterday too.

FIELDBO.

Well, yesterday there was some excuse for it; but to-day——

ASLAKSEN.

What about your friends in there, then ? Aren't they drinking too?

FIELDBO.

Yes, my dear Aslaksen; that's a fair retort ; but circumstances differ so in this world.

ASLAKSEN.

I didn't choose my circumstances.

FIELDBO.

No; God chose them for you.

ASLAKSEN.

No, he didn't—men chose them. Daniel Heire
chose, when he took me from the printing-house
and sent me to college. And Chamberlain Bratsberg chose, when he ruined Daniel Heire and
sent me back to the printing-house.

FIELDBO.

Now you know that's not true. The Chamberlain did not ruin Daniel Heire; Daniel Heire
ruined himself.

ASLAKSEN.

Perhaps! But how dared Daniel Heire ruin
himself, in the face of his responsibilities towards
me? God's partly to blame too, of course. Why
should he give me talent and ability? Well, of
course I could have turned them to account as a
respectable handicraftsman; but then comes that
tattling old fool——

FIELDBO.

It's base of you to say that. Daniel Heire acted
with the best intentions.

ASLAKSEN.

What good do his "best intentions" do me?
You hear them in there, clinking glasses and
drinking healths? Well, I too have sat at that
table in my day, dressed in purple and fine linen,
like the best of them——! That was just the thing
for me, that was—for me, that had read so much

and had thirsted so long to have my share in all the good things of life. Well, well; how long was Jeppe in Paradise ?[1] Smash, crash ! down you go—and my fine fortunes fell to pie, as we printers say.

FIELDBO.

But, after all, you were not so badly off; you had your trade to fall back upon.

ASLAKSEN.

That's easily said. After getting out of your class you can't get into it again. They took the ground from under my feet, and shoved me out on the slippery ice—and then they abuse me because I stumble.

FIELDBO.

Well, far be it from me to judge you harshly——

ASLAKSEN.

No ; you have no right to.—What a queer jumble it is ! Daniel Heire, and Providence, and the Chamberlain, and Destiny, and Circumstance —and I myself in the middle of it ! I've often thought of unravelling it all and writing a book about it ; but it's so cursedly entangled that—— [*Glances towards the door on the left.*] Ah ! They're rising from table.

> [*The party, ladies and gentlemen, pass from the dining-room into the garden, in lively conversation. Among the guests is* STENSGÅRD, *with* THORA *on his left arm and* SELMA *on his right.* FIELDBO *and* ASLAKSEN *stand beside the door at the back.*

[1] An allusion to Holberg's comedy, *Jeppe på Bierget,* which deals with the theme of Abou Hassan, treated by Shakespeare in the Induction to *The Taming of the Shrew,* and by Hauptmann in *Schluck und Jau.*

STENSGÅRD.

I don't know my way here yet ; you must tell me where I am to take you, ladies.

SELMA.

Out into the air ; you must see the garden.

STENSGÅRD.

Oh, that will be delightful.
  [*They go out by the foremost glass door on the right.*

FIELDBO.

Why, by all that's wonderful, there's Stensgård!

ASLAKSEN.

It's him I want to speak to. I've had a fine chase after him ; fortunately I met Daniel Heire——

DANIEL HEIRE *and* ERIK BRATSBERG *enter from the dining-room.*

HEIRE.

Hee-hee! Excellent sherry, upon my word. I've tasted nothing like it since I was in London.

ERIK.

Yes, it's good, isn't it ? It puts life into you.

HEIRE.

Well, well—it's a real pleasure to see one's money so well spent.

ERIK.

How so ? [*Laughing.*] Oh, yes ; I see, I see.
  [*They go into the garden.*

FIELDBO.

You want to speak to Stensgård, you say ?

ASLAKSEN.
Yes.

FIELDBO.
On business ?

ASLAKSEN.

Of course ; the report of the fête——

FIELDBO.

Well, then, you must wait out there in the meantime.

ASLAKSEN.
In the passage ?

FIELDBO.

In the anteroom.   This is scarcely the time or place—but the moment I see Stensgård alone, I'll tell him——

ASLAKSEN.

Very well ; I'll bide my time.

[*Goes out by the back.*

CHAMBERLAIN BRATSBERG, LUNDESTAD, RINGDAL,
*and one or two other gentlemen come
out of the dining-room.*

THE CHAMBERLAIN.

[*Conversing with* LUNDESTAD.] Violent, you say ? Well, perhaps the form wasn't all that could be desired ; but there were real gems in the speech, I can assure you.

LUNDESTAD.

Well, if you are satisfied, Chamberlain, I have no right to complain.

THE CHAMBERLAIN.

Why should you? Ah, here's the Doctor! Starving, I'll be bound.

FIELDBO.

It doesn't matter, Chamberlain. The servants will attend to me. I feel myself almost at home here, you know.

THE CHAMBERLAIN.

Oh, you do, do you? I wouldn't be in too great a hurry.

FIELDBO.

What? Am I taking too great a liberty? You yourself permitted me to——

THE CHAMBERLAIN.

What I permitted, I permitted. Well, well, make yourself at home, and forage for something to eat. [*Slaps him lightly on the shoulder and turns to* LUNDESTAD.] Now, here's one you may call an adventurer and—and the other thing I can't remember.

FIELDBO.

Why, Chamberlain——!

LUNDESTAD.

No, I assure you——

THE CHAMBERLAIN.

No arguments after dinner; it's bad for the digestion. They'll serve the coffee outside presently.   [*Goes with the guests into the garden.*

LUNDESTAD.

[*To* FIELDBO.] Did you ever see the Chamberlain so strange as he is to-day?

FIELDBO.

I noticed it yesterday evening.

LUNDESTAD.

He will have it that I called Mr. Stensgård an
adventurer and something else of that sort.

FIELDBO.

Oh, well, Mr. Lundestad, what if you did?
Excuse me; I must go and talk to the ladies.
[*Goes out to the right.*

LUNDESTAD.

[*To* RINGDAL, *who is arranging a card table.*]
How do you account for Mr. Stensgård's appearance here to-day?

RINGDAL.

Yes, how?   He wasn't on the original list.

LUNDESTAD.

An afterthought, then?   After his attack on
the Chamberlain yesterday——?

RINGDAL

Yes, can you understand it?

LUNDESTAD.

Understand it?   Oh yes, I suppose I can.

RINGDAL.

[*More softly.*] You think the Chamberlain is
afraid of him?

LUNDESTAD.

I think he is prudent—that's what I think.

[*They go up to the back conversing, and so out into the garden. At the same time* SELMA *and* STENSGÅRD *enter by the foremost door on the right.*

SELMA.

Yes, just look—over the tops of the trees you can see the church tower and all the upper part of the town.

STENSGÅRD.

So you can; I shouldn't have thought so.

SELMA.

Don't you think it's a beautiful view?

STENSGÅRD.

Everything is beautiful here : the garden, and the view, and the sunshine, and the people ! Great heaven, how beautiful it all is! And you live here all the summer ?

SELMA.

No, not my husband and I ; we come and go. We have a big, showy house in town, much finer than this ; you'll see it soon.

STENSGÅRD.

Perhaps your family live in town ?

SELMA.

My family ?   Who are my family ?

STENSGÅRD.

Oh, I didn't know——

SELMA.

We fairy princesses have no family.

STENSGÅRD.

Fairy princesses?

SELMA.

At most we have a wicked stepmother——

STENSGÅRD.

A witch, yes!   So you are a princess!

SELMA.

Princess of all the sunken palaces, whence you hear the soft music on midsummer nights. Doctor Fieldbo thinks it must be pleasant to be a princess; but I must tell you——

ERIK BRATSBERG.

[*Coming from the garden.*]   Ah, at last I find the little lady!

SELMA.

The little lady is telling Mr. Stensgård the story of her life.

ERIK.

Oh, indeed.   And what part does the husband play in the little lady's story?

SELMA.

The Prince, of course.   [*To* STENSGÅRD.]   You know the prince always comes and breaks the spell, and then all ends happily, and every one calls and congratulates, and the fairy-tale is over.

STENSGÅRD.

Oh, it's too short.

SELMA.

Perhaps—in a way.

ERIK.

[*Putting his arm round her waist.*] But a new fairy-tale grows out of the old one, and in it the Princess becomes a Queen !

SELMA.

On the same condition as real Princesses ?

ERIK.

What condition ?

SELMA.

They must go into exile—to a foreign kingdom.

ERIK.

A cigar, Mr. Stensgård ?

STENSGÅRD.

Thank you, not just now.

DOCTOR FIELDBO *and* THORA *enter from the garden.*

SELMA.

[*Going towards them.*]   Is that you, Thora dear ? I hope you're not ill ?

THORA.

I ?   No.

SELMA.

Oh, but I'm sure you must be ; you seem to be always consulting the doctor of late.

THORA.

No, I assure you——

SELMA.

Nonsense ; let me feel your pulse ! You are burning. My dear Doctor, don't you think the fever will pass over ?

FIELDBO.

Everything has its time.

THORA.

Would you rather have me freezing—— ?

SELMA.

No, a medium temperature is the best—ask my husband.

THE CHAMBERLAIN.

[*Enters from the garden.*] The whole family gathered in secret conclave ? That's not very polite to the guests.

THORA.

I am just going, father dear——

THE CHAMBERLAIN.

Aha, it is you the ladies are paying court to, Mr. Stensgård ! I must look to this.

THORA.

[*Softly to* FIELDBO.] Remain here !
[*She goes into the garden.*

ERIK.

[*Offers* SELMA *his arm.*] Has Madame any objection—— ?

SELMA.

Come !   [*They go out to the right.*

THE CHAMBERLAIN.

[*Looking after them.*] It's impossible to get these two separated.

FIELDBO.

It would be sinful to try.

THE CHAMBERLAIN.

Fools that we are! How Providence blesses us in spite of ourselves. [*Calls out.*] Thora, Thora, do look after Selma! Get a shawl for her, and don't let her run about so: she'll catch cold! How short-sighted we mortals are, Doctor! Do you know any cure for that disease?

FIELDBO.

The spectacles of experience; through them you will see more clearly a second time.

THE CHAMBERLAIN.

You don't say so! Thanks for the advice. But since you feel yourself at home here, you must really pay a little attention to your guests.

FIELDBO.

Certainly; come, Stensgård, shall we——?

THE CHAMBERLAIN.

Oh, no, no—there's my old friend Heire out there——

FIELDBO.

He thinks himself at home here too.

THE CHAMBERLAIN.

Ha ha ha! So he does.

FIELDBO.

Well, we two will join forces, and do our best.
[*Goes into the garden.*

STENSGÅRD.

You were speaking of Daniel Heire, Chamberlain. I must say I was rather surprised to see
him here.

THE CHAMBERLAIN.

Were you ? Mr. Heire and I are old school and
college friends. Besides, we have had a good deal
to do with each other in many ways since——

STENSGÅRD.

Yes, Mr. Heire was good enough to give his
own account of some of these transactions, yesterday evening.

THE CHAMBERLAIN.

H'm !

STENSGÅRD.

Had it not been for him, I certainly should not
have let myself boil over as I did. But he has a
way of speaking of people and things, that—in
short, he has a vile tongue in his head.

THE CHAMBERLAIN.

My dear young friend—Mr. Heire is my guest ;
you must not forget that. My house is liberty
hall, with only one reservation : my guests must
not be discussed to their disadvantage.

STENSGÅRD.

I beg your pardon, I'm sure—— !

THE CHAMBERLAIN.

Oh, never mind ; you belong to the younger
generation, that's not so punctilious.   As for Mr.
Heire, I don't think you really know him.   I, at
any rate, owe Mr. Heire a great deal.

STENSGÅRD.

Yes, so he gave one to understand ; but I didn't
think——

THE CHAMBERLAIN.

I owe him the best part of our domestic happiness, Mr. Stensgård !   I owe him my daughter-in-
law.   Yes, that is really so.   Daniel Heire was kind
to her in her childhood.   She was a youthful
prodigy ; she gave concerts when she was only ten
years old.   I daresay you have heard her spoken
of—Selma Sjöblom.[1]

STENSGÅRD.

Sjöblom ?   Yes, of course ; her   father   was
Swedish ?

THE CHAMBERLAIN.

Yes, a music-teacher.   He came here many years
ago.   Musicians, you know, are seldom millionaires;
and their habits are not always calculated to—— ;
in short, Mr. Heire has always had an eye for
talent ; he was struck with the child, and had her
sent to Berlin ; and then, when her father was
dead and Heire's fortunes were on the wane, she
returned to Christiania, where she was of course
taken up by the best people.   That was how my
son happened to fall in with her.

[1] Pronounce "Shöblom"—the modified " ö " much as in
German.

STENSGÅRD.

Then in that way old Daniel Heire has indeed
been an instrument for good——

THE CHAMBERLAIN.

That is how one thing leads to another in this
life, you see.   We are all instruments, Mr. Stensgård ; you, like the rest of us ; an instrument of
wrath, I suppose——

STENSGÅRD.

Oh, don't speak of it, Chamberlain.   I am
utterly ashamed——

THE CHAMBERLAIN.

Ashamed ?

STENSGÅRD.

It was most unbecoming——

THE CHAMBERLAIN.

The form was perhaps open to criticism, but the
intention was excellent.   And now I want to ask
you, in future, when you are contemplating any
move of the sort, just to come to me and tell me of
it openly, and without reserve.   You know we all
want to act for the best ; and it is my duty——

STENSGÅRD.

You will permit me to speak frankly to you ?

THE CHAMBERLAIN.

Of course I will.   Do you think I haven't long
realised that matters here have in some ways taken
a most undesirable turn ?   But what was I to do ?
In the late King's time I lived for the most part in
Stockholm.   I am old now ; and besides, it is not
in my nature to take the lead in reforms, or to

throw myself personally into the turmoil of public affairs. You, on the other hand, Mr. Stensgård, have every qualification for them ; so let us hold together.

STENSGÅRD.

Thanks, Chamberlain ; many, many thanks !

RINGDAL *and* DANIEL HEIRE *enter from the garden.*

RINGDAL.

And I tell you it must be a misunderstanding.

HEIRE.

Indeed ? I like that ! How should I misunderstand my own ears ?

THE CHAMBERLAIN.

Anything new, Heire ?

HEIRE.

Only that Anders Lundestad is going over to the Stonelee party.

THE CHAMBERLAIN.

Oh, you're joking !

HEIRE.

I beg your pardon, my dear sir ; I have it from his own lips. Mr. Lundestad intends, on account of failing health, to retire from political life ; you can draw your own conclusions from that.

STENSGÅRD.

He told you so himself ?

HEIRE.

Of course he did.   He made the momentous
announcement to an awe-struck circle down in the
garden ; hee-hee !

THE CHAMBERLAIN.

Why, my dear Ringdal, what can be the meaning
of this ?

HEIRE.

Oh, it's not difficult to guess.

THE CHAMBERLAIN.

Indeed it is though.   This is a most important
affair for the district.   Come along, Ringdal; we
must find the man himself.

> [*He and* RINGDAL *go down the garden.*

FIELDBO.

[*Entering by the furthest back garden-door.*]   Has
the Chamberlain gone out ?

HEIRE.

Sh !   The sages are deliberating !   Great news,
Doctor !   Lundestad is going to resign.

FIELDBO.

Oh, impossible !

STENSGÅRD.

Can you understand it ?

HEIRE.

Ah, now we may look out for real sport.   It's
the League of Youth that's beginning to work,
Mr. Stensgård.   Do you know what you should
call your League ?   I'll tell you some other time.

STENSGÅRD.

Do you think it's really our League—— ?

HEIRE.

Not the least doubt about it.   So we're to have
the pleasure of sending our respected friend Mr.
Mons Monsen to Parliament !   I wish he were off
already ;—I'd give him a lift with pleasure——
I say no more ; hee-hee !

[*Goes into the garden.*

STENSGÅRD.

Tell me, Fieldbo—how do you explain all this ?

FIELDBO.

There are other things still more difficult to
explain.   How come you to be here ?

STENSGÅRD.

I ?   Like the rest, of course—by invitation.

FIELDBO.

I hear you were invited yesterday evening—
after your speech——

STENSGÅRD.

What then ?

FIELDBO.

How could you accept the invitation ?

STENSGÅRD.

What the deuce was I to do ?   I couldn't insult
these good people.

FIELDBO.

Indeed !   You couldn't ?   What about your
speech then ?

STENSGÅRD.

Nonsense !   It was principles I attacked in my speech, not persons.

FIELDBO.

And how do you account for the Chamberlain's invitation ?

STENSGÅRD.

Why, my dear friend, there can only be one way of accounting for it.

FIELDBO.

Namely, that the Chamberlain is afraid of you ?

STENSGÅRD.

By heaven, he shall have no reason to be !   He is a gentleman.

FIELDBO.

That he is.

STENSGÅRD.

Isn't it touching the way the old man has taken this affair ?   And how lovely Miss Bratsberg looked when she brought me the letter !

FIELDBO.

But look here—they haven't mentioned the scene of yesterday, have they ?

STENSGÅRD.

Not a word ; they have far too much tact for that.   But I am filled with remorse ; I must find an opportunity of apologising——

FIELDBO.

I strongly advise you not to !   You don't know the Chamberlain——

STENSGÅRD.

Very well; then my acts shall speak for me.

FIELDBO.

You won't break with the Stonelee party?

STENSGÅRD.

I shall bring about a reconciliation.   I have my
League; it's a power already, you see.

FIELDBO.

By-the-bye, while I remember — we were
speaking of Miss Monsen—I advised you to go
in and win——

STENSGÅRD.

Oh, there's no hurry——

FIELDBO.

But listen; I have been thinking it over : you
had better put all that out of your head.

STENSGÅRD.

I believe you are right.   If you marry into an
underbred family, you marry the whole tribe of
them.

FIELDBO.

Yes, and there are other reasons——

STENSGÅRD.

Monsen is an underbred fellow ; I see that now.

FIELDBO.

Well, polish is not his strong point.

STENSGÅRD.

No, indeed it's not ! He goes and speaks ill of
his guests ; that's ungentlemanly. His rooms all
reek of stale tobacco——

FIELDBO.

My dear fellow, how is it you haven't noticed
the stale tobacco before ?

STENSGÅRD.

It's the contrast that does it. I made a false
start when I settled here. I fell into the clutches
of a clique, and they bewildered me with their
clamour. But there shall be an end to that ! I
won't go and wear my life out as a tool in the
hands of self-interest or coarse stupidity.

FIELDBO.

But what will you do with your League ?

STENSGÅRD.

The League shall remain as it is ; it's founded
on a pretty broad basis. Its purpose is to counter-
act noxious influences ; and I am just beginning
to realise what side the noxious influences come
from.

FIELDBO.

But do you think the " Youth " will see it in
the same light ?

STENSGÅRD.

They shall ! I have surely a right to expect
fellows like that to bow before my superior insight.

FIELDBO.

But if they won't ?

STENSGÅRD.

Then they can go their own way. I have done
with them. ·You don't suppose I am going to let
my life slip into a wrong groove, and never reach
the goal, for the sake of mere blind, pig-headed
consistency !

FIELDBO.

What do you call the goal ?

STENSGÅRD.

A career that gives scope for my talents, and
fulfils my aspirations.

FIELDBO.

No vague phrases ! What do you mean by your
goal ?

STENSGÅRD.

Well, to you I can make a clean breast of it.
My goal is this : in the course of time to get into
Parliament, perhaps into the Ministry, and to
marry happily into a family of means and position.

FIELDBO.

Oh, indeed ! And by help of the Chamberlain's social connections you intend to——?

STENSGÅRD.

I intend to reach the goal by my own exertions ! I must and will reach it ; and without
help from any one. It will take time, I daresay ; but never mind ! Meanwhile I shall enjoy
life here, drinking in beauty and sunshine——

FIELDBO.

Here ?

STENSGÅRD.

Yes, here ! Here there are fine manners ; life moves gracefully here ; the very floors seem laid to be trodden only by lacquered shoes. Here the arm-chairs are deep and the ladies sink exquisitely into them. Here conversation moves lightly and elegantly, like a game at battledore ; here no blunders come plumping in to make an awkward silence. Oh, Fieldbo—here I feel for the first time what distinction means ! Yes, we have indeed an aristocracy of our own ; a little circle ; an aristocracy of culture ; and to it I will belong. Don't you yourself feel the refining influence of this place ? Don't you feel that wealth here loses its grossness ? When I think of Monsen's money, I seem to see piles of fetid bank-notes and greasy mortgages—but here ! here it is shimmering silver ! And the people are the same. Look at the Chamberlain — what a fine high-bred old fellow !

FIELDBO.

He is indeed.

STENSGÅRD.

And the son—alert, straightforward, capable !

FIELDBO.

Certainly.

STENSGÅRD.

And then the daughter-in-law ! Isn't she a pearl ? Good God, what a rich, what a fascinating nature !

FIELDBO.

Thora—Miss Bratsberg has that too.

STENSGÅRD.

Oh yes; but she is less remarkable.

FIELDBO.

Oh, you don't know her.   You don't know how deep, and steadfast, and true her nature is.

STENSGÅRD.

But oh, the daughter-in-law !   So frank, almost reckless; and yet so appreciative, so irresistible——

FIELDBO.

Why, I really believe you're in love with her.

STENSGÅRD.

With a married woman ? Are you crazy ? What good would that do me ?   No, but I am falling in love—I can feel that plainly.   Yes, she is indeed deep, and steadfast, and true.

FIELDBO.

Who ?

STENSGÅRD.

Miss Bratsberg, of course.

FIELDBO.

What ?   You're never thinking of——?

STENSGÅRD.

Yes, by heaven I am !

FIELDBO.

I assure you it's quite out of the question.

STENSGÅRD.

Ho-ho !   Will rules the world, my dear fellow ! We shall see if it doesn't.

FIELDBO.

Why, this is the merest extravagance ! Yesterday it was Miss Monsen——

STENSGÅRD.

Oh, I was too hasty about that; besides, you
yourself advised me not to——

FIELDBO.

I advise you most emphatically to dismiss all
thought of either of them.

STENSGÅRD.

Indeed !   Perhaps you yourself think of throwing the handkerchief to one of them ?

FIELDBO.

I ?   No, I assure you——

STENSGÅRD.

Well, it wouldn't have mattered if you had.   If
people stand in my way and want to balk me of
my future, why, I stick at nothing.

FIELDBO.

Take care I don't say the same !

STENSGÅRD.

You ! What right have you to pose as guardian
and protector to Chamberlain Bratsberg's family ?

FIELDBO.

I have at least the right of a friend.

STENSGÅRD.

Pooh ! that sort of talk won't do with me. Your
motive is mere self-interest ! It gratifies your petty
vanity to imagine yourself cock-of-the-walk in this
house ; and so I am to be kept outside the pale.

FIELDBO.

That is the best thing that could happen to you.
Here you are standing on hollow ground.

STENSGÅRD.

Am I indeed ?   Many thanks !   I shall manage
to prop it up.

FIELDBO.

Try ; but I warn you, it will fall through with
you first.

STENSGÅRD.

Ho-ho ! So you are intriguing against me, are
you ?   I'm glad I have found it out.   I know you
now ; you are my enemy, the only one I have here.

FIELDBO.

Indeed I am not.

STENSGÅRD.

Indeed you are ! You have always been so, ever
since our school-days.   Just look around here and
see how every one appreciates me, stranger as I
am.   You, on the other hand, you who know me,
have never appreciated me.   That is the radical
weakness of your character—you can never appreciate any one.   What did you do in Christiania but
go about from tea-party to tea-party, spreading
yourself out in little witticisms ?   That sort of
thing brings its own punishment !   You dull your
sense for all that makes life worth living, for all

that is ennobling and inspiring ; and presently you
get left behind, fit for nothing.

FIELDBO.

Am I fit for nothing ?

STENSGÅRD.

Have you ever been fit to appreciate me ?

FIELDBO.

What was I to appreciate in you?

STENSGÅRD.

My will, if nothing else. Every one else appreciates it — the crowd at the fête yesterday—
Chamberlain Bratsberg and his family——

FIELDBO.

Mr. Mons Monsen and his ditto—— !   And by-
the-bye, that reminds me—there's some one out
here waiting for you——

STENSGÅRD.

Who ?

FIELDBO.

[*Going towards the back.*]   One who appreciates
you.   [*Opens the door and calls.*]   Aslaksen, come
in !

STENSGÅRD.

Aslaksen ?

ASLAKSEN.

[*Entering.*]   Ah, at last !

FIELDBO.

Good-bye for the present ; I won't intrude upon
friends in council.   [*Goes into the garden.*

STENSGÅRD.

What in the devil's name do you want here ?

ASLAKSEN.

I must speak to you. You promised me yesterday an account of the founding of the League,
and——

STENSGÅRD.

I can't give it you ; it must wait till another
time.

ASLAKSEN.

Impossible, Mr. Stensgård ; the paper appears
to-morrow morning.

STENSGÅRD.

Nonsense ! It has all to be altered. The matter
has entered on a new phase ; new forces have
come into play. What I said about Chamberlain
Bratsberg must be entirely recast before it can
appear.

ASLAKSEN.

Oh, that about the Chamberlain, that's in type
already.

STENSGÅRD.

Then it must come out of type again.

ASLAKSEN.

Not go in ?

STENSGÅRD.

I won't have it published in that form. Why
do you stare at me ? Do you think I don't know
how to manage the affairs of the League ?

ASLAKSEN.

Oh, certainly ; but you must let me tell you——

STENSGÅRD.

No arguing, Aslasken; that I can't and won't
stand!

ASLAKSEN.

Do you know, Mr. Stensgård, that you are doing
your best to take the bread out of my mouth? Do
you know that?

STENSGÅRD.

No; I know nothing of the sort.

ASLAKSEN.

But you are.   Last winter, before you came here,
my paper was looking up.   I edited it myself, I
must tell you, and I edited it on a principle.

STENSGÅRD.

You?

ASLAKSEN.

Yes, I!—I said to myself: it's the great public
that supports a paper; now the great public is the
bad public—that comes of the local situation; and
the bad public will have a bad paper.   So you see
I edited it——

STENSGÅRD.

Badly!   Yes, that's undeniable.

ASLAKSEN.

Well, and I prospered by it.   But then you came
and brought ideas into the district.   The paper
took on a colour, and then Lundestad's supporters
all fell away.   The subscribers that are left won't
pay their subscriptions——

STENSGÅRD.

Ah, but the paper has become a good one.

ASLAKSEN.

I can't live on a good paper. You were to make
things lively ; you were to grapple with abuses, as
you promised yesterday. The bigwigs were to be
pilloried ; the paper was to be filled with things
people were bound to read—and now, you leave
me in the lurch——

STENSGÅRD.

Ho-ho ! You think I am going to keep you
supplied with libels ! No, thank you, my good sir !

ASLAKSEN.

Mr. Stensgård, you musn't drive me to desperation, or you'll repent it.

STENSGÅRD.

What do you mean ?

ASLAKSEN.

I mean that I must make the paper pay in
another way. Heaven knows I should be sorry to
do it. Before you came I made an honest living
out of accidents and suicides and other harmless
things, that often hadn't even happened. But
now you have turned everything topsy-turvy;
people now want very different fare——

STENSGÅRD.

Just let me tell you this : if you break loose in
any way, if you go a single step beyond my orders,
and try to exploit the movement in your own dirty
interests, I'll go to the opposition printer and start
a new paper. We have money, you must know !
We can bring your rag to ruin in a fortnight.

ASLAKSEN.

[*Pale.*] You wouldn't do that!

STENSGÅRD.

Yes, I would; and you'll see I can edit a paper so as to appeal to the great public.

ASLAKSEN.

Then I'll go this instant to Chamberlain Bratsberg——

STENSGÅRD.

You? What have you to do with him?

ASLAKSEN.

What have you to do with him? Do you think I don't know why you are invited here? It's because he is afraid of you, and of what you may do; and you are making capital of that. But if he's afraid of what you may do, he'll be no less afraid of what I may print; and *I* will make capital of that!

STENSGÅRD.

Would you dare to? A wretched creature like you——!

ASLAKSEN.

I'll soon show you. If your speech is to be kept out of the paper, the Chamberlain shall pay me for keeping it out.

STENSGÅRD.

Try it; just try it! You're drunk, fellow——!

ASLAKSEN.

Only in moderation. But I'll fight like a lion if you try to take my poor crust out of my mouth.

Little you know what sort of a home mine is : a
bedridden wife, a crippled child——

STENSGÅRD.

Off with you ! Do you think I want to be soiled
with your squalor ? What are your bedridden
wives and deformed brats to me ? If you stand in
my way, if you dare so much as to obstruct a single
one of my prospects, you shall be on the parish
before the year's out !

ASLAKSEN.

I'll wait one day——

STENSGÅRD.

Ah, you're coming to your senses.

ASLAKSEN.

I shall announce to the subscribers in a hand-
bill that in consequence of an indisposition con-
tracted at the fête, the editor——

STENSGÅRD.

Yes, do so ; I daresay, later on, we shall come
to an understanding.

ASLAKSEN.

I trust we may.—Remember this, Mr. Stensgård : that paper is my one ewe lamb.

[*Goes out by the back.*

LUNDESTAD.

[*At the foremost garden door.*] Ah, Mr. Stensgård !

STENSGÅRD.

Ah, Mr. Lundestad !

LUNDESTAD.

You here alone ?   If you have no objection, I
should like to have a little talk with you.

STENSGÅRD.

With pleasure.

LUNDESTAD.

In the first place, let me say that if any one has
told you that I have said anything to your disadvantage, you musn't believe it.

STENSGÅRD.

To my disadvantage ?   What do you mean ?

LUNDESTAD.

Oh, nothing ; nothing, I assure you.   You see,
there are so many busybodies here, that go about
doing nothing but setting people by the ears.

STENSGÅRD.

Well, on the whole—I'm afraid our relations a r e
a little strained.

LUNDESTAD.

They are quite natural relations, Mr. Stensgård:
the relation of the old to the new ; it is always so.

STENSGÅRD.

Oh, come, Mr. Lundestad, you are not so old as
all that.

LUNDESTAD.

Yes indeed, I'm getting old.   I have held my seat
ever since 1839.   It's time I should be relieved.

STENSGÅRD.

Relieved ?

LUNDESTAD.

Times change, you see. New problems arise,
and for their solution we want new forces.

STENSGÅRD.

Now, frankly, Mr. Lundestad—are you really
going to give up your seat to Monsen?

LUNDESTAD.

To Monsen? No, certainly not to Monsen.

STENSGÅRD.

Then I don't understand——

LUNDESTAD.

Suppose, now, I did retire in Monsen's favour:
do you think he would be elected?

STENSGÅRD.

It's hard to say. As the preliminary election
comes on the day after to-morrow, there may
scarcely be time to prepare the public mind;
but——

LUNDESTAD.

I don't believe he would manage it. The
Chamberlain's party, my party, would not vote for
him. Of course " my party " is a figure of speech:
I mean the men of property, the old families. who
are settled on their own land and belong to it.
They won't have anything to do with Monsen.
Monsen is a newcomer; no one really knows anything about Monsen and his affairs. And then he
has had to cut down so much to clear a place for
himself—to fell both trees and men, you may
say.

STENSGÅRD.

Well then, if you think he has no chance——

LUNDESTAD.

H'm! You are a man of rare gifts, Mr. Stensgård. Providence has dealt lavishly with you. But it has made one little oversight : it ought to have given you one thing more.

STENSGÅRD.

And what may that be?

LUNDESTAD.

Tell me—why do you never think of yourself? Why have you no ambition?

STENSGÅRD.

Ambition? I?

LUNDESTAD.

Why do you waste all your strength on other people? In one word—why not go into Parliament yourself?

STENSGÅRD.

I? You are not serious?

LUNDESTAD.

Why not? You have qualified, I hear. And if you don't seize this opportunity, then some one else will come in; and when once he is firm in the saddle, it may not be so easy to unseat him.

STENSGÅRD.

Great heavens, Mr. Lundestad! do you really mean what you say?

LUNDESTAD.

Oh, I don't want to commit you ; if you don't
care about it——

STENSGÅRD.

Not care about it! Well, I must confess I'm
not so utterly devoid of ambition as you suppose.
But do you really think it possible ?

LUNDESTAD.

Oh, there's nothing impossible about it. I
should do my best, and so, no doubt, would the
Chamberlain ; he knows your oratorical gifts. You
have the young men on your side——

STENSGÅRD.

Mr. Lundestad, by heaven, you are my true
friend !

LUNDESTAD.

Oh, you don't mean much by that. If you really
looked upon me as a friend, you would relieve me
of this burden. You have young shoulders ; you
could bear it so easily.

STENSGÅRD.

I place myself entirely at your disposal ; I will
not fail you.

LUNDESTAD.

Then you are really not disinclined to——

STENSGÅRD.

Here's my hand on it !

LUNDESTAD.

Thanks! Believe me, Mr. Stensgård, you will
not regret it. But now we must go warily to work.

We must both of us take care to be on the electoral
college—I to propose you as my successor, and
put you through your facings before the rest; and
you to give an account of your views——

STENSGÅRD.

If we once get so far, we are safe.   In the
electoral college you are omnipotent.

LUNDESTAD.

There is a limit to omnipotence.   You must of
course bring your oratory into play ; you must take
care to explain away anything that might seem
really awkward or objectionable——

STENSGÅRD.

You don't mean that I am to break with my
party ?

LUNDESTAD.

Now just look at the thing reasonably.   What
do we mean when we talk of two parties?   We
have, on the one hand, certain men or families
who are in possession of the common civic advantages—I mean property, independence, and power.
That is the party I belong to.   On the other hand,
we have the mass of our younger fellow citizens
who want to share in these advantages.   That is
your party.   But that party you will quite naturally
and properly pass out of when you get into power
—to say nothing of taking up a solid position as a
man of property—for of course that is essential,
Mr. Stensgård.

STENSGÅRD.

Yes, I believe it is.   But the time is short ; an
such a position is not to be attained in a day.

LUNDESTAD.

That's true ; but perhaps the prospect of such a position would be enough——

STENSGÅRD.

The prospect—— ?

LUNDESTAD.

Have you any rooted objection to a good marriage, Mr. Stensgård ?   There are heiresses in the country-side. A man like you, with a future before him—a man who can reckon on attaining the highest offices—believe me, you needn't fear a repulse if you play your cards neatly.

STENSGÅRD.

Then, for heaven's sake, help me in the game ! You open wide vistas to me—great visions !   All that I have hoped and longed for, and that seemed so dreamlike and far away, stands suddenly before me in living reality—to lead the people forward towards emancipation, to——

LUNDESTAD.

Yes, we must keep our eyes open, Mr. Stensgård. I see your ambition is already on the alert. That's well.   The rest will come of itself.—In the meantime, thanks ! I shall never forget your readiness to take the burden of office from my old shoulders.

> [*The whole party gradually enters from the garden. Two maid-servants bring in candles and hand round refreshments during the following scene.*

SELMA.

[*Goes towards the piano at the back, left.*]   Mr.
Stensgård, you must join us; we are going to have
a game of forfeits.

STENSGÅRD.

With pleasure ; I am just in the mood.
[*Follows her towards the back, makes
arrangements with her, places chairs,
etc. etc.*

ERIK BRATSBERG.

[*In an undertone.*]   What the deuce is this my
father is saying, Mr. Heire ? What speech has Mr.
Stensgård been making yesterday ?

HEIRE.

Hee-hee !   Don't you know about it ?

ERIK.

No ; we townspeople had our dinner and ball at
the Club.   My father declares Mr. Stensgård has
entirely broken with the Stonelee gang—that he
was frightfully rude to Monsen——

HEIRE.

To Monsen !   No, you must have misunderstood
him, my dear sir.

ERIK.

Well, there were a whole lot of people about, so
that I couldn't quite follow what he said ; but I
certainly heard——

HEIRE.

Wait till to-morrow—— I say no more.   You'll
have the whole story with your coffee, in
Aslaksen's paper.   [*They separate.*

THE CHAMBERLAIN.

Well, my dear Lundestad, are you sticking to those crotchets of yours?

LUNDESTAD.

They are no crotchets, Chamberlain; rather than be ousted, one should give way gracefully.

THE CHAMBERLAIN.

Nonsense; who is dreaming of ousting you?

LUNDESTAD.

H'm; I'm an old weather-prophet. There has been a change in the wind. Besides, I have my successor ready. Mr. Stensgård is willing——

THE CHAMBERLAIN.

Mr. Stensgård?

LUNDESTAD.

Wasn't that what you meant? I took it for a hint when you said he was a man we must make friends with and support.

THE CHAMBERLAIN.

I meant in his onslaught upon all the corruption and swindling that goes on at Stonelee.

LUNDESTAD.

But how could you count so confidently upon his breaking with that crew?

THE CHAMBERLAIN.

He did it openly enough last evening, my dear fellow.

LUNDESTAD.

Last evening?

THE CHAMBERLAIN.

Yes, when he spoke of Monsen's deplorable influence in the district.

LUNDESTAD.

[*Open-mouthed.*]   Of Monsen's—— ?

THE CHAMBERLAIN.

Of course; that time on the table——

LUNDESTAD.

On the table?   Yes?

THE CHAMBERLAIN.

He was frightfully rude; called him a money-
bag, and a griffin or a basilisk, or something.
Ha-ha!—it was great sport to hear him.

LUNDESTAD.

Great sport, was it?

THE CHAMBERLAIN.

Yes, I own I'm not sorry to see these people a
little roughly handled.   But now we must back
him up; for after such a savage attack——

LUNDESTAD.

As that of yesterday, you mean?

THE CHAMBERLAIN.

Of course.

LUNDESTAD.

Upon the table?

THE CHAMBERLAIN.

Yes, upon the table.

LUNDESTAD.

Against Monsen ?

THE CHAMBERLAIN.

Yes, against Monsen and his set. Of course
they'll try to have their revenge ; you can't blame
them——

LUNDESTAD.

[*Decidedly.*]   Mr. Stensgård must be supported
—that is clear !

THORA.

Father dear, you must join in the game.

THE CHAMBERLAIN.

Oh, nonsense, child——

THORA.

Yes, indeed you must ; Selma insists upon it.

THE CHAMBERLAIN.

Very well, I suppose I must give in.   [*In an
undertone as they go towards the back.*]   I'm quite
distressed about Lundestad ; he is really failing ;
fancy, he didn't in the least understand what
Stensgård——

THORA.

Oh, come, come ; they've begun the game.
[*She drags him into the circle of young
people where the game is in full swing.*

ERIK.

[*Calls from his place.*]   Mr. Heire, you are
appointed forfeit-judge.

HEIRE.

Hee-hee! It's the first appointment I ever had.

STENSGÅRD.

[*Also in the circle.*] On account of your legal experience, Mr. Heire.

HEIRE.

Oh, my amiable young friends, I should be delighted to sentence you all—— I say no more!

STENSGÅRD.

[*Slips up to* LUNDESTAD, *who stands in front on the left.*] You were speaking to the Chamberlain. What about? Was it about me?

LUNDESTAD.

Unfortunately it was — about that affair of yesterday evening——

STENSGÅRD.

[*Writhing.*] Oh, confound it all!

LUNDESTAD.

He said you had been frightfully **rude**.

STENSGÅRD.

Do you think it isn't a torture to me?

LUNDESTAD.

Now is your chance to atone for it.

ERIK.

[*Calls.*] Mr. Stensgård, it's your turn.

STENSGÅRD.

Coming! [*Quickly to* LUNDESTAD.] What do you mean?

LUNDESTAD.

Find an opportunity and apologise to the Chamberlain.

STENSGÅRD.

By heaven, I will!

SELMA.

Make haste, make haste!

STENSGÅRD.

I'm coming! Here I am!
[*The game goes on with noise and laughter.
Some elderly gentlemen play cards on the
right.* LUNDESTAD *takes a seat on the
left;* DANIEL HEIRE *near him.*

HEIRE.

That whelp twits me with my legal experience,
does he?

LUNDESTAD.

He's rather free with his tongue, that's certain.

HEIRE.

And so the whole family goes and fawns upon
him. Hee-hee! They're pitifully afraid of him.

LUNDESTAD.

No, there you are wrong, Mr. Heire; the
Chamberlain is not afraid of him.

HEIRE.

Not afraid? Do you think I'm blind, my good
sir?

LUNDESTAD.

No, but—I can trust you to keep the secret?
Well, I'll tell you all about it.   The Chamberlain
thinks it was Monsen he was attacking.

HEIRE.

Monsen?   Oh, absurd!

LUNDESTAD.

Fact, Mr. Heire!   Ringdal or Miss Thora must
have got him persuaded that——-

HEIRE.

And so he goes and asks him to a state dinner-
party!   Deuce take me, if that isn't the best thing
I've heard for long!   No, really now, I can't keep
that bottled up.

LUNDESTAD.

Sh, sh!   Remember your promise.   The Chamberlain's your old school-fellow ; and even if he
has been a little hard upon you——

HEIRE.

Hee-hee!   I'll pay him back with interest!

LUNDESTAD.

Take care!   The Chamberlain is powerful.
Don't play tricks in the lion's den !

HEIRE.

Bratsberg a lion?   Pooh, he's a blockhead, sir,
and I am not.   Oh, won't I get a rare crop of
taunts, and jibes, and innuendoes out of this, when
once our great suit comes on !

SELMA.

[*Calls from the circle.*] Learned judge, what shall the owner of this forfeit do ?

ERIK.

[*Unnoticed, to* HEIRE.]   It's Stensgård's ! Think of something amusing.

HEIRE.

That forfeit ? Hee-hee, let me see ; he might, for example—yes—he shall make a speech !

SELMA.

It's Mr. Stensgård's forfeit.

ERIK.

Mr. Stensgård is to make a speech.

STENSGÅRD.

Oh no, spare me that ; I came off badly enough last night.

THE CHAMBERLAIN.

Excellently, Mr. Stensgård ; I know something of public speaking.

LUNDESTAD.

[*To* HEIRE.] If only he doesn't put his foot in it now.

HEIRE.

Put his foot in it ? Hee-hee ! You're a sharp one ! That's an inspiration ! [*In an undertone to* STENSGÅRD.] If you came off badly last night, why not put yourself right again to-night ?

STENSGÅRD.

[*Seized with a sudden idea.*] Lundestad, here is the opportunity !

LUNDESTAD.

⌐*Evasively.*⌐]   Play your cards neatly.
[*Looks for his hat and slips quietly towards
the door.*

STENSGÅRD.

Yes, I will make a speech !

THE YOUNG LADIES.

Bravo !   Bravo !

STENSGÅRD.

Fill your glasses, ladies and gentlemen !   I am
going to make a speech which shall begin with a
fable ; for here I seem to breathe the finer air of
fable-land.

ERIK.

[*To the* LADIES.]   Hush !   Listen !
[*The* CHAMBERLAIN *takes his glass from the
card-table on the right, beside which he
remains standing.* RINGDAL, FIELDBO,
*and one or two other gentlemen come in
from the garden.*

STENSGÅRD.

It was in the spring time.   There came a young
cuckoo flying over the uplands.   Now the cuckoo
is an adventurer.   There was a great Bird-Parlia-
ment on the meadow beneath him, and both wild
and tame fowl flocked to it.   They came tripping
out of the hen-yards ; they waddled up from the
goose-ponds ; down from Stonelee hulked a fat
capercailzie, flying low and noisily ; he settled
down, and ruffled his feathers and flapped his wings,
and made himself even broader than he was ; and
every now and then he crowed : " Krak, krak,

krak !" as much as to say : I'm the game-cock from
Stonelee, I am !

THE CHAMBERLAIN.

Capital !   Hear, hear !

STENSGÅRD.

And then there was an old woodpecker.   He
bustled up and down the tree-trunks, pecking with
his pointed beak, and gorging himself with grubs
and everything that turns to gall.   To right and
left you heard him going : prik, prik, prik !   And
that was the woodpecker.

ERIK.

Excuse me, wasn't it a stork, or a—— ? [1]

HEIRE.

Say no more !

STENSGÅRD.

That was the old woodpecker.   But now there
came life into the crew ; for they found something
to cackle evil about.   And they flustered together,
and cackled in chorus, until at last the young
cuckoo began to join in the cackling——

FIELDBO.

[*Unnoticed.*]   For God's sake, man, be quiet !

STENSGÅRD.

Now it was an eagle they cackled about—an
eagle who dwelt in lonely dignity upon a beetling

[1] As before stated, " Heire " means a heron.

cliff.[1] They were all agreed about him. "He's a bugbear to the neighbourhood," croaked a hoarse raven. But the eagle swooped down into their midst, seized the cuckoo, and bore him aloft to his eyrie.—Heart conquered heart! From that clear summit the adventurer-cuckoo looked far and wide over the lowlands; there he found sunshine and peace; and there he learned to judge aright the swarm from the hen-yards and the clearings——

FIELDBO.

[*Loudly.*] Bravo, bravo! And now some music.

THE CHAMBERLAIN.

Hush! Don't interrupt him.

STENSGÅRD.

Chamberlain Bratsberg—here my fable ends; and here I stand before you, in the presence of every one, to beg your forgiveness for last night.

THE CHAMBERLAIN.

[*Falls a step backwards.*] Mine——?

STENSGÅRD.

I thank you for the magnanimous vengeance you have taken for my senseless words. In me you have henceforth a faithful champion. And now, ladies and gentlemen, I drink the health of the eagle on the mountain-top—the health of Chamberlain Bratsberg.

THE CHAMBERLAIN.

[*Clutching at the table.*] Thank you, Mr.—Mr. Stensgård.

[1] " Et brat fjeld "—an allusion to the name Bratsberg.

THE GUESTS.

[*For the most part in painful embarrassment.*]
The Chamberlain! Chamberlain Bratsberg!

THE CHAMBERLAIN.

Ladies! Gentlemen! [*Softly.*] Thora!

THORA.

Father!

THE CHAMBERLAIN.

Oh, Doctor, Doctor, what have you done

STENSGÅRD.

[*With his glass in his hand, radiant with self-satisfaction.*] Now to our places again! Hullo,
Fieldbo! Come, join in—join in the League of
Youth! The game's going merrily!

HEIRE.

[*In front, on the left.*] Yes, on my soul, the
game's going merrily!

[LUNDESTAD *slips out by the door in the
back.*

ACT THIRD.

*An elegant morning-room, with entrance-door in the
    back. On the left, the door of the* CHAMBERLAIN'S
    *study ; further back, a door leading to the draw-
    ing-room. On the right, a door leading to* RING-
    DAL'S *offices ; further forward, a window.*
THORA *is seated on the sofa, left, weeping. The*
    CHAMBERLAIN *paces angrily up and down.*

THE CHAMBERLAIN.
Yes, now we have the epilogue—tears and
lamentations——

THORA.
Oh, that we had never seen that man !

THE CHAMBERLAIN.
What man ?

THORA.
That wretched Mr. Stensgård, of course.

THE CHAMBERLAIN.
You should rather say : Oh, that we had never
seen that wretched Doctor.

THORA.
Doctor Fieldbo ?

THE CHAMBERLAIN.

Yes, Fieldbo, Fieldbo! Wasn't it he that palmed off a parcel of lies upon me—— ?

THORA.

No, my dear father, it was I.

THE CHAMBERLAIN.

You? Well, then, both of you! You were his accomplice—behind my back. A nice state of affairs!

THORA.

Oh, father, if you only knew——

THE CHAMBERLAIN.

Oh, I know enough; more than enough; much more!

DR. FIELDBO *enters from the back.*

FIELDBO.

Good morning, Chamberlain! Good morning, Miss Bratsberg!

THE CHAMBERLAIN.

[*Still pacing the room.*] So you are there, are you—bird of evil omen!

FIELDBO.

Yes, it was a very unpleasant affair.

THE CHAMBERLAIN.

[*Looking out at the window.*] Oh, you think so?

FIELDBO.

You must have noticed how I kept my eye upon Stensgård all the evening. Unfortunately,

when I heard there was to be a game of forfeits,
I thought there was no danger——

THE CHAMBERLAIN.

[*Stamping on the floor.*] To be made a laughing-
stock by such a windbag ! What must my guests
have thought of me ? That I was mean enough
to want to buy this creature, this—this —— as
Lundestad calls him !

FIELDBO.

Yes, but——

THORA.

[*Unnoticed by her father.*] Don't speak !

THE CHAMBERLAIN.

[*After a short pause, turns to* FIELDBO.] Tell me
frankly, Doctor:—Am I really denser than the
general run of people ?

FIELDBO.

How can you ask such a question, Chamberlain?

THE CHAMBERLAIN.

Then how did it happen that I was probably
the only person there who didn't understand that
that confounded speech was meant for me ?

FIELDBO.

Shall I tell you why ?

THE CHAMBERLAIN.

Certainly.

FIELDBO.

It is because you yourself regard your position
in the district differently from other people.

THE CHAMBERLAIN.

I regard my position as my father before me
regarded his.   No one would ever have ventured
to treat h i m so.

FIELDBO.

Your father died about the year 1830.

THE CHAMBERLAIN.

Oh, yes; many a barrier has broken down since
that time.   But, after all, it's my own fault.   I
have mixed myself up too much with these good
people.   So now I must be content to have my
name coupled with Anders Lundestad's!

FIELDBO.

Well, frankly, I see no disgrace in that.

THE CHAMBERLAIN.

Oh, you know quite well what I mean.   Of
course I don't plume myself on rank, or titles, or
anything of that sort.   But what I hold in
honour, and expect others to hold in honour, is
the integrity handed down in our family from
generation to generation.   What I mean is that
when a man like Lundestad goes into public life,
he cannot keep his character and his conduct
entirely free from stain.   In the general mud-
throwing, he is sure to find himself bespattered.
But they might leave m e in peace; I stand outside their parties.

FIELDBO.

Not so entirely, Chamberlain; at least you were
delighted so long as you thought it was Monsen
that was attacked.

THE CHAMBERLAIN.

Don't mention that fellow !—It is he that has
relaxed the moral sense of the district.   And
now he has gone and turned my son's head,
confound him !

THORA.

Erik's ?

FIELDBO.

Your son's ?

THE CHAMBERLAIN.

Yes ; what tempted him to go and set up in
business ?   It leads to nothing.

FIELDBO.

Why, my dear Chamberlain, he must live
and——

THE CHAMBERLAIN.

Oh, with economy he could quite well live on
the money that came to him from his mother.

FIELDBO.

He might perhaps live o n it ; but what could
he live for ?

THE CHAMBERLAIN.

For ?   Well, if he absolutely must have something to live for, hasn't he qualified as a lawyer ?
He might live for his profession.

FIELDBO.

No, that he couldn't do ; it is against his nature.
Then there was no official appointment he could
well hope for ; you have kept the management of
your property in your own hands ; and your son
has no children to educate.   Under these circumstances, when he sees tempting examples around

him—people who have started from nothing and are worth their half million——

THE CHAMBERLAIN.

Their half million! Oh, come now, let us keep to the hundred thousands. But neither the half million nor the hundred thousands can be scraped together with perfectly clean hands;—I don't mean in the eyes of the world; Heaven knows it is easy enough to keep within the law; but in respect to one's own conscience. Of course my son cannot descend to anything questionable; so you may be quite sure Mr. Erik Bratsberg's financial operations won't bring in any half millions.

SELMA, *in walking dress, enters from the back.*

SELMA.

Good-morning! Is Erik not here?

THE CHAMBERLAIN.

Good-morning, child! Are you looking for your husband?

SELMA.

Yes, he said he was coming here. Mr. Monsen called upon him early this morning, and then——

THE CHAMBERLAIN.

Monsen? Does Monsen come to your house?

SELMA.

Now and then; generally on business. Why, my dear Thora, what's the matter? Have you been crying?

THORA.

Oh, it's nothing.

SELMA.

No, it's n o t nothing! At home Erik was out of
humour, and here——— I can see it in your looks :
there is something wrong.   What is it?

THE CHAMBERLAIN.

Nothing you need trouble about, at any rate.
You are too dainty to carry burdens, my little
Selma.   Go into the drawing-room for the present.
If Erik said he was coming, he will be here soon,
no doubt.

SELMA.

Come, Thora—and be sure you don't let me sit
in a draught!   [*Embracing her.*]   Oh, I could hug
the life out of you, my sweet Thora!

[*The two ladies go off to the left.*

THE CHAMBERLAIN.

So they are hand in glove, are they, the two
speculators!   They should go into partnership.
Monsen and Bratsberg—how nice it would sound!
[*A knock at the door in the back.*]   Come in!

STENSGÅRD *enters.*

THE CHAMBERLAIN.

[*Recoiling a step.*]   What is this?

STENSGÅRD.

Yes, here I am again, Chamberlain!

THE CHAMBERLAIN.

So I see.

FIELDBO.

Are you mad, Stensgård?

STENSGÅRD.

You retired early yesterday evening. When Fieldbo had explained to me how matters stood, you had already——

THE CHAMBERLAIN.

Excuse me—all explanations are superfluous——

STENSGÅRD.

I understand that ; therefore I have not come to make any.

THE CHAMBERLAIN.

Oh, indeed ?

STENSGÅRD.

I know I have insulted you.

THE CHAMBERLAIN.

I know that too ; and before I have you turned out, perhaps you will be good enough to tell me why you are here.

STENSGÅRD.

Because I love your daughter, Chamberlain !

FIELDBO.

What—— !

THE CHAMBERLAIN.

What does he say, Doctor ?

STENSGÅRD.

Ah, you can't grasp the idea, Chamberlain. You are an old man ; you have nothing to fight for——

THE CHAMBERLAIN.

And you presume to—— ?

STENSGÅRD.

I am here to ask for your daughter's hand, Chamberlain.

THE CHAMBERLAIN.

You—— you——? Won't you sit down?

STENSGÅRD.

Thanks, I prefer to stand.

THE CHAMBERLAIN.

What do you say to this, Doctor?

STENSGÅRD.

Oh, Fieldbo is on my side; he is my friend; the only true friend I have.

FIELDBO.

No, no, man! Never in this world, if you——

THE CHAMBERLAIN.

Perhaps it was with this view that Doctor Fieldbo secured his friend's introduction into my house?

STENSGÅRD.

You know me only by my exploits of yesterday and the day before. That is not enough. Besides, I am not the same man to-day that I was then. My intercourse with you and yours has fallen like spring showers upon my spirit, making it put forth new blossoms in a single night! You must not hurl me back into my sordid past. Till now, I have never been at home with the beautiful in life; it has always been beyond my reach——

THE CHAMBERLAIN.

But my daughter——?

STENSGÅRD.

Oh, I shall win her.

THE CHAMBERLAIN.

Indeed ? H'm !

STENSGÅRD.

Yes, for I have will on my side. Remember
what you told me yesterday. You were opposed
to your son's marriage—and see how it has turned
out ! You must put on the glasses of experience,
as Fieldbo said——

THE CHAMBERLAIN.

Ah, that was what you meant ?

FIELDBO.

Not in the least ! My dear Chamberlain, let
me speak to him alone——

STENSGÅRD.

Nonsense ; I have nothing to speak to y o u
about. Now, pray be reasonable, Chamberlain !
A family like yours needs new alliances, or its
brains stagnate——

THE CHAMBERLAIN.

Oh, this is too much !

STENSGÅRD.

Now, now, don't get angry ! These high-and-
mighty airs are unworthy of you—of course you
know they are all nonsense at bottom. You shall
see how much you'll value me when you come to
know me. Yes, yes ; you s h a l l value me—both
you and your daughter ! I will make her——

THE CHAMBERLAIN.

What do you think of this, Doctor?

FIELDBO.

I think it's madness.

STENSGÅRD.

Yes, it would be in you; but I, you see— I have
a mission to fulfil on God's beautiful earth ;—I am
not to be deterred by nonsensical prejudices

THE CHAMBERLAIN.

Mr. Stensgård, there is the door.

STENSGÅRD.

You show me—— ?

THE CHAMBERLAIN.

The door!

STENSGÅRD.

Don't do that!

THE CHAMBERLAIN.

Out with you! You are an adventurer an
a—a—confound my memory! You're a——

STENSGÅRD.

What am I?

THE CHAMBERLAIN.

You are—that other thing—it's on the tip of
my tongue——

STENSGÅRD.

Beware how you block my career!

THE CHAMBERLAIN.

Beware? Of what?

STENSGÅRD.

I will attack you in the papers, persecute you,
libel you, do all I can to undermine your reputation. You shall shriek under the lash. You
shall seem to see spirits in the air raining blows
upon you. You shall huddle together in dread,
and crouch with your arms bent over your head
to ward off the strokes—you shall try to creep
into shelter——

THE CHAMBERLAIN.

Creep into shelter yourself—in a madhouse;
that is the proper place for you!

STENSGÅRD.

Ha-ha; that is a cheap retort; but you know
no better, Mr. Bratsberg! I tell you the wrath of
the Lord is in me. It is His will you are oppos-
ing. He has destined me for the light—beware
how you cast a shadow!—Well, I see I shall
make no way with you to-day : but that matters
nothing. I only ask you to speak to your daughter
—to prepare her—to give her the opportunity of
choosing! Reflect, and look around you. Where
can you expect to find a son-in-law among these
plodding dunces? Fieldbo says she is deep and
steadfast and true. So now you know just how
matters stand. Good-bye, Chamberlain—I leave
you to choose between my friendship and my
enmity. Good-bye!   [*Goes out by the back.*

THE CHAMBERLAIN.

So it has come to this! This is how they dare
to treat me in my own house!

FIELDBO.

Stensgård dares; no one else would.

THE CHAMBERLAIN.

He to-day; others to-morrow.

FIELDBO.

Let them come; I shall keep them off; I would
go through fire and water for you——

THE CHAMBERLAIN.

Yes, you who have caused all the mischief!—
H'm; that Stensgård is the most impudent scoundrel I have ever known! And yet, after all—deuce
take me if there isn't something I like about him.

FIELDBO.

He has possibilities——

THE CHAMBERLAIN.

He has openness, Dr Fieldbo! He doesn't go
playing his own game behind one's back, like so
many other people; he—he——!

FIELDBO.

It's not worth disputing about. Only be firm,
Chamberlain; no, and no again, to Stensgård——!

THE CHAMBERLAIN.

Oh, keep your advice to yourself! You may
rely upon it that neither he nor any one else——

RINGDAL.

[*Enters by the door on the right.*] Excuse me,
Chamberlain; one word——   [*Whispers.*

THE CHAMBERLAIN.

What? In your room?

RINGDAL.

He came in by the back way, and begs you to see him.

THE CHAMBERLAIN.

H'm.—Oh, Doctor, just go into the drawing-room for a moment; there's some one here who—— But don't say a word to Selma of Mr. Stensgård and his visit. She must be kept outside all this business. As for my daughter, I should prefer that you should say nothing to her either; but—— Oh, what's the use——? Please go now.

[FIELDBO *goes into the drawing-room.* RINGDAL *has, in the meantime, gone back to his office, whence* MONSEN *presently enters.*

MONSEN.

[*At the door.*] I beg ten thousand pardons, sir——

THE CHAMBERLAIN.

Oh, come in, come in!

MONSEN.

I trust your family is in good health?

THE CHAMBERLAIN.

Thank you. Is there anything you want?

MONSEN.

I can't quite put it that way. Thank heaven, I'm one of those that have got pretty nearly all they can want.

THE CHAMBERLAIN.

Oh, indeed? That is a good deal to say.

MONSEN.

But I've had to work for it, Chamberlain. Oh,
I know you regard my work with no very friendly
eye.

THE CHAMBERLAIN.

I cannot suppose that your work is in any way
affected by my way of regarding it.

MONSEN.

Who knows? At any rate, I'm thinking of
gradually withdrawing from business

THE CHAMBERLAIN.

Really?

MONSEN.

The luck has been on my side, I may tell you.
I've gone ahead as far as I care to; so now I
think it's about time to slack off a little——

THE CHAMBERLAIN.

Well, I congratulate both you—and other
people.

MONSEN.

And if I could at the same time do you a
service, Chamberlain——

THE CHAMBERLAIN.

Me?

MONSEN.

When the Langerud woods were put up to
auction five years ago, you made a bid for
them——

THE CHAMBERLAIN.

Yes, but you outbade me, and they were
knocked down to you.

MONSEN.

You can have them now, with the saw-mills and
all appurtenances——

THE CHAMBERLAIN.

After all your sinful cutting and hacking—— !

MONSEN.

Oh, they're worth a good deal still ; and with
your method of working, in a few years——

THE CHAMBERLAIN.

Thank you ; unfortunately I must decline the
proposal.

MONSEN.

There's a great deal of money in it, Chamberlain. As for me,—I may tell you I have a
great speculation on hand ; the stakes are large ;
I mean there's a big haul to be made—a hundred
thousand or so——

THE CHAMBERLAIN.

A hundred thousand ? That is certainly no
trifle.

MONSEN.

Ha ha ha ! A nice round sum to add to the pile.
But when you're going into a great battle you
need reserve forces, as the saying goes. There's
not much ready money about ; the names that
are worth anything are rather used up——

THE CHAMBERLAIN.

Yes, certain people have taken care of that.

MONSEN.

It's a case of you scratch me, I scratch you.
Well, Chamberlain, is it to be a bargain ?   You
shall have the woods at your own figure——

THE CHAMBERLAIN.

I will not have them at any figure, Mr. Monsen.

MONSEN.

Well, one good offer deserves another.   Will
you help me, sir ?

THE CHAMBERLAIN.

What do you mean ?

MONSEN.

Of course I'll give good security.   I have plenty
of property.   Look here — these papers — just let
me explain my position to you.

THE CHAMBERLAIN.

[*Waving the papers aside.*]   Is it pecuniary aid
you want ?

MONSEN.

Not ready money ; oh, no '   But your support,
Chamberlain.   Of course I'll pay for it—and give
security, and——

THE CHAMBERLAIN.

And you come to me with such a proposal as
this ?

MONSEN.

Yes, precisely to you.   I know you've often let
bygones be bygones when a man was in **real**
straits.

THE CHAMBERLAIN.

Well, in a way, I must thank you for your good
opinion—especially at a time like this ; but never ·
theless——

MONSEN.

Won't you tell me, Chamberlain, what sets you
against me ?

THE CHAMBERLAIN.

Oh, what would be the use ?

MONSEN.

It might lead to a better understanding between us.　I've never stood in your way that I
know of.

THE CHAMBERLAIN.

You think not ?　Then let me tell you of one
case in which you have stood in my way.　I
founded the Iron-works Savings Bank for the
benefit of my employees and others.　But then
you must needs set up as a banker; people take
their savings to you——

MONSEN.

Naturally, sir, for I give higher interest.

THE CHAMBERLAIN.

Yes, but you charge higher interest on loans.

MONSEN.

But I don't make so many difficulties about
security and so forth.

THE CHAMBERLAIN.

That is just the mischief of it ; for now we have
people making bargains to the tune of ten or

twenty thousand dollars,[1] though neither of the
parties has so much as a brass farthing. That is
what sets me against you, Mr. Monsen. And
there is another thing too that touches me still
more nearly. Do you think it was with my good
will that my son flung himself into all these wild
speculations ?

MONSEN.

But how can I help that ?

THE CHAMBERLAIN.

It was your example that infected him, as it
did the others. Why could you not stick to your
last ?

MONSEN.

Remain a lumberman, like my father ?

THE CHAMBERLAIN.

Was it a disgrace to be in my employment ?
Your father made his bread honourably, and was
respected in his own class.

MONSEN.

Yes, until he'd almost worked his life out, and
at last went over the waterfall with his raft. Do
you know anything of life in that class, Chamberlain ? Have you ever realised what the men have
to endure who toil for you deep in the forests, and
along the river-reaches, while you sit comfortably
at home and fatten on the profits ? Can you blame
such a man for struggling to rise in the world ? I
had had a little more schooling than my father ;
perhaps I had rather more brains too——

---

[1] The dollar = four crowns = four-and-sixpence, was the unit
of coinage at the time this play was written. It has since
been replaced by the crown .

THE CHAMBERLAIN.

Very likely. But by what means have you
risen in the world ? You began by selling brandy.
Then you bought up doubtful debts, and enforced
them mercilessly ;—and so you got on and on.
How many people have you not ruined to push
yourself forward !

MONSEN.

That's the course of business ; one up, another
down.

THE CHAMBERLAIN.

But there are different methods of business.   I
know of respectable families whom you have
brought to the workhouse.

MONSEN.

Daniel Heire is not very far from the workhouse.

THE CHAMBERLAIN.

I understand you ; but I can justify my conduct
before God and man ! When the country was in
distress, after the separation from Denmark, my
father made sacrifices beyond his means. Thus
part of our property came into the hands of the
Heire family. What was the result ? The people
who lived upon the property suffered under
Daniel Heire's incompetent management. He
cut down timber to the injury, I may even say to
the ruin, of the district. Was it not my obvious
duty to put a stop to it if I was able ? And it
happened that I was able ; I had the law on my
side ; I was well within my rights when I re-
entered upon my family property.

MONSEN.

I, too, have always had the law on my side.

THE CHAMBERLAIN.

But what about your sense of right, your conscience, if you have such a thing ?   And how you have broken down all social order !   How you have impaired the respect that should attach to wealth !   People never think of asking nowadays how such and such a fortune was made, or how long it has been in such and such a family ; they only ask : how much is so-and-so worth ?—and they esteem him accordingly.   Now I suffer by all this ; I find myself regarded as a sort of associate of yours ; people speak of us in one breath, because we are the two largest proprietors in the neighbourhood.   This state of things I cannot endure !   I tell you once for all : that is why I am set against you.

MONSEN.

This state of things shall come to an end. sir ; I will give up business, and make way for you at every point ; but I beg you, I implore you, to help me !

THE CHAMBERLAIN.

I will not.

MONSEN.

I'm willing to pay what you like——

THE CHAMBERLAIN.

To pay !   And you dare to—— !

MONSEN.

If not for my sake, then for your son's !

THE CHAMBERLAIN.

My son's!

MONSEN.

Yes, he's in it.   I reckon he stands to win some twenty thousand dollars.

THE CHAMBERLAIN.

Stands to win?

MONSEN.

Yes.

THE CHAMBERLAIN.

Then, good God, who stands to lose all this money?

MONSEN.

How do you mean?

THE CHAMBERLAIN.

If my son wins, some one or other must lose!

MONSEN.

It's a good stroke of business; I'm not in a position to say more.   But I need a solid name; only just your endorsement——

THE CHAMBERLAIN.

Endorsement!   On a bill——?

MONSEN.

Only for ten or fifteen thousand dollars.

THE CHAMBERLAIN.

Do you suppose for a moment that——?   My name!   In such an affair!   My name?   As surety, no doubt?

MONSEN.

A mere matter of form——

THE CHAMBERLAIN.

A matter of swindling !   My name !   Not upon any consideration.   I have never put my name on other men's paper.

MONSEN.

Never ?   That's an exaggeration, Chamberlain.

THE CHAMBERLAIN.

It is the literal truth.

MONSEN.

No, not literal ; I've seen it with my own eyes.

THE CHAMBERLAIN.

What have you seen ?

MONSEN.

Your name—on one bill at least.

THE CHAMBERLAIN.

It is false, I tell you !   You have never seen it !

MONSEN.

I have !   On a bill for two thousand dollars. Think again !

THE CHAMBERLAIN.

Neither for two thousand nor for ten thousand ! On my sacred word of honour, never !

MONSEN.

Then it's a forgery.

THE CHAMBERLAIN.

Forgery ?

MONSEN.

Yes, a forgery—for I have seen it.

THE CHAMBERLAIN.

Forgery? Forgery! Where did you see it?
In whose hands?

MONSEN.

That I won't tell you.

THE CHAMBERLAIN.

Ha-ha! We shall soon find that out

MONSEN.

Listen to me—— !

THE CHAMBERLAIN

Silence! It has come to this then! Forgery.
They must mix me up in their abominations! No
wonder, then, that people bracket me with the
rest of you. But it is my turn now!

MONSEN.

Chamberlain—for your own sake and for the
sake of others——

THE CHAMBERLAIN.

Off with you! Out of my sight! It is you
that are at the root of it all!—Yes you are! Woe
unto him from whom offences come. Your home-
life is scandalous. What sort of society do you
get about you? Persons from Christiania and elsewhere, who think only of eating and drinking, and
do not care in what company they gorge themselves. Silence! I have seen with my own eyes
your distinguished guests tearing along the roads
at Christmas-time like a pack of howling wolves.
And there is worse behind. You have had scandals
with your own maid-servants. You drove your

wife out of her mind by your ill-treatment and debauchery.

MONSEN.

Come, this is going too far! You shall pay for these words!

THE CHAMBERLAIN.

Oh, to the deuce with your threats! What harm can you do to me? Me? You asked what I had to say against you. Well, I have said it. Now you know why I have kept you out of decent society.

MONSEN.

Yes, and now I'll drag your decent society down——

THE CHAMBERLAIN.

That way!

MONSEN.

I know my way, Chamberlain!

[*Goes out by the back.*

THE CHAMBERLAIN.

[*Opens the door on the right and calls.*] Ringdal, Ringdal—come here!

RINGDAL.

What is it, sir?

THE CHAMBERLAIN.

[*Calls into the drawing room.*] Doctor, please come this way!—Now, Ringdal, now you shall see my prophecies fulfilled.

FIELDBO.

[*Entering.*] What can I do for you, Chamberlain?

RINGDAL.

What prophecies, sir?

THE CHAMBERLAIN.

What do you say to this, Doctor? You have always accused me of exaggerating when I said that Monsen was corrupting the neighbourhood.

FIELDBO.

Well, what then?

THE CHAMBERLAIN.

We are getting on, I can tell you! What do you think? There are forgeries going about.

RINGDAL.

Forgeries?

THE CHAMBERLAIN.

Yes, forgeries! And whose name do you think they have forged? Why, mine!

FIELDBO.

Who in the world can have done it?

THE CHAMBERLAIN.

How can I tell? I don't know all the scoundrels in the district. But we shall soon find out.— Doctor, do me a service. The papers must have come into the hands either of the Savings Bank or the Iron-works Bank. Drive up to Lundestad; he is the director who knows most about things. Find out whether there is any such paper——

FIELDBO.

Certainly; at once.

RINGDAL.

Lundestad is here at the works to-day; there s
a meeting of the school committee.

THE CHAMBERLAIN.

So much the better. Find him; bring him
here.

FIELDBO.

I'll go at once. *[Goes out at the back.*

THE CHAMBERLAIN.

And you, Ringdal, make inquiries at the Iron-
works. As soon as we have got to the bottom of
the matter, we'll lay an information. No mercy
to the scoundrels!

RINGDAL.

Very good, sir. Bless me, who'd have thought
of such a thing? *[Goes out to the right
[The* CHAMBERLAIN *paces the room once or
twice, and is then about to go into his
study. At that instant* ERIK BRATSBERG
enters from the back.

ERIK.

My dear father——!

THE CHAMBERLAIN.

Oh, are you there?

ERIK.

I want so much to speak to you.

THE CHAMBERLAIN.

H'm; I'm not much in the humour for speaking
to any one. What do you want?

ERIK.

You know I have never mixed you up in my affairs, father.

THE CHAMBERLAIN.

No; that is an honour I should certainly have declined.

ERIK.

But now I am forced to——

THE CHAMBERLAIN.

What are you forced to do?

ERIK.

Father, you must help me!

THE CHAMBERLAIN.

With money! You may be very sure that——

ERIK.

Only this once! I swear I'll never again——
The fact is, I am under certain engagements to
Monsen of Stonelee——

THE CHAMBERLAIN.

I know that. You have a brilliant speculation on hand.

ERIK.

A speculation? We? No! Who told you so?

THE CHAMBERLAIN.

Monsen himself.

ERIK.

Has Monsen been here?

THE CHAMBERLAIN.

He has just gone.   I showed him the door.

ERIK.

If you don't help me, father, I am ruined.

THE CHAMBERLAIN.

You ?

ERIK.

Yes.   Monsen has advanced me money.   I had
to pay terribly dear for it ; and now the bills
have fallen due——

THE CHAMBERLAIN.

There we have it !   What did I tell you—— ?

ERIK.

Yes, yes ; it's too late now——

THE CHAMBERLAIN.

Ruined !   In two years !   But how could you
expect anything else ?   What had you to do
among these charlatans that go about dazzling
people's eyes with wealth that never existed !
They were no company for you.   Among people
of that sort you must meet cunning with cunning,
or you'll go to the wall ; you have learnt that
now.

ERIK.

Father, will you save me or will you not ?

THE CHAMBERLAIN.

No ; for the last time, no.   I will not.

ERIK.

My honour is at stake——

THE CHAMBERLAIN.

Oh, let us have no big phrases! There's no
honour involved in commercial success nowadays;
quite the opposite, I had almost said. Go home
and make up your accounts; pay every man his
due, and have done with it, the sooner the better.

ERIK.

Oh, you don't know——

SELMA *and* THORA *enter from the drawing-room.*

SELMA.

Is that Erik's voice?—Good heavens, what is
the matter?

THE CHAMBERLAIN.

Nothing.   Go into the drawing-room again.

SELMA.

No, I won't go. I will know. Erik, what is
it? Tell me!

ERIK.

It's only that I am ruined!

THORA.

Ruined!

THE CHAMBERLAIN.

There, you see!

SELMA.

What is ruined?

ERIK.

Everything.

SELMA.

Do you mean you have lost your money?

ERIK.

Money, house, inheritance—everything!

SELMA.

Is that what you call everything?

ERIK.

Come, let us go, Selma. You are all I have left
me. We must bear the blow together.

SELMA.

The blow? Bear it together? [*With a cry.*] Do
you think I am fit for that, now?

THE CHAMBERLAIN.

For heaven's sake—— !

ERIK.

What do you mean?

THORA.

Oh, Selma, take care!

SELMA.

No, I won't take care! I cannot go on lying
and shamming any longer! I must speak the
truth. I will not "bear" anything!

ERIK.

Selma!

THE CHAMBERLAIN.

Child, what are you saying?

SELMA.

Oh, how cruel you have been to me! Shamefully
—all of you! It was my part always to accept—

never to give. I have been like a pauper among
you. You never came and demanded a sacrifice of
me; I was not fit to bear anything. I hate you!
I loathe you!

ERIK.

What can this mean?

THE CHAMBERLAIN.

She is ill; she is out of her mind!

SELMA.

How I have thirsted for a single drop of your
troubles, your anxieties! But when I begged for
it you only laughed me off. You have dressed me
up like a doll; you have played with me as you
would play with a child. Oh, what a joy it would
have been to me to take my share in your burdens! How I longed, how I yearned, for a large,
and high, and strenuous part in life! Now you
come to me, Erik, now that you have nothing else
left. But I will not be treated simply as a last re-
source. I will have nothing to do with your
troubles now. I won't stay with you! I will rather
play and sing in the streets——! Let me be!
Let me be!   [*She rushes out by the back.*

THE CHAMBERLAIN.

Thora, was there any meaning in all that,
or——

THORA.

Oh, yes, there was meaning in it; if only I had
seen it sooner.   [*Goes out by the back.*

ERIK.

No! All else I can lose, but not her ! Selma,
Selma !   [*Follows* THORA *and* SELMA.

RINGDAL.
[*Enters from the right.*]   Chamberlain !

THE CHAMBERLAIN.
Well, what is it ?

RINGDAL.
I have been to the Bank——

THE CHAMBERLAIN.
The Bank ? Oh, yes, about the bill——

RINGDAL.
It's all right ; they have never had any bill
endorsed by you——

FIELDBO *and* LUNDESTAD *enter by the back.*

FIELDBO.
False alarm, Chamberlain !

THE CHAMBERLAIN.
Indeed ? Not at the Savings Bank either ?

LUNDESTAD.
Certainly not. During all the years I've been
a director I have never once seen your name ;
except, of course, on your son's bill.

THE CHAMBERLAIN.
My son's bill ?

LUNDESTAD.

Yes, the bill you accepted for him early this spring.

THE CHAMBERLAIN.

My son? My son? Do you dare to tell me——?

LUNDESTAD.

Why, bless me, just think a moment; the bill for two thousand dollars drawn by your son——

THE CHAMBERLAIN.

[*Groping for a chair.*] Oh, my God——!

FIELDBO.

For heaven's sake——'

RINGDAL.

It's not possible that——!

THE CHAMBERLAIN.

[*Who has sunk down on a chair.*] Quietly, quietly! Drawn by my son, you say? Accepted by me? For two thousand dollars?

FIELDBO.

[*To* LUNDESTAD.] And this bill is in the Savings Bank?

LUNDESTAD.

Not now; it was redeemed last week by Monsen——

THE CHAMBERLAIN.

By Monsen——?

RINGDAL.

Monsen may still be at the works; I'll go——

THE CHAMBERLAIN.

Stop here !

DANIEL HEIRE *enters by the back.*

HEIRE.

Good-morning, gentlemen! Good-morning, Chamberlain! Thank you so much for the delightful evening we spent yesterday. What do you think I've just heard——?

RINGDAL.

Excuse me ; we are busy——

HEIRE.

So are other people, I can tell you ; our friend from Stonelee, for example——

THE CHAMBERLAIN.

Monsen ?

HEIRE.

Hee-hee ; it's a pretty story ! The electioneering intrigues are in full swing. And what do you think is the last idea ? They are going to bribe you, Chamberlain !

LUNDESTAD.

To bribe—— ?

THE CHAMBERLAIN.

They judge the tree by its fruit.

HEIRE.

Deuce take me if it isn't the most impudent thing I ever heard of! I just looked in at Madam Rundholmen's to have a glass of bitters. There

sat Messrs. Monsen and Stensgård drinking port—
filthy stuff! I wouldn't touch it; but they might
have had the decency to offer me a glass, all the
same. However, Monsen turned to me and said,
"What do you bet that Chamberlain Bratsberg
won't go with our party at the preliminary election
to-morrow?" "Indeed," said I, "how's that to
be managed?" "Oh," he said, "this bill will
persuade him——"

FIELDBO.

Bill——?

LUNDESTAD.

At the election——?

THE CHAMBERLAIN.

Well? What then?

HEIRE

Oh, I know no more. They said something
about two thousand dollars. That's the figure
they rate a gentleman's conscience at! Oh, it's
abominable, I say!

THE CHAMBERLAIN.

A bill for two thousand dollars?

RINGDAL.

And Monsen has it?

HEIRE.

No, he handed it over to Stensgård.

LUNDESTAD.

Indeed!

FIELDBO.

To Stensgård?

THE CHAMBERLAIN.

Are you sure of that ?

HEIRE.

Quite certain. " You can make what use you
please of it," he said   But I don't understand——

LUNDESTAD.

I want to speak to you, Mr. Heire—and you
too, Ringdal

[*The three converse in a whisper at the
back.*

FIELDBO.

Chamberlain !

THE CHAMBERLAIN.

Well ?

FIELDBO.

Your son's bill is genuine, of course—— ?

THE CHAMBERLAIN.

One would suppose so

FIELDBO.

Of course.   But now if the forged bill were to
turn up—— ?

THE CHAMBERLAIN.

I will lay no information.

FIELDBO.

Naturally not ;—but you must do more.

THE CHAMBERLAIN.

[*Rising.*]   I can do no more.

FIELDBO.

Yes, for heaven's sake, you can and must.   You
must save the poor fellow——

THE CHAMBERLAIN.
In what way?

FIELDBO.
Quite simply: by acknowledging the signature.

THE CHAMBERLAIN.
Then you think, Doctor, that we stick at nothing
in our family?

FIELDBO.
I am trying to think for the best, Chamberlain.

THE CHAMBERLAIN.
And do you believe for a moment that I can
tell a lie?—that I can play into the hands of
forgers?

FIELDBO.
And do you realise what will be the consequences if you do not?

THE CHAMBERLAIN.
The offender must settle that with the law.
                    [*He goes out to the left.*

ACT FOURTH.

A public room in MADAM RUNDHOLMEN'S *hotel.
Entrance door in the back ; a smaller door on
either side. A window on the right ; before it, a
table with writing materials ; further back, in the
middle of the room, another table.*

MADAM RUNDHOLMEN.

[*Within, on the left, heard talking loudly.*] Oh,
let them go about their business ! Tell them
they've come here to vote and not to drink. If
they won't wait, they can do the other thing.

STENSGÅRD.

[*Enters by the back.*] Good-morning ! H'm, h'm,
Madam Rundholmen ! [*Goes to the door on the
left and knocks.*] Good-morning, Madam Rundholmen !

MADAM RUNDHOLMEN.

[*Within.*] Oh ! Who's there ?

STENSGÅRD.

It is I—Stensgård. May I come in ?

MADAM RUNDHOLMEN.

No, indeed you mustn't ! No ! I'm not dress'd.

STENSGÅRD.

What ? Are you so late to-day ?

MADAM RUNDHOLMEN.

Oh, I can tell you I've been up since all hours;
but one must look a little decent, you know.
[*Peeps out, with a kerchief over her head.*]   Well,
what is it ?   No, you really mustn't look at me,
Mr. Stensgård.—Oh, there's some one else !
                    [*Disappears, slamming the door to.*

ASLAKSEN.

[*Enters from the back with a bundle of papers.*]
Good morning, Mr. Stensgård.

STENSGÅRD.

Well, is it in ?

ASLAKSEN.

Yes, here it is.   Look—" The Independence
Day Celebrations—From our Special Correspon-
dent."   Here's the founding of the League on
the other side, and your speech up here.   I've
leaded all the abuse.

STENSGÅRD.

It seems to me it's all leaded.

ASLAKSEN.

Pretty nearly.

STENSGÅRD.

And the extra number was of course distributed
yesterday ?

ASLAKSEN.

Of course; all over the district, both to subscribers and others.   Would you like to see it ?
                              [*Hands him a copy.*

STENSGÅRD.

[*Running his eye over the paper.*]   " Our respected member, Mr. Lundestad, proposes to resign . . . long and faithful service . . . in the words of the poet: ' Rest, patriot, it is thy due ! ' "   H'm ! " The association founded on Independence Day: the League of Youth . . . Mr. Stensgård, the guiding intelligence of the League . . . timely reforms, credit on easier terms."   Ah, that's very good.   Has the polling begun ?

ASLAKSEN.

It's in full swing.   The whole League is on the spot—both voters and others.

STENSGÅRD.

Oh, deuce take the others—between ourselves, of course.   Well, you go down and talk to the waverers.

ASLAKSEN.

All right.

STENSGÅRD.

You can tell them that I am pretty much at one with Lundestad——

ASLAKSEN.

Trust to me ; I know the local situation.

STENSGÅRD.

One thing more ; just to oblige me, Aslaksen, don't drink to-day.

ASLAKSEN.

Oh, what do you mean—— !

STENSGÅRD.

We'll have a jolly evening when it's all over;
but remember what you, as well as I, have at
stake ; your paper—— Come, now, my good
fellow, let me see that you can——

ASLAKSEN.

There, that's enough now ; I'm old enough to
look after myself.   [*Goes out to the right.*

MADAM RUNDHOLMEN.

[*Enters from the left, elaborately dressed.*]   Now,
Mr. Stensgård, I'm at your service.   Is it anything of importance—— ?

STENSGÅRD.

No, only that I want you to be good enough to
let me know when Mr. Monsen comes.

MADAM RUNDHOLMEN.

He won't be here to-day.

STENSGÅRD.

Not to-day ?

MADAM RUNDHOLMEN.

No ; he drove past here at four this morning ;
he's always driving about nowadays.   What's
more, he came in and roused me out of bed—he
wanted to borrow money, you must know.

STENSGÅRD.

Monsen did ?

MADAM RUNDHOLMEN.

Yes.   He's a tremendous man to get through
money is Monsen.   I hope things may turn out

all right for him. And I say the same to you;
for I hear you're going into Parliament.

STENSGÅRD.

I ? Nonsense. Who told you so ?

MADAM RUNDHOLMEN.

Oh, some of Mr. Lundestad's people.

DANIEL HEIRE.

[*Enters from the back.*] Hee-hee ! Good-morning ! I'm not in the way, am I ?

MADAM RUNDHOLMEN.

Gracious, no !

HEIRE.

Good God, how resplendent ! Can it be for
me that you've got yourself up like this ?

MADAM RUNDHOLMEN.

Of course. It's for you bachelors we get ourselves up, isn't it ?

HEIRE.

For marrying men, Madam Rundholmen; for
marrying men ! Unfortunately, my law-suits take
up all my time——

MADAM RUNDHOLMEN.

Oh, nonsense; you've always plenty of time to
get married.

HEIRE.

No ; deuce take me if I have ! Marriage is a
thing you've got to give your whole mind to.
Well, well—if you can't have me, you must put
up with somebody else. For you ought to marry
again.

MADAM RUNDHOLMEN.

Now, do you know, I'm sometimes of the same opinion.

HEIRE.

Naturally; when once one has tasted the joys of matrimony—— Of course, poor Rundholmen was one in a thousand——

MADAM RUNDHOLMEN.

Well, I won't go so far as that; he was a bit rough, and rather too fond of his glass; but a husband's always a husband.

HEIRE.

Very true, Madam Rundholmen; a husband's a husband, and a widow's a widow——

MADAM RUNDHOLMEN.

And business is business. Oh, when I think of all I've got to attend to, I don't know whether I'm on my heels or my head. Every one wants to buy; but when it comes to paying, I've got to go in for summonses and executions, and Lord knows what. Upon my word, I'll soon have to engage a lawyer all to myself.

HEIRE.

I'll tell you what, Madam Rundholmen, you should retain Mr. Stensgård; he's a bachelor.

MADAM RUNDHOLMEN.

Oh, how you do talk! I won't listen to a word more.   [Goes out to the right.

HEIRE.

A substantial woman, sir! Comfortable and
well-preserved ; no children up to date ; money
well invested. Education too ; she's widely read,
sir.

STENSGÅRD.

Widely read, eh ?

HEIRE.

Hee-hee ; she ought to be ; she had charge of
Alm's circulating library for a couple of years.
But your head's full of other things to-day, I
daresay.

STENSGÅRD

Not at all ; I don't even know that I shall vote.
Who are you going to vote for, Mr. Heire ?

HEIRE.

Haven't got a vote, sir. There was only one
kennel that would qualify in the market, and that
you bought.

STENSGÅRD.

If you're at a loss for a lodging, I'll give it up
to you.

HEIRE.

Hee-hee, you're joking. Ah, youth, youth !
What a pleasant humour it has ! But now I must
be off and have a look at the menagerie. I'm
told your whole League is afoot. [*Sees* FIELDBO,
who enters from the back.] Here's the Doctor too '
I suppose you have come on a scientific mission ?

FIELDBO.

A scientific mission ?

HEIRE.

Yes, to study the epidemic; you've heard of the virulent *rabies agitatoria* that has broken out? God be with you, my dear young friends?

[*Goes out to the right.*

STENSGÅRD.

Tell me quickly—have you seen the Chamberlain to-day?

FIELDBO.

Yes.

STENSGÅRD.

And what did he say?

FIELDBO.

What did he say?

STENSGÅRD.

Yes; you know I have written to him.

FIELDBO.

Have you? What did you write?

STENSGÅRD.

That I am still of the same mind about his daughter; that I want to talk the matter over with him; and that I propose to call on him to-morrow.

FIELDBO.

If I were you, I should at least defer my visit. It is the Chamberlain's birthday to-morrow; a crowd of people will be there——

STENSGÅRD.

That's all right; the more the better.   hold big cards in my hand, let me tell you.

FIELDBO.

And perhaps you have bluffed a little with your big cards ?

STENSGÅRD.

How do you mean ?

FIELDBO.

I mean you have perhaps embellished your declaration of love with a few little threats or so ?

STENSGÅRD.

Fieldbo, you have seen the letter !

FIELDBO.

No, I assure you——

STENSGÅRD.

Well then, frankly—I have threatened him.

FIELDBO.

Ah !   Then I have, in a way, an answer to your letter.

STENSGÅRD.

An answer ?   Out with it, man !

FIELDBO.

[Shows him a sealed paper.]   Look here—the Chamberlain's proxy.

STENSGÅRD.

And who does he vote for ?

FIELDBO.

Not for you, at any rate.

STENSGÅRD.

For whom then ?   For whom ?

FIELDBO.

For the Sheriff and the Provost.[1]

STENSGÅRD.

What!   Not even for Lundestad?

FIELDBO.

No. And do you know why? Because Lundestad
is going to propose you as his successor.

STENSGÅRD.

He dares to do this!

FIELDBO.

Yes, he does. And he added : " If you see
Stensgård, you can tell him how I am voting ; it
will show him on what footing we stand."

STENSGÅRD.

Good ; since he will have it so!

FIELDBO.

Take care; it's dangerous to tug at an old
tower—it may come down on your head.

STENSGÅRD.

Oh, I have learnt wisdom in these two days.

FIELDBO.

Indeed? You're not so wise but that you let
old Lundestad lead you by the nose.

[1] "Amtmanden og provsten." The "Amtmand" is the
chief magistrate of an "Amt" or county ; the "Provst" is an
ecclesiastical functionary, perhaps equivalent to a rural dean.

STENSGÅRD.

Do you think I haven't seen through Lundestad ?
Do you think I don't understand that he took me
up because he thought I had won over the Chamberlain, and because he wanted to break up our
League and keep Monsen out ?

FIELDBO.

But now that he knows you haven't won over
the Chamberlain——

STENSGÅRD.

He has gone too far to draw back ; and I've
made good use of the time, and scattered an-
nouncements broadcast.   Most of his supporters
will abstain from voting ; mine are all here——

FIELDBO.

It's a big stride from the preliminary election
to the final election.

STENSGÅRD.

Lundestad knows very well that if he fails me
in the College of Electors, I'll soon agitate him
out of the Town Council.

FIELDBO.

Not a bad calculation.   And to succeed in all
this, you feel that you must strike root here more
firmly than you have as yet done ?

STENSGÅRD.

Yes, these people always demand material
guarantees, community of interests——

FIELDBO.

Just so ; and therefore Miss Bratsberg is to be
sacrificed ?

STENSGÅRD.

Sacrificed ? If that were so, I should be
no better than a scoundrel. But it will be for
her happiness, that I'm convinced. What now ?
Fieldbo, why do you look like that ? You have
some underhand scheme of your own——

FIELDBO.

I ?

STENSGÅRD.

Yes, you have ! You are intriguing against
me, behind my back. Why do you do that ? Be
open with me—will you ?

FIELDBO.

Frankly, I won't. You are so dangerous, so
unscrupulous—well, so reckless at any rate, that
one dare not be open with you. Whatever you
know, you make use of without hesitation. But
this I say to you as a friend : put Miss Bratsberg
out of your head.

STENSGÅRD.

I cannot. I must extricate myself from these
sordid surroundings. I can't go on living in this
hugger-mugger way. Here have I got to be hail-
fellow-well-met with Dick, Tom, and Harry ; to
whisper in corners with them, to hob-nob with
them, to laugh at their beery witticisms ; to be
hand in glove with hobbledehoys and unlicked
cubs. How can I keep my love of the People un-
tarnished in the midst of all this ? I feel as if all
the electricity went out of my words. I have no

elbow-room, no fresh air to breathe.   Oh, a longing comes over me at times for exquisite women !
I want something that brings beauty with it !   I
lie here in a sort of turbid eddy, while out there
the clear blue current sweeps past me——   But
what can you understand of all this '

LUNDESTAD.

[*Enters from the back.*]   Ah, here we are.   Good-
morning, gentlemen.

STENSGÅRD.

I have news for you, Mr. Lundestad !   Do you
know who the Chamberlain is voting for ?

FIELDBO.

Silence !   It's dishonourable of you.

STENSGÅRD.

What do I care ?   He is voting for the Sheriff
and the Provost.

LUNDESTAD.

Oh, that was to be expected.   You went and
ruined your chances with him—though I implored
you to play your cards neatly.

STENSGÅRD.

I shall play them neatly enough—in future.

FIELDBO.

Take care—two can play at that game.
                    [*Goes out to the right.*

STENSGÅRD.

That fellow has something up his sleeve.   Have
you any idea what it can be ?

LUNDESTAD.

No, I haven't.   But, by-the-bye, I see you are
flourishing in the paper to-day.

STENSGÅRD.

I ?

LUNDESTAD.

Yes, with a nice little epitaph on me.

STENSGÅRD.

Oh, that's that beast Aslaksen, of course——

LUNDESTAD.

Your attack on the Chamberlain is in too.

STENSGÅRD.

I don't know anything about that.   If it's to
be war between the Chamberlain and me, I have
sharper weapons.

LUNDESTAD.

Indeed !

STENSGÅRD.

Have you ever seen this bill ?   Look at it.   Is
it good ?

LUNDESTAD.

Good, you say ?   This bill here ?

STENSGÅRD.

Yes   look closely at it.

HEIRE.

[*Enters from the right.*]   Why, what the deuce
can be the meaning of—— Ah, how interesting !
Do remain as you are, gentlemen, I beg ! Do you

know what you irresistibly remind me of ?   Of a
summer night in the Far North.

LUNDESTAD.

That's a curious simile.

HEIRE.

A very obvious one—the setting and the rising
sun together.   Delightful, delightful !   But, talking of that, what the deuce is the matter outside
there ?   Your fellow citizens are scuttling about
like frightened fowls, cackling and crowing and
not knowing what perch to settle on.

STENSGÅRD.

Well, it's an occasion of great importance.

HEIRE.

Oh, you and your importance !   No, it's something quite different, my dear friends.   There are
whispers of a great failure ; a bankruptcy—oh,
not political, Mr. Lundestad ; I don't mean that !

STENSGÅRD.

A bankruptcy ?

HEIRE.

Hee-hee !   That puts life into our legal friend.
Yes, a bankruptcy ; some one is on his last legs ;
the axe is laid to the root of the tree——   I say
no more !   Two strange gentlemen have been seen
driving past ; but where to ?   To whose address ?
Do you know anything, Mr. Lundestad ?

LUNDESTAD.

I know how to hold my tongue, Mr. Heire.

HEIRE.

Of course; you are a statesman, a diplomatist.
But I must be off and find out all I can about it.
It's such sport with these heroes of finance : they
are like beads on a string—when one slips off, all
the rest follow.   [*Goes out by the back.*

STENSGÅRD.

Is there any truth in all this gossip ?

LUNDESTAD.

You showed me a bill ; I thought I saw young
Mr. Bratsberg's name upon it ?

STENSGÅRD.

The Chamberlain's too.

LUNDESTAD.

And you asked me if it was good ?

STENSGÅRD.

Yes ; just look at it.

LUNDESTAD.

It's perhaps not so good as it might be.

STENSGÅRD.

You see it then ?

LUNDESTAD.

What ?

STENSGÅRD.

That it is a forgery.

LUNDESTAD.

A forgery? Forged bills are often the safest; people redeem them first.

STENSGÅRD.

But what do you think? Isn't it a forgery?

LUNDESTAD.

I don't much like the look of it.

STENSGÅRD.

How so?

LUNDESTAD.

I'm afraid there are too many of these about, Mr. Stensgård.

STENSGÅRD.

What! It's not possible that—— ?

LUNDESTAD.

If young Mr. Bratsberg slips off the string, those nearest him are only too likely to follow.

STENSGÅRD.

[Seizes his arm.] What do you mean by those nearest him?

LUNDESTAD.

Who can be nearer than father and son?

STENSGÅRD.

Why, good God—— !

LUNDESTAD.

Remember, I say nothing! It was Daniel Heire that was talking of failure and bankruptcy and——

STENSGÅRD.

This is a thunderbolt to me.

LUNDESTAD.

Oh, many a man that seemed solid enough has gone to the wall before now. Perhaps he's too good-natured; goes and backs bills; ready money isn't always to be had; property has to be sold for an old song——

STENSGÅRD.

And of course this falls on—falls on the children as well.

LUNDESTAD.

Yes, I'm heartily grieved for Miss Bratsberg. She didn't get much from her mother; and heaven knows if even the little she has is secured.

STENSGÅRD.

Oh, now I understand Fieldbo's advice ! He's a true friend, after all.

LUNDESTAD.

What did Doctor Fieldbo say ?

STENSGÅRD.

He was too loyal to say anything, but I understand him all the same. And now I understand you too, Mr. Lundestad.

LUNDESTAD.

Have you not understood me before ?

STENSGÅRD.

Not thoroughly. I forgot the proverb about the rats and the sinking ship.

LUNDESTAD.

That's not a very nice way to put it. But what's the matter with you? You look quite ill. Good God, I haven't gone and blasted your hopes, have I?

STENSGÅRD.

How do you mean?

LUNDESTAD.

Yes, yes—I see it all. Old fool that I am! My dear Mr. Stensgård, if you really love the girl, what does it matter whether she is rich or poor?

STENSGÅRD.

Matter? No, of course——

LUNDESTAD.

Good Lord, we all know happiness isn't a matter of money.

STENSGÅRD.

Of course not.

LUNDESTAD.

And with industry and determination you'll soon be on your feet again. Don't let poverty frighten you. I know what love is; I went into all that in my young days. A happy home; a faithful woman——! My dear young friend, beware how you take any step that may involve you in life-long self-reproach.

STENSGÅRD.

But what will become of your plans?

LUNDESTAD.

Oh, they must go as best they can. I couldn't think of demanding the sacrifice of your heart!

STENSGÅRD.

But I will make the sacrifice. Yes, I will show
you that I have the strength for it. Think of the
longing multitude out there : they claim me with
a sort of voiceless pathos. I cannot, I dare not,
fail them !

LUNDESTAD.

Yes, but the stake in the district—— ?

STENSGÅRD.

I shall take measures to fulfil the demands of
my fellow citizens in that respect, Mr. Lundestad.
I see a way, a new way; and I will follow it up.
I renounce the happiness of toiling in obscurity
for the woman I love. I say to my fellow
countrymen : " Here I am—take me ! "

LUNDESTAD.

[*Looks at him in quiet admiration and presses his
hand.*] You are indeed a man of rare gifts, Mr.
Stensgård.   [*Goes out to the right.*
[STENSGÅRD *paces the room several times,
now stopping for a moment at the window,
now running his fingers through his hair.
Presently* BASTIAN MONSEN *enters from
the back.*

BASTIAN.

Here I am, my dear friend.[1]

STENSGÅRD.

Where have you come from?

BASTIAN.

From the Nation.

[1] Bastian now says "thou" (du) to Stensgård—*il le tutoie.*

STENSGÅRD.

The Nation? What does that mean?

BASTIAN.

Don't you know what the Nation means? It means the People; the common people; those who have nothing, and are nothing; those who lie chained——

STENSGÅRD

What monkey-tricks are these, I should like to know?

BASTIAN.

Monkey-tricks?

STENSGÅRD.

I have noticed lately that you go about mimicking me; you imitate even my clothes and my handwriting. Be kind enough to stop that.

BASTIAN.

What do you mean? Don't we belong to the same party?

STENSGÅRD.

Yes, but I won't put up with this—you make yourself ridiculous——

BASTIAN.

By being like you?

STENSGÅRD.

By aping me. Be sensible now, Monsen, and give it up. It's quite disgusting. But look here —can you tell me when your father is coming back?

BASTIAN.

I have no idea. I believe he's gone to Christiania; he may not be back for a week or so.

STENSGÅRD.

Indeed ? I'm sorry for that. He has a big stroke of business on hand, I hear.

BASTIAN.

I have a big stroke of business on hand too. Look here, Stensgård, you must do me a service.

STENSGÅRD.

Willingly.   What is it ?

BASTIAN.

I feel so full of energy. I have to thank you for that; you have stimulated me. I feel I must do something, Stensgård :—I want to get married.

STENSGÅRD.

To get married ? To whom ?

BASTIAN.

Sh ! Some one in this house.

STENSGÅRD.

Madam Rundholmen ?

BASTIAN.

Sh ! Yes, it's her. Put in a good word for me, do ! This sort of thing is just the thing for me. She's in the swim, you know ; she's on the best of terms with the Chamberlain's people, ever since her sister was housekeeper there. If I get her, perhaps I shall get the town-contracts too. So that on the whole—damn it, I love her !

STENSGÅRD.

Oh, love, love ! Have done with that sickening hypocrisy.

BASTIAN.

Hypocrisy !

STENSGÅRD.

Yes; you are lying to yourself, at any rate. You
talk in one breath of town-contracts and of love.
Why not call a spade a spade ? There's something
sordid about all this; I will have nothing to do
with it.

BASTIAN.

But listen—— !

STENSGÅRD.

Do your dirty work yourself, I say ! [*To* FIELDBO,
who enters from the right.]   Well, how goes the
election ?

FIELDBO.

Excellently for you, it appears. I saw Lundestad
just now ; he said you were getting all the votes.

STENSGÅRD.

Am I indeed ?

FIELDBO.

But what good will they do you ? Since you're
not a man of property——

STENSGÅRD.

[*Between his teeth.*]   Isn't it confounded !

FIELDBO.

Well, you can't do two things at once.   If you ·
win on the one side, you must be content to lose
on the other.   Good-bye !   [*Goes out by the back.*

BASTIAN.

What did he mean by winning and losing ?

STENSGÅRD.

I'll tell you afterwards. But now, my dear
Monsen—to return to what we were talking about
—I promised to put in a good word for you——

BASTIAN.

You promised? On the contrary, I thought you
said—— ?

STENSGÅRD.

Oh, nonsense; you didn't let me explain myself
fully. What I meant was that there is something
sordid in mixing up your love with town-contracts
and so forth; it is an offence against all that is
noblest in your nature. So, my dear friend, if you
really love the girl——

BASTIAN.

The widow——

STENSGÅRD.

Yes, yes; it's all the same. I mean when one
really loves a woman, that in itself should be a
conclusive reason——

BASTIAN.

Yes, that's just what I think. So you'll speak
for me, will you?

STENSGÅRD.

Yes, with great pleasure—but on one condition.

BASTIAN.

What's that?

STENSGÅRD.

Tit for tat, my dear Bastian—you must put in a
word for me too.

BASTIAN.

I ? With whom ?

STENSGÅRD.

Have you really not noticed anything ? Yet it's before your very nose.

BASTIAN.

You surely don't mean—— ?

STENSGÅRD.

Your sister Ragna ? Yes, it is she. Oh, you don't know how I have been moved by the sight of her quiet, self-sacrificing devotion to her home——

BASTIAN.

Do you really mean to say so ?

STENSGÅRD.

And you, with your penetrating eye, have suspected nothing ?

BASTIAN.

Yes, at one time I did think——; but now people are talking of your hanging about the Chamberlain's——

STENSGÅRD.

Oh, the Chamberlain's ! Well, Monsen, I'll tell you frankly that for a moment I did hesitate ; but, thank goodness, that is over ; now I see my way quite clear before me.

BASTIAN.

There's my hand. I'll back you up, you may be sure. And as for Ragna—why, she daren't do anything but what I and father wish.

STENSGÅRD.

Yes, but your father—that's just what I wanted to say——

BASTIAN.

Sh! There—I hear Madam Rundholmen. Now's your chance to speak for me, if she's not too busy; for then she's apt to be snappish. You do your best, my dear fellow, and leave the rest to me. Do you happen to have seen Aslaksen?

STENSGÅRD.

He's probably at the polling-booth.

[BASTIAN *goes out by the back, as* MADAM RUNDHOLMEN *enters from the right.*

MADAM RUNDHOLMEN.

Things are going as smooth as possible, Mr. Stensgård; every one is voting for you.

STENSGÅRD.

That's very odd.

MADAM RUNDHOLMEN.

Goodness knows what Monsen of Stonelee will say.

STENSGÅRD.

I want a word with you, Madam Rundholmen.

MADAM RUNDHOLMEN.

Well, what is it?

STENSGÅRD.

Will you listen to me?

MADAM RUNDHOLMEN.

Lord yes, that I will.

STENSGÅRD.

Well then : you were talking just now about being alone in the world——

MADAM RUNDHOLMEN.

Oh, it was that horrid old Heire——

STENSGÅRD.

You were saying how hard it is for an unprotected widow——

MADAM RUNDHOLMEN.

Yes, indeed; you should just try it, Mr. Stensgård !

STENSGÅRD.

But now if there came a fine young man——

MADAM RUNDHOLMEN.

A fine young man ?

STENSGÅRD.

One who had long loved you in secret——

MADAM RUNDHOLMEN.

Oh, come now, Mr. Stensgård, I won't hear any more of your nonsense.

STENSGÅRD.

You must ! A young man who, like yourself, finds it hard to be alone in the world——

MADAM RUNDHOLMEN.

Well, what then ? I don't understand you at all.

STENSGÅRD.

If you could make two people happy, Madam Rundholmen—yourself and——

MADAM RUNDHOLMEN.

And a fine young man?

STENSGÅRD.

Just so; now, answer me——

MADAM RUNDHOLMEN.

Mr. Stensgård, you can't be in earnest?

STENSGÅRD.

You don't suppose I would jest on such a subject? Should you be disposed——?

MADAM RUNDHOLMEN.

Yes, that I am, the Lord knows! Oh, you dear, sweet——

STENSGÅRD.

[*Recoiling a step.*]   What is this?

MADAM RUNDHOLMEN.

Bother, here comes some one!

RAGNA MONSEN *enters hastily, and in evident disquietude, from the back.*

RAGNA.

I beg your pardon—isn't my father here?

MADAM RUNDHOLMEN.

Your father? Yes; no;—I—I don't know—excuse me——

RAGNA.

Where is he?

MADAM RUNDHOLMEN.

Your father? Oh, he drove past here——

STENSGÅRD.

Towards Christiania.

RAGNA.

No; it's impossible——

MADAM RUNDHOLMEN.

Yes, I know for certain he drove down the road.
Oh, my dear Miss Monsen, you can't think how
happy I am! Wait a moment—I'll just run
to the cellar, and fetch up a bottle of the real
thing.   *[Goes out to the left.*

STENSGÅRD.

Tell me, Miss Monsen—is it really your father
you are looking for?

RAGNA.

Yes, of course it is.

STENSGÅRD.

And you didn't know that he had gone away?

RAGNA.

Oh, how should I know? They tell me nothing.
But to Christiania—— ? That's impossible; they
would have met him. Good-bye!

STENSGÅRD.

[*Intercepts her.*] Ragna! Tell me! Why are
you so changed towards me?

RAGNA.

I? Let me pass! Let me go!

STENSGÅRD.

No, you shall not go! I believe Providence guided you here at this moment. Oh, why do you shrink from me? You used not to.

RAGNA.

Ah, that is all over, thank God!

STENSGÅRD.

But why?

RAGNA.

I have learnt to know you better; it is well that I learned in time.

STENSGÅRD.

Oh, that is it? People have been lying about me? Perhaps I am to blame too; I have been lost in a maze of perplexities. But that is past now. Oh, the very sight of you makes a better man of me. It is you I care for, deeply and truly; it is you I love, Ragna—you and no other!

RAGNA.

Let me pass! I am afraid of you——

STENSGÅRD.

Oh, but to-morrow, Ragna—may I come and speak to you to morrow?

RAGNA.

Yes, yes, if you must; only for heaven's sake not to-day.

STENSGÅRD.

Only not to-day! Hurrah! I have won; now I am happy!

MADAM RUNDHOLMEN.

[*Enters from the left with cake and wine.*]   Come
now, we must drink a glass for luck.

STENSGÅRD

For luck in love!   Here's to love and happiness!   Hurrah for to-morrow!   [*He drinks*

HELLE.

[*Entering from the right, to* RAGNA.]   Have you
found him?

RAGNA.

No, he is not here.   Come, come!

MADAM RUNDHOLMEN.

Heaven help us, what's the matter?

HELLE.

Nothing; only some visitors have arrived at
Stonelee——

RAGNA.

Thanks for all your kindness, Madam Rundholmen——

MADAM RUNDHOLMEN.

Oh, have you got visitors on your hands again?

RAGNA.

Yes, yes; excuse me; I must go home.   Good-
bye!

STENSGÅRD.

Good-bye—till to-morrow!

        [RAGNA *and* HELLE *go out by the back*

DANIEL HEIRE *enters from the right.*

HEIRE.

Ha-ha! It's going like a house on fire! They're all cackling Stensgård, Stensgård, Stensgård! They're all plumping for you. Now you should plump for him too, Madam Rundholmen!

MADAM RUNDHOLMEN.

Hey, that's an idea! Are they all voting for him?

HEIRE.

Unanimously—Mr. Stensgård enjoys the confidence of the constituency, as the saying is. Old Lundestad is going about with a face like a pickled cucumber. Oh, it's a pleasure to see it all.

MADAM RUNDHOLMEN.

They shan't regret having voted for him. If I can't vote, I can stand treat. [*Goes out to the left.*

HEIRE.

Ah, you are the man for the widows, Mr. Stensgård! I'll tell you what—if you can only get hold of her, you're a made man, sir!

STENSGÅRD.

Get hold of Madam Rundholmen?

HEIRE.

Yes, why not? She's a substantial woman in every sense of the word. She'll be mistress of the situation as soon as the Stonelee card-castle has come to grief.

STENSGÅRD.

There's nothing wrong at Stonelee, is there?

HEIRE.

Isn't there?   You have a short memory, my
dear sir.   Didn't I tell you there were rumours
of failure, and bankruptcy, and——?

STENSGÅRD.

Well, what then?

HEIRE.

What then?   That's just what we want to know.
There's a hue and cry after Monsen; two men
have come to Stonelee——

STENSGÅRD.

Yes, I know—a couple of visitors——

HEIRE.

Uninvited visitors, my dear young friend; there
are whispers of the police and infuriated creditors
—there's something queer about the accounts, you
must know!   Talking of that—what paper was
that Monsen gave you yesterday?

STENSGÅRD.

Oh, just a paper—— Something queer about
the accounts, you say?   Look here! you know
Chamberlain Bratsberg's signature?

HEIRE.

Hee-hee!   I should rather think I did.

STENSGÅRD.

[*Produces the bill.*]   Well, look at this.

HEIRE.

Give it here—I'm rather short-sighted, you know. [*After examining it.*] That, my dear sir? That's not the Chamberlain's hand.

STENSGÅRD.

Not? Then it is—— ?

HEIRE.

And it's drawn by Monsen?

STENSGÅRD.

No, by young Mr. Bratsberg.

HEIRE.

Nonsense! Let me see. [*Looks at the paper and hands it back again.*] You can light your cigar with this.

STENSGÅRD.

What! The drawer's name too—— ?

HEIRE.

A forgery, young man; a forgery, as sure as my name's Daniel. You have only to look at it with the keen eye of suspicion——

STENSGÅRD.

But how can that be? Monsen can't have known——

HEIRE.

Monsen? No, he knows nothing about either his own paper or other people's. But I'm glad it has come to an end, Mr. Stensgård !—It's a satisfaction to one's moral sense. Ah, I have often glowed with a noble indignation, if I may say so, at

having to stand by and see—— I say no more
But the best of it all is that now Monsen is down
he'll drag young Bratsberg after him ; and the son
will bring the father down——

STENSGÅRD.

Yes, so Lundestad said.

HEIRE.

But of course there's method even in bankruptcy. You'll see ; I am an old hand at prophecy·
Monsen will go to prison; young Bratsberg will
compound with his creditors; and the Chamberlain will be placed under trustees; that's to say,
his creditors will present him with an annuity of a
couple of thousand dollars. That's how things go,
Mr. Stensgård ; I know it, I know it! What says
the classic? *Fiat justitia, pereat mundus ;* which
means : Fie on what's called justice in this wicked
world, sir !

STENSGÅRD.

[*Pacing the room.*]   One after the other!   Both
ways barred !

HEIRE.

What the deuce—— ?

STENSGÅRD.

And now too ! Just at this moment !

ASLAKSEN.

[*Enters from the right.*]   I congratulate you,
chosen of the people !

STENSGÅRD.

Elected !

ASLAKSEN.

Elected by 117 votes, and Lundestad by 53.
The rest all nowhere.

HEIRE.

Your first step on the path of glory, Mr. Stens-.
gård.

ASLAKSEN.

And it shall cost you a bowl of punch——

HEIRE.

Well, it's the first step that costs, they say.

ASLAKSEN.

[*Goes off to the left, shouting.*] Punch, Madam
Rundholmen ! A bowl of punch ! The chosen of
the people stands treat !

LUNDESTAD, *and after him several* ELECTORS,
enter from the right.

HEIRE.

[*In a tone of condolence to* LUNDESTAD.] Fifty-
three ! That's the grey-haired patriot's reward !

LUNDESTAD.

[*Whispers to* STENSGÅRD.] Are you firm in your
resolve ?

STENSGÅRD.

What's the use of being firm when everything
is tumbling about your ears ?

LUNDESTAD.

Do you think the game is lost ?

ASLAKSEN.

[*Returning by the left.*] Madam Rundholmen
stands treat herself. She says she has the best
right to.

STENSGÅRD.

· [*Struck by an idea.*] Madam Rundholmen .—has
the best right to—— !

LUNDESTAD.

What ?

STENSGÅRD.

The game is not lost, Mr. Lundestad !
[*Sits at the right-hand table and writes.*

LUNDESTAD.

[*In a low voice.*] Oh, Aslaksen—can you get
something into your next paper for me ?

ASLAKSEN.

Of course I can.   Is it libellous ?

LUNDESTAD.

No, certainly not !

ASLAKSEN.

Well, never mind ; I'll take it all the same.

LUNDESTAD.

It is my political last will and testament ; I shall
write it to-night.

A MAID-SERVANT.

[*Enters from the left.*]   The punch, with Madam
Rundholmen's compliments.

ASLAKSEN.

Hurrah! Now there's some life in the local situation.

[*He places the punch-bowl on the middle table, serves the others, and drinks freely himself during the following scene.* BASTIAN MONSEN *has meanwhile entered from the right.*

BASTIAN.

[*Softly.*] You won't forget my letter?

ASLAKSEN.

Don't be afraid. [*Taps his breast pocket.*] I have it here.

BASTIAN.

You'll deliver it as soon as you can—when you see she's disengaged, you understand.

ASLAKSEN.

I understand. [*Calls.*] Come, now, the glasses are filled.

BASTIAN.

You shan't do it for nothing, I promise you.

ASLAKSEN.

All right, all right. [*To the servant.*] A lemon, Karen—quick as the wind! [BASTIAN *retires.*

STENSGÅRD.

A word, Aslaksen; shall you be passing here to-morrow evening?

ASLAKSEN.

To-morrow evening? I can, if you like.

STENSGÅRD.

Then you might look in and give Madam Rundholmen this letter.

ASLAKSEN.

From you?

STENSGÅRD.

Yes.   Put it in your pocket.   There now.   To-
morrow evening, then?

ASLAKSEN.

All right; trust to me.
        [*The servant brings the lemon ;* STENSGÅRD
        goes towards the window.

BASTIAN.

Well — have you spoken to Madam Rundholmen?

STENSGÅRD.

Spoken?   Oh yes, I said a word or two——

BASTIAN.

And what do you think?

STENSGÅRD.

Oh—well—we were interrupted   I can't say
anything definite.

BASTIAN.

I'll take my chance all the same; she's always
complaining of her loneliness.   My fate shall be
sealed within an hour.

STENSGÅRD.

Within an hour?

BASTIAN.

[*Sees* MADAM RUNDHOLMEN, *who enters from the left.*] Sh ! Not a word to any one !
[*Goes towards the back.*

STENSGÅRD.

[*Whispers to* ASLAKSEN.] Give me back the letter.

ASLAKSEN.

Do you want it back ?

STENSGÅRD.

Yes, at once ; I shall deliver it myself.

ASLAKSEN.

Very well; here it is.
[STENSGÅRD *thrusts the letter into his pocket, and mixes with the rest.*

MADAM RUNDHOLMEN.

[*To* BASTIAN.] What do you say to the election, Mr. Bastian ?

BASTIAN.

I'm delighted. Stensgård and I are bosom friends, you know. I shouldn't be surprised if he got into Parliament.

MADAM RUNDHOLMEN.

But your father wouldn't much like that.

BASTIAN.

Oh, father has so many irons in the fire. Besides, if Stensgård's elected, it will still be all in the family, I daresay.

MADAM RUNDHOLMEN.

How so ?

BASTIAN.

He wants to marry——

MADAM RUNDHOLMEN.

Lord! Has he said anything?

BASTIAN.

Yes; and I've promised to put in a word for him. It'll be all right. I'm sure Ragna likes him.

MADAM RUNDHOLMEN.

Ragna!

LUNDESTAD.

[*Approaching.*] What is interesting you so deeply, Madam Rundholmen?

MADAM RUNDHOLMEN.

What do you think he says? Why, that Mr. Stensgård's making up to——

LUNDESTAD.

Yes, but he won't find the Chamberlain so easy to deal with.

BASTIAN.

The Chamberlain?

LUNDESTAD.

He probably thinks her too good a match for a mere lawyer——

MADAM RUNDHOLMEN.

Who? Who?

LUNDESTAD.

Why, his daughter, Miss Bratsberg, of course.

BASTIAN.

He's surely not making love to Miss Bratsberg?

LUNDESTAD.

Yes, indeed he is.

MADAM RUNDHOLMEN.

You are quite sure of that?

BASTIAN.

And he told me—— ! Oh, I want to say a word to you!

[LUNDESTAD *and* BASTIAN *go towards the back.*

MADAM RUNDHOLMEN.

[*Approaching* STENSGÅRD.] You must be on your guard, Mr. Stensgård.

STENSGÅRD.

Against whom?

MADAM RUNDHOLMEN.

Against malicious people who are slandering you.

STENSGÅRD.

Why, let them—so long as one person doesn't believe their slanders.

MADAM RUNDHOLMEN.

And who may that one person be?

STENSGÅRD.

[*Slips the letter into her hand.*] Take this; read it when you are alone.

MADAM RUNDHOLMEN.

Ah, I knew it!   [*Goes off to the left.*

RINGDAL.

[*Enters from the right.*] Well, I hear you have
won a brilliant victory, Mr. Stensgård.

STENSGÅRD.

Yes, I have, Mr. Ringdal, in spite of your noble
chief's endeavours.

RINGDAL.

His endeavours? What to do?

STENSGÅRD.

To keep me out.

RINGDAL.

Like other people, he has a right to vote as he
pleases.

STENSGÅRD.

It's a pity he is not likely to retain that right
for long.

RINGDAL.

What do you mean?

STENSGÅRD.

I mean, since his affairs are not so straight as
they might be——

RINGDAL.

His affairs! What affairs? What have you got
into your head?

STENSGÅRD.

Oh, you needn't pretend ignorance. Isn't there
a storm brewing?—a great crash impending?

RINGDAL.

Yes, so I hear on all sides.

STENSGÅRD.

And aren't both the Bratsbergs involved in it ?

RINGDAL.

My dear sir, are you crazy ?

STENSGÅRD.

Oh, you naturally want to keep it dark.

RINGDAL.

What good would that be ?   That sort of thing can't be kept dark.

STENSGÅRD.

Is it not true then ?

RINGDAL.

Not a word of it, so far as the Chamberlain is concerned.   How could you believe such nonsense ?   Who has been humbugging you ?

STENSGÅRD.

I won't tell you just yet.

RINGDAL.

Well, you needn't; but whoever it was must have had a motive.

STENSGÅRD.

A motive—— !

RINGDAL.

Yes, just think : is there no one who has an interest in keeping you and the Chamberlain apart ?

STENSGÅRD.

Yes, on my soul, but there is though !

RINGDAL.

The Chamberlain in reality thinks very highly
of you——

STENSGÅRD.

Does he ?

RINGDAL.

Yes, and that's why people want to make
mischief between you. They reckon on your
ignorance of the situation, on your impulsive-
ness and your confiding disposition——

STENSGÅRD.

Oh, the vipers ! And Madam Rundholmen has
my letter !

RINGDAL.

What letter ?

STENSGÅRD.

Oh, nothing. But it's not too late ! My dear
Mr. Ringdal, shall you see the Chamberlain this
evening ?

RINGDAL.

In all probability.

STENSGÅRD.

Then tell him to think no more of those
threats—he will understand ; tell him I shall
call to-morrow and explain everything.

RINGDAL.

You'll call ?

STENSGÅRD.

Yes, to prove to him—— Ah! a proof! Look here, Mr. Ringdal; will you give the Chamberlain this bill from me?

RINGDAL.

This bill——?

STENSGÅRD.

Yes; it's a matter I can't explain to you; but just you give it to him——

RINGDAL.

Upon my word, Mr. Stensgård——

STENSGÅRD.

And just add these words from me : This is how I treat those who vote against me!

RINGDAL.

I shan't forget.   [Goes out at the back.

STENSGÅRD.

I say, Mr. Heire—how could you go and palm off that story about the Chamberlain upon me?

HEIRE.

How could I palm it off on you——?

STENSGÅRD.

Yes—it's a lie from beginning to end.

HEIRE.

No! Is it indeed? I'm delighted to hear it. Do you hear, Mr. Lundestad? It's all a lie about the Chamberlain.

LUNDESTAD.

Sh! We were on a false scent; it's nearer at hand.

STENSGÅRD.

How nearer at hand?

LUNDESTAD.

I know nothing for certain; but they talk of Madam Rundholmen——

STENSGÅRD.

What!

HEIRE.

Haven't I prophesied it! She has been too much mixed up with our friend at Stonelee——

LUNDESTAD.

He drove off this morning before daylight——

HEIRE.

And his family is out hunting for him——

LUNDESTAD.

And the son has been doing all he knows to get his sister provided. for——

STENSGÅRD.

Provided for! "To-morrow" she said; and then her anxiety about her father——!

HEIRE.

Hee-hee! You'll see he's gone and hanged himself, sir!

ASLASKEN.

Has any one hanged himself?

LUNDESTAD.

Mr. Heire says Monsen of Stonelee——

MONSEN.

[*Enters from the back.*]   A dozen of champagne '

ASLAKSEN AND OTHERS.

Monsen !

MONSEN.

Yes, Monsen !   Champagne-Monsen !   Money-
Monsen !   Let's have the wine, confound it all !

HEIRE.

But, my dear sir——

STENSGÅRD.

Why, where have you dropped from ?

MONSEN.

I've been doing a stroke of business, sir !
Cleared a hundred thousand !   Hei !   To-morrow
I'll give a thundering dinner at Stonelee.   I invite
you all.   Champagne, I say !   I congratulate you,
Stensgård !   I hear you're elected.

STENSGÅRD. .

Yes ; I must explain to you——

MONSEN.

Pooh ; what does it matter to me ?   Wine, I
say !   Where is Madam Rundholmen ?
[*Makes a motion to go out to the left.*

THE MAID-SERVANT.

[*Who has just entered, intercepts him.*]   No one can
see the mistress just now ; she's got a letter——

BASTIAN.

Oh, damn it all !   [*Goes out by the back.*

STENSGÅRD.

Is she reading it ?

SERVANT.

Yes ; and it seems quite to have upset her.

STENSGÅRD.

Good-bye, Mr. Monsen ; dinner at Stonelee to-
morrow—— ?

MONSEN.

Yes, to-morrow.   Good-bye !

STENSGÅRD.

[*Whispers.*] Mr. Heire, will you do me a service ?

HEIRE.

Certainly, certainly.

STENSGÅRD.

Then just run me down a little to Madam Rundholmen; indulge in an innuendo or two at my
expense.   You are so good at that sort of thing.

HEIRE.

What the deuce is the meaning of this ?

STENSGÅRD.

I have my reasons.   It's a joke, you know—a
wager with—with some one you have a grudge
against.

HEIRE.

Aha, I understand.   I say no more !

STENSGÅRD.

Don't go too far, you know. Just place me in
a more or less equivocal light—make her a little
suspicious of me, for the moment.

HEIRE.

Rely upon me ; it will be a real pleasure to me.

STENSGÅRD.

Thanks, thanks in advance. [*Goes towards the
table.*] Mr. Lundestad, we shall meet to-morrow
forenoon at the Chamberlain's.

LUNDESTAD.

Have you hopes ?

STENSGÅRD.

A threefold hope.

LUNDESTAD.

Threefold ? I don't understand——

STENSGÅRD.

You needn't. Henceforth I will be my own
counsellor.   [*Goes out by the back.*

MONSEN.

[*At the punch-bowl.*] Another glass, Aslaksen !
Where's Bastian ?

ASLAKSEN.

He's just gone out. But I have a letter to
deliver for him.

MONSEN.

Have you ?

ASLAKSEN.

To Madam Rundholmen.

MONSEN.

Ah, at last !

ASLAKSEN.

But not till to-morrow evening, he said; to-
morrow evening, neither sooner nor later. Here's
to you !

HEIRE.

[*To* LUNDESTAD.]   What the deuce is all
this business between Stensgård and Madam
Rundholmen ?

LUNDESTAD.

[*Whispers.*]   He's courting her.

HEIRE.

I suspected as much !   But he asked me to run
him down a bit—to cast a slur on his character——

LUNDESTAD.

And you said you would ?

HEIRE.

Yes, of course.

LUNDESTAD.

I believe he says of you that your word is as
good as your bond—and no better.

HEIRE.

Hee-hee—the dear fellow !   He shall find out
his mistake this time.

MADAM RUNDHOLMEN.

[*With an open letter in her hand, at the door on the
left.*]   Where is Mr. Stensgård ?

HEIRE.

He kissed your chambermaid and went, Madam
Rundholmen !

ACT FIFTH.

Large reception-room at the CHAMBERLAIN'S. *Entrance
door at the back.   Doors right and left.*
RINGDAL *stands at a table looking through some
papers.   A knock.*

RINGDAL.

Come in.

FIELDBO.

[*From the back.*]   Good-morning.

RINGDAL.

Good-morning, Doctor.

FIELDBO

All well, eh?

RINGDAL.

Oh, yes, well enough ; but——

FIELDBO.

What?

RINGDAL.

Of course you've heard the great news?

FIELDBO.

No.   What is it?

RINGDAL.

Do you mean to say you haven't heard what
has happened at Stonelee.

FIELDBO.

No.

RINGDAL.

Monsen has absconded.

FIELDBO.

Absconded!   Monsen ?

RINGDAL.

Absconded.

FIELDBO.

Great heavens——!

RINGDAL.

There were ugly rumours yesterday ; but then
Monsen turned up again ; he managed to throw
dust in people's eyes——

FIELDBO.

But the reason ?   The reason ?

RINGDAL.

Enormous losses in timber, they say.   Several
houses in Christiania have stopped payment, and
so——

FIELDBO.

And so he has gone off!

RINGDAL.

To Sweden, probably.   The authorities took
possession at Stonelee this morning.   Things are
being inventoried and sealed up——

FIELDBO.

And the unfortunate children——?

RINGDAL.

The son seems to have kept clear of the business ; at least I hear he puts a bold face on it.

FIELDBO.

But the daughter ?

RINGDAL.

Sh! The daughter is here.

FIELDBO.

Here?

RINGDAL.

The tutor brought her and the two little ones here this morning. Miss Bratsberg is looking after them, quietly you know.

FIELDBO.

And how does she bear it?

RINGDAL.

Oh, pretty well, I fancy. You may guess, after the treatment she has met with at home—— And, besides, I may tell you she is——. Ah, here's the Chamberlain.

THE CHAMBERLAIN.

[*From the left.*] So you are there, my dear Doctor?

FIELDBO.

Yes, I am pretty early astir. Let me wish you many happy returns of the day, Chamberlain.

THE CHAMBERLAIN.

Oh, as for happiness——! But thank you, all the same; I know you mean it kindly.

FIELDBO.

And may I ask, Chamberlain——?

THE CHAMBERLAIN.

One word: be good enough to drop that title

FIELDBO.

What do you mean?

THE CHAMBERLAIN.

I am an ironmaster, and nothing more.

FIELDBO.

Why, what strange notion is this?

THE CHAMBERLAIN.

I have renounced my post and my title.   I am sending in my resignation to-day.

FIELDBO.

You should sleep upon that.

THE CHAMBERLAIN.

When his Majesty was graciously pleased to assign me a place in his immediate circle, he did so because of the unblemished honour of my family through long generations.

FIELDBO.

Well, what then?

THE CHAMBERLAIN.

My family is disgraced, just as much as Mr. Monsen's.   Of course you have heard about Monsen?

FIELDBO.

Yes, I have.

THE CHAMBERLAIN.

[*To* RINGDAL.]   Any further news about him?

RINGDAL.

Only that he brings down with him a good many of the younger men.

THE CHAMBERLAIN.

And my son?

RINGDAL.

Your son has sent me his balance-sheet.   He
will be able to pay in full; but there will be
nothing over.

THE CHAMBERLAIN.

H'm. Then will you get my resignation copied?

RINGDAL.

I'll see to it.

[*Goes out by the foremost door on the right.*

FIELDBO.

Have you reflected what you are doing? Things
can be arranged without any one being a bit the
wiser.

THE CHAMBERLAIN.

Indeed!   Can I make myself ignorant of what
has happened?

FIELDBO.

Oh, after all, what has happened?   Has not he
written to you, acknowledged his fault, and
begged for your forgiveness? This is the only
time he has done anything of the sort; why not
simply blot it out?

THE CHAMBERLAIN.

Would you do what my son has done?

FIELDBO.

He won't repeat it; that is the main point.

THE CHAMBERLAIN.

How do you know he will not repeat it?

FIELDBO.

If for no other reason, because of what you
yourself told me—the scene with your daughter-

in-law.   Whatever else comes of it, that will
steady him.

THE CHAMBERLAIN.

[*Pacing the room.*]   My poor Selma! Our peace
and happiness gone !

FIELDBO.

There are higher things than peace and happiness.   Your happiness has been an illusion.   Yes,
I must speak frankly to you : in that, as in many
other things, you have built on a hollow foundation.   You have been shortsighted and over-
weening, Chamberlain !

THE CHAMBERLAIN.

[*Stops short.*]   I ?

FIELDBO.

Yes, you !   You have plumed yourself on your
family honour; but when has that honour been
tried ?   Are you sure it would have stood the test ?

THE CHAMBERLAIN.

You can spare your sermons, Doctor.   Do you
think I have not learnt a lesson from the events
of these days?

FIELDBO.

I daresay you have ; but prove it, by showing
greater tolerance and clearer insight.   You reproach your son; but what have you done for
him ? You have taken care to develop his faculties,
but not to form his character.   You have lectured
him on what he owed to the honour of his family ;
but you have not guided and moulded him so that
honour became to him an irresistible instinct.

THE CHAMBERLAIN.

Do you think so ?

FIELDBO.

I not only think, I know it. But that is generally the way here : people are bent on learning,
not on living. And you see what comes of it;
you see hundreds of men with great gifts, who
never seem to be more than half ripe; who are
one thing in their ideas and feelings, and something quite different in their habits and acts.
Just look at Stensgård——

THE CHAMBERLAIN.

Ah, Stensgård now ! What do you make of
Stensgård ?

FIELDBO.

A patchwork. I have known him from childhood. His father was a mere rag of a man, a
withered weed, a nobody. He kept a little
huckster's shop, and eked things out with pawn-
broking ; or rather his wife did for him. She was a
coarse-grained woman, the most unwomanly I ever
knew. She had her husband declared incapable ;[1]
she had not an ounce of heart in her. And in that
home Stensgård passed his childhood. Then he
went to the grammar-school. " He shall go to
college," said his mother; " I'll make a smart
solicitor of him." Squalor at home, high-pressure
at school ; soul, temperament, will, talents, all
pulling in different ways—what could it lead to
but disintegration of character?

THE CHAMBERLAIN.

What could it lead to, eh ? I should like to
know what is good enough for you. We are to
expect nothing of Stensgård ; nothing of my son ;
but we may look to you, I suppose—to you—— ?

[1] " Gjort umyndig "=placed under a legal interdict.

FIELDBO.

Yes, to me—precisely. Oh, you needn't laugh ;
I take no credit to myself; but my lot has been
one that begets equilibrium and firmness of character. I was brought up amid the peace and
harmony of a modest middle-class home. My
mother is a woman of the finest type ; in our
home we had no desires that outstripped our
opportunities, no cravings that were wrecked on
the rocks of circumstance ; and death did not
break in upon our circle, leaving emptiness and
longing behind it. We were brought up in the
love of beauty, but it informed our whole view of
life, instead of being a side-interest, a thing apart.
We were taught to shun excesses, whether of the
intellect or of the feelings——

THE CHAMBERLAIN.

Bless me ! So that accounts for your being the
pink of perfection ?

FIELDBO.

I am far from thinking so. I only say that fate
had been infinitely kind to me, and that I regard
its favours in the light of obligations.

THE CHAMBERLAIN.

Very well ; but if Stensgård is under no such
obligations, it is all the more to his credit that
he——

FIELDBO.

What ? What is to his credit?

THE CHAMBERLAIN.

You have misjudged him, my good Doctor.
Look here. What do you say to this ?

FIELDBO.

Your son's bill!

THE CHAMBERLAIN.

Yes ; he has sent it to me.

FIELDBO.

Of his own accord ?

THE CHAMBERLAIN.

Of his own accord, and unconditionally.   It is
fine ; it is noble.   From this day forth, my house
is open to him.

FIELDBO.

Think again!   For your own sake, for your
daughter's——

THE CHAMBERLAIN.

Oh, let me alone!   He is better than you in
many ways.   At any rate he is straightforward,
while you are underhand in your dealings.

FIELDBO.

I ?

THE CHAMBERLAIN.

Yes, you !   You have made yourself the master
of this house ; you come and go as you please; I
consult you about everything—and yet——

FIELDBO.

Well ?—And yet?

THE CHAMBERLAIN.

And yet there's always something confoundedly
close about you ; yes, and something—something
uppish that I cannot endure !

FIELDBO.

Please explain yourself !

THE CHAMBERLAIN.

I ? No, it is you that ought to explain yourself! But now you must take the consequences.

' FIELDBO.

We don't understand each other, Chamberlain.
I have no bill to give up to you ; yet, who knows
but I may be making a greater sacrifice for your
sake ?

THE CHAMBERLAIN.

Indeed ! How so ?

FIELDBO.

By holding my tongue.

THE CHAMBERLAIN.

Holding your tongue, indeed ! Shall I tell you
what I am tempted to do ? To forget my manners,
use bad language, and join the League of Youth.
You are a stiff-necked Pharisee, my good Doctor ;
and that sort of thing is out of place in our free
society. Look at Stensgård ; he is not like that ;
so he shall come here whenever he likes ; he
shall—he shall—— ! Oh, what's the use of talking—— ! You must take the consequences ; as
you make your bed, so you must lie.

LUNDESTAD.

[*Enters from the back.*] My congratulations,
Chamberlain ! May you long enjoy the respect
and——

THE CHAMBERLAIN.

Oh, go to the devil—I'm almost inclined to
say ! That's all humbug, my dear Lundestad.
There's nothing but humbug in this world.

LUNDESTAD.

That is what Mr. Monsen's creditors are saying.

THE CHAMBERLAIN.

Ah, about Monsen—didn't it come upon you
like a thunderbolt?

LUNDESTAD.

Oh, you have often prophesied it, Chamberlain.

THE CHAMBERLAIN.

H'm, h'm ;—yes, to be sure I have. I prophesied
it only the day before yesterday ; he came here
trying to get money out of me——

FIELDBO.

It might have saved him.

LUNDESTAD.

Impossible ; he was too deep in the mire; and
whatever is, is for the best.

THE CHAMBERLAIN.

That is your opinion ?   Was it for the best, then,
that you were beaten at the poll yesterday ?

LUNDESTAD.

I wasn't beaten ; everything went just as I
wanted. Stensgård is not a man to make an
enemy of ; he has got what we others have to
whistle for.

THE CHAMBERLAIN.

I don't quite understand what you mean——?

LUNDESTAD.

He has the power of carrying people away with
him. And then he has the luck to be unhampered
by either character, or conviction, or social position ;
so that Liberalism is the easiest thing in the world
to him.

THE CHAMBERLAIN.

Well, really, I should have thought we were all Liberals.

LUNDESTAD.

Yes, of course we are Liberals, Chamberlain ; not a doubt of it.   But the thing is that we are Liberal only on our own behalf, whereas Stensgård's Liberalism extends to other people.   That's the novelty of the thing.

THE CHAMBERLAIN.

And you are going over to these subversive ideas ?

LUNDESTAD.

I've read in old story-books about people who could summon up spirits, but could not lay them again.

THE CHAMBERLAIN.

Why, my dear Lundestad, how can a man of your enlightenment—— ?

LUNDESTAD.

I know it's mere popish superstition, Chamberlain.   But new ideas are like those spirits : it's not so easy to lay them ; the best plan is to compromise with them as best you can.

THE CHAMBERLAIN.

But now that Monsen has fallen, and no doubt his crew of agitators with him——

LUNDESTAD.

If Monsen's fall had come two or three days ago, things would have been very different.

THE CHAMBERLAIN.

Yes, unfortunately.   You have been too hasty.

LUNDESTAD.

Partly out of consideration for you, Chamberlain

THE CHAMBERLAIN.

For me ?

LUNDESTAD.

Our party must keep up its reputation in the eyes of the people. We represent the old, deep-rooted Norse sense of honour. If I had deserted Stensgård, you know he holds a paper——

THE CHAMBERLAIN.

Not now.

LUNDESTAD.

What ?

THE CHAMBERLAIN.

Here it is.

LUNDESTAD.

He has given it up to you?

THE CHAMBERLAIN.

Yes. Personally, he is a gentleman ; so much I must say for him.

LUNDESTAD.

[*Thoughtfully.*]   Mr. Stensgård has rare abilities.

STENSGÅRD.

[*At the back, standing in the doorway.*]   May I come in ?

THE CHAMBERLAIN.

[*Going to meet him.*]   I am delighted to see you.

STENSGÅRD.

And you will accept my congratulations ?

THE CHAMBERLAIN.

With all my heart.

STENSGÅRD.

Then with all my heart I wish you happiness!
And you must forget all the stupid things I have
written.

THE CHAMBERLAIN.

I go by deeds, not words, Mr. Stensgård.

STENSGÅRD.

How good of you to say so!

The CHAMBERLAIN.

And henceforth—since you wish it—you must
consider yourself at home here.

STENSGÅRD.

May I? May I really?   [*A knock at the door.*

THE CHAMBERLAIN.

Come in.

Several LEADING MEN *of the neighbourhood,* TOWN
COUNCILLORS, *etc., enter.* THE CHAMBERLAIN
*goes to receive them, accepts their congratulations,
and converses with them.*

THORA.

[*Who has meantime entered by the second door on
the left.*]   Mr. Stensgård, let me thank you.

STENSGÅRD.

You, Miss Bratsberg!

THORA.

My father has told me how nobly you have
acted.

STENSGÅRD.

But——?

THORA.

Oh, how we have misjudged you!

STENSGÅRD.

Have you—— ?

THORA.

It was your own fault—— No, no; it was ours.
Oh, what would I not do to atone for our error.

STENSGÅRD.

Would you? You yourself? Would you
really—— ?

THORA.

All of us would; if we only knew——

THE CHAMBERLAIN.

Refreshments for these gentlemen, my child.

THORA.

They are just coming.

> [*She retires towards the door again, where a*
> SERVANT *at the same moment appears
> with cake and wine, which are handed
> round.*

STENSGÅRD.

Oh, my dear Lundestad! I feel like a con-
quering god.

LUNDESTAD.

So you must have felt yesterday, I suppose.

STENSGÅRD.

Pooh! This is something quite different; the
final triumph; the crown of all! There is a glory,
a halo, over my life.

LUNDESTAD.

Oho; dreams of love!

STENSGÅRD.

Not dreams!   Realities, glorious realities!

LUNDESTAD.

So brother Bastian has brought you the answer?

STENSGÅRD.

Bastian——?

LUNDESTAD.

Yes, he gave me a hint yesterday; he had promised to plead your cause with a certain young lady.

STENSGÅRD.

Oh, what nonsense——

LUNDESTAD.

Why make a mystery of it? If you haven't heard already, I can give you the news. You have won the day, Mr. Stensgård; I have it from Ringdal.

STENSGÅRD.

What have you from Ringdal?

LUNDESTAD.

Miss Monsen has accepted you.

STENSGÅRD.

What?

LUNDESTAD.

Accepted you, I say.

STENSGÅRD.

Accepted me!   And the father has bolted!

LUNDESTAD.

But the daughter hasn't.

STENSGÅRD.

Accepted me! In the midst of all this family trouble! How unwomanly! How repellant to any man with the least delicacy of feeling! But the whole thing is a misunderstanding. I never commissioned Bastian—— How could that idiot——? However, it doesn't matter to me; he must answer for his follies himself.

DANIEL HEIRE.

[*Enters from the back.*] Hee-hee! Quite a gathering! Of course, of course! We are paying our respects, propitiating the powers that be, as the saying goes. May I, too——

THE CHAMBERLAIN.

Thanks, thanks, old friend!

HEIRE.

Oh, I protest, my dear sir? That is too much condescension. [*New* GUESTS *arrive.*] Ah, here we have the myrmidons of justice—the executive—— I say no more. [*Goes over to* STENSGÅRD.] Ah, my dear fortunate youth, are you there? Your hand! Accept the assurance of an old man's unfeigned rejoicing.

STENSGÅRD.

At what?

HEIRE.

You asked me yesterday to run you down a little to her—you know——

STENSGÅRD.

Yes, yes; what then?

HEIRE.

It was a heartfelt pleasure to me to oblige you——

STENSGÅRD.

Well—and what happened then? How did she take it?

HEIRE.

Like a loving woman, of course—burst into tears; locked herself into her room; would neither answer nor show herself——

STENSGÅRD.

Ah, thank goodness!

HEIRE.

It's barbarous to subject a widow's heart to such cruel tests, to go and gloat over her jealous agonies! But love has cat's eyes—— I say no more! For to-day, as I drove past, there stood Madam Rundholmen, brisk and buxom, at her open window, combing her hair. She looked like a mermaid, if you'll allow me to say so. Oh, she's a fine woman!

STENSGÅRD.

Well, and then?

HEIRE.

Why, she laughed like one possessed, sir, and waved a letter in the air, and called out "A proposal, Mr. Heire! I'm engaged to be married."

STENSGÅRD.

What! Engaged?

HEIRE.

My hearty congratulations, young man; I'm inexpressibly pleased to be the first to announce to you ——

STENSGÅRD.

It's all rubbish! It's nonsense!

HEIRE.

What is nonsense?

STENSGÅRD.

You have misunderstood her; or else she has
misunderstood —— Engaged! Preposterous!
Now that Monsen's down, she'll probably——

HEIRE.

Not at all, sir, not at all! Madam Rundholmen
has solid legs to stand on.

STENSGÅRD.

No matter! I have quite other intentions. All
that about the letter was only a joke—a wager,
as I told you. My dear Mr. Heire, do oblige me
by not saying a word to any one of this silly
affair.

HEIRE.

I see, I see! It's to be kept secret; it's to be
a romance. Ah, youth, youth! it's nothing if not
poetical.

STENSGÅRD.

Yes, yes; mum's the word. You shan't regret
it—I'll take up your cases—— Sh! I rely upon
you.   [He retires.

THE CHAMBERLAIN.

[Who has meanwhile been talking to LUNDESTAD.]
No, Lundestad—that I really cannot believe!

LUNDESTAD.

I assure you, Chamberlain—Daniel Heire told
me so himself.

HEIRE.

What did I tell you, may I inquire?

THE CHAMBERLAIN.

Did Mr. Stensgård show you a bill yesterday?

HEIRE.

Yes, by-the-bye——! What on earth was the meaning of all that?

THE CHAMBERLAIN.

I'll tell you afterwards. And you told him——

LUNDESTAD.

You persuaded him it was a forgery?

HEIRE.

Pooh, a mere innocent jest, to bewilder him a little in the hour of triumph.

LUNDESTAD.

And you told him both signatures were forged?

HEIRE.

Oh yes; why not both while I was about it?

THE CHAMBERLAIN.

So that was it!

LUNDESTAD.

[*To the* CHAMBERLAIN.] And when he heard that——

THE CHAMBERLAIN.

He gave the bill to Ringdal!

LUNDESTAD.

The bill that was useless as a weapòn of offence.

THE CHAMBERLAIN.

He shams magnanimity! Makes a fool of me a second time! Gains admission to my house, and makes me welcome him and thank him—this—this——! And this is the fellow——

HEIRE.

Why, what are you going on about, my dear sir?

THE CHAMBERLAIN.

I'll tell you all about it afterwards. [*Takes*
LUNDESTAD *apart.*] And this is the fellow you
protect, push forward, help to rise!

LUNDESTAD.

Well, he took you in, too!

THE CHAMBERLAIN.

Oh, I should like to——!

LUNDESTAD.

[*Pointing to* STENSGÅRD, *who is speaking to* THORA.]
Look there! What will people be fancying!

THE CHAMBERLAIN.

I shall soon put a stop to these fancies.

LUNDESTAD.

Too late, Chamberlain; he'll worm himself
forward by dint of promises and general plausi-
bility——

THE CHAMBERLAIN.

I, too, can manœuvre, Mr. Lundestad.

LUNDESTAD.

What will you do?

THE CHAMBERLAIN.

Just watch. [*Goes over to* FIELDBO.] Doctor
Fieldbo, will you do me a service?

FIELDBO.

With pleasure.

THE CHAMBERLAIN.

Then turn that fellow out of my house.

FIELDBO.

Stensgård?

THE CHAMBERLAIN.

Yes, the adventurer; I hate his very name; turn him out!

FIELDBO.

But how can I—— ?

THE CHAMBERLAIN.

That is your affair; I give you a free hand.

FIELDBO.

A free hand! Do you mean it? Entirely free?

THE CHAMBERLAIN.

Yes, yes, by all means.

FIELDBO.

Your hand on it, Chamberlain!

THE CHAMBERLAIN.

Here it is.

FIELDBO.

' So be it, then; now or never! [*Loudly.*]   May I request the attention of the company for a moment?

THE CHAMBERLAIN.

Silence for Doctor Fieldbo!

FIELDBO.

With Chamberlain Bratsberg's consent, I have the pleasure of announcing my engagement to his daughter.

[*An outburst of astonishment.* THORA *utters a slight scream.* THE CHAMBERLAIN *is on the point of speaking, but refrains. Loud talk and congratulations.*

STENSGÅRD.

Engagement!   Your engagement——

HEIRE.

With the Chamberlain's——?   With your——
What does it mean?

LUNDESTAD.

Is the Doctor out of his mind?

STENSGÅRD.

But, Chamberlain——?

THE CHAMBERLAIN.

What can I do?   I am a Liberal.   I join the
League of Youth!

FIELDBO.

Thanks, thanks—and forgive me!

THE CHAMBERLAIN.

Associations are the order of the day, Mr.
Stensgård.   There is nothing like free compe-
tition!

THORA.

Oh, my dear father!

LUNDESTAD.

Yes, and engagements are the order of the day
I have another to announce.

STENSGÅRD.

A mere invention!

LUNDESTAD.

No, not a bit of it; Miss Monsen is engaged
to——

STENSGÅRD.

False, false, I say!

THORA.

No, father, it's true; they are both here.

THE CHAMBERLAIN.

Who ?   Where ?

THORA.

Ragna and Mr. Helle.   They are in here——

[*Goes towards the second door on the right.*

LUNDESTAD.

Mr. Helle!   Then it's he——!

THE CHAMBERLAIN.

Here ?   In my house ?   [*Goes towards the door.*]
Come in, my dear child.

RAGNA.

[*Shrinking back shyly.*]   Oh, no, no ; there are
so many people.

THE CHAMBERLAIN.

Don't be bashful ; you couldn't help what has
happened.

HELLE.

She is homeless now, Chamberlain.

RAGNA.

Oh, you must help us !

THE CHAMBERLAIN.

I will, indeed ; and thank you for giving me
the opportunity.

HEIRE.

You may well say engagements are the order
of the day.   I have one to add to the list.

THE CHAMBERLAIN.

What ?   You ?   At your age ?—How rash of
you !

HEIRE.

Oh—!   I say no more.

LUNDESTAD.

The game is up, Mr. Stensgård.

STENSGÅRD.

Indeed ? [*Loudly.*] *I* have one to add to the
list, Mr. Heire ! An announcement, gentlemen :
I too have cast anchor for life.

THE CHAMBERLAIN.

What ?

STENSGÅRD.

One is now and then forced to play a double
game, to conceal one's true intentions. I regard
this as permissible when the general weal is at
stake. My life-work lies clear before me, and is
all in all to me. I consecrate my whole energies
to this district; I find here a ferment of ideas
which I must strive to clarify. But this task
cannot be accomplished by a mere adventurer.
The men of the district must gather round one of
themselves. Therefore I have determined to unite
my interests indissolubly with yours—to unite
them by a bond of affection. If I have awakened
any false hopes, I must plead for forgiveness. I
too am engaged.

THE CHAMBERLAIN.

You ?

FIELDBO.

Engaged ?

HEIRE.

I can bear witness.

THE CHAMBERLAIN.

But how—— ?

FIELDBO.

Engaged ? To whom ?

LUNDESTAD.

It surely can't be—— ?

STENSGÅRD.

It is a union both of the heart and of the understanding. Yes, my fellow citizens, I am engaged to Madam Rundholmen.

FIELDBO.

To Madam Rundholmen!

THE CHAMBERLAIN.

The storekeeper's widow!

LUNDESTAD.

H'm.   Indeed!

THE CHAMBERLAIN.

Why, my head's going round!   How could you—— ?

STENSGÅRD.

A manœuvre, Mr. Bratsberg!

LUNDESTAD.

He has rare abilities!

ASLAKSEN.

[*Looks in at the door, back.*]   I humbly beg pardon——

THE CHAMBERLAIN.

Oh, come in, Aslaksen!   A visit of congratulation, eh ?

ASLAKSEN.

Oh, not at all ; I wouldn't presume—— But I have something very important to say to Mr. Stensgård.

STENSGÅRD.

Another time ; you can wait outside.

ASLAKSEN.

No, confound it ; I must tell you——

STENSGÅRD.

Hold your tongue ! What instrusiveness is this ?—Yes, gentlemen, strange are the ways of destiny. The district and I required a bond that should bind us firmly together ; and I found on my path a woman of ripened character who could make a home for me. I have put off the adventurer, gentlemen, and here I stand in your midst, as one of yourselves. Take me ; I am ready to stand or fall in any post your confidence may assign me.

LUNDESTAD.

You have won.

THE CHAMBERLAIN.

Well, really, I must say—— [*To the* MAID, *who has entered from the back.*] Well, what is it ? What are you giggling about ?

THE SERVANT.

Madam Rundholmen——?

THE COMPANY.

Madam Rundholmen ?

THE CHAMBERLAIN.

What about her ?

THE SERVANT.

Madam Rundholmen is waiting outside with her young man——

THE COMPANY.

[*To each other.*] Her young man ? Madam Rundholmen ! How's this ?

STENSGÅRD.

What nonsense!

ASLAKSEN.

Yes, I was just telling you——

THE CHAMBERLAIN.

[*At the door.*] Come along, come along!

BASTIAN MONSEN, *with* MADAM RUNDHOLMEN *on his arm, enters from the back. A general movement.*

MADAM RUNDHOLMEN.

I hope I'm not intruding, sir——

THE CHAMBERLAIN.

Not at all, not at all.

MADAM RUNDHOLMEN.

But I couldn't resist bringing up my young man to show him to you and Miss Bratsberg.

THE CHAMBERLAIN.

Yes, I hear you are engaged; but——

THORA.

We didn't know——

STENSGÅRD.

[*To* ASLAKSEN.] How is all this——?

ASLAKSEN.

I had so much in my head yesterday; so much to think about, I mean——

STENSGÅRD.

But I gave her my letter, and——

ASLAKSEN.

No, you gave her Bastian Monsen's; here is yours.

STENSGÅRD.

Bastian's? And here——? [*Glances at the address, crumples the letter together, and crams it into his pocket.*] Oh, curse you for a blunderer!

MADAM RUNDHOLMEN.

Of course I was willing enough. There's no trusting the men folk, I know; but when you have it in black and white that their intentions are honourable—— Why, there's Mr. Stensgård, I declare. Well, Mr. Stensgård, won't you congratulate me?

HEIRE.

[*To* LUNDESTAD.] How hungrily she glares at him.

THE CHAMBERLAIN.

Of course he will, Madam Rundholmen; but won't you congratulate your sister-in-law to be?

MADAM RUNDHOLMEN.

Who?

THORA.

Ragna; she is engaged too.

BASTIAN.

Are you, Ragna?

MADAM RUNDHOLMEN.

Indeed? Yes, Bastian told me there was something in the wind. I wish you both joy; and welcome into the family, Mr. Stensgård!

FIELDBO.

No, no; not Stensgård!

THE CHAMBERLAIN.

No, it's Mr. Helle; an excellent choice. And, by-the-bye, you may congratulate my daughter too.

MADAM RUNDHOLMEN.

Miss Bratsberg ! Ah, so Lundestad was right, after all. I congratulate you, Miss Thora; and you too, Mr. Stensgård.

FIELDBO.

You mean Doctor Fieldbo.

MADAM RUNDHOLMEN.

What ?

FIELDBO.

I am the happy man.

MADAM RUNDHOLMEN.

Well, now, I don't in the least know where I am.

THE CHAMBERLAIN.

And we have just found out where we are.

STENSGÅRD.

Excuse me ; I have an appointment——

THE CHAMBERLAIN.

[*Aside.*] Lundestad, what was the other word ?

LUNDESTAD.

What other ?

THE CHAMBERLAIN.

Not adventurer, but the other—— ?

LUNDESTAD.

Demagogue.

STENSGÅRD.

I take my leave.

THE CHAMBERLAIN.

One word—only one word, Mr. Stensgård—a word which has long been on the tip of my tongue.

STENSGÅRD.

At the door.] Excuse me; I'm in a hurry.

THE CHAMBERLAIN.

[*Following him.*] Demagogue!

STENSGÅRD.

Good-bye; good-bye!   [*Goes out by the back.*

THE CHAMBERLAIN.

[*Coming forward again.*] Now the air is pure again, my friends.

BASTIAN.

I hope you don't blame me, sir, for what has happened at home?

THE CHAMBERLAIN.

Every one must bear his own burden.

BASTIAN.

I had really no part in it.

SELMA.

[*Who, during the preceding scene, has been listening at the second door on the right.*] Father! Now you are happy;—may he come now?

THE CHAMBERLAIN.

Selma! You! You plead for him? After what happened two days ago——

SELMA.

Oh, two days are a long time   All is well now. I know now that he can go astray——

THE CHAMBERLAIN.

And that pleases you?

SELMA.

Yes, that he can ; but in future I won't let him.

THE CHAMBERLAIN.

Bring him in then.

[SELMA *goes out again to the right.*

RINGDAL.

[*Enters by the foremost door on the right.*]   Here is your resignation.

THE CHAMBERLAIN.

Thanks ; but you can tear it up.

RINGDAL.

Tear it up ?

THE CHAMBERLAIN.

Yes, Ringdal ; I have found another way.   I can make atonement without that; I shall set to work in earnest——

ERIK.

[*Enters with* SELMA *from the right.*]   Can you forgive me ?

THE CHAMBERLAIN.

[*Hands him the bill.*]   I cannot be less merciful than fate.

ERIK.

Father !   I shall retire this very day from the business you dislike so much.

THE CHAMBERLAIN.

No, indeed ; you must stick to it.   No cowardice ! No running away from temptation !   But I will stand at your side.   [*Loudly.*]   News for you, gentlemen !   I have entered into partnership with my son.

SEVERAL GENTLEMEN.

What ?   You, Chamberlain ?

HEIRE.

You, my dear sir ?

THE CHAMBERLAIN.

Yes ; it is a useful and honourable calling ; or
at any rate it can be made so.   And now I have
no reason to hold aloof any longer.

LUNDESTAD.

Well, I'll tell you what, Chamberlain—since
you are going to set to work for the good of the
district, it would be a shame and disgrace if an old
soldier like me were to sulk in his tent.

ERIK.

Ah, what is this ?

LUNDESTAD.

I cannot, in fact.   After the disappointments
in love that have befallen Mr. Stensgård to-day,
Heaven forbid we should force the poor fellow
into the political mill.   He must rest and recover ;
a change of air is what he wants, and I shall see
that he gets it.   So if my constituents want me,
why, they can have me.

THE GENTLEMEN.

[*Shaking hands with him enthusiastically.*]   Thanks,
Lundestad !   That's a good fellow !   You won't
fail us ?

THE CHAMBERLAIN.

Now, this is as it should be ; things are settling
down again.   But whom have we to thank for all
this ?

FIELDBO.

Come, Aslaksen, you can explain——?

ASLAKSEN.

[*Alarmed.*] I, Doctor ? I'm as innocent as the
babe unborn !

FIELDBO.

What about that letter, then——— ?

ASLAKSEN.

It wasn't my fault, I tell you ! It was the
election and Bastian Monsen, and chance, and
destiny, and Madam Rundholmen's punch—there
was no lemon in it—and there was I, with the
whole responsibility of the press upon me———

THE CHAMBERLAIN.

[*Approaching.*] What ? What's that ?

ASLAKSEN.

The press, sir !

THE CHAMBERLAIN.

The press ! That's just it ! Haven't I always
said that the press has marvellous influence in
these days ?

ASLAKSEN.

Oh, Chamberlain———

THE CHAMBERLAIN.

No false modesty, Mr. Aslaksen ! I haven't
hitherto been in the habit of reading your paper,
but henceforth I will. I shall subscribe for ten
copies.

ASLAKSEN.

Oh, you can have twenty, Chamberlain !

THE CHAMBERLAIN.

Very well, then ; let me have twenty. And if
you need money, come to me ; I mean to support

the press; but I tell you once for all—I won't write for it.

RINGDAL.

What's this I hear? Your daughter engaged?

THE CHAMBERLAIN.

Yes; what do you say to that?

RINGDAL.

I am delighted! But when was it arranged?

FIELDBO.

[*Quickly*.] I'll tell you afterwards——

THE CHAMBERLAIN.

Why, it was arranged on the Seventeenth of May.

FIELDBO.

What?

THE CHAMBERLAIN.

The day little Miss Ragna was here.

THORA.

Father, father; did you know——?

THE CHAMBERLAIN.

Yes, my dear; I have known all along.

FIELDBO.

Oh, Chamberlain——!

THORA.

Who can have——?

THE CHAMBERLAIN.

Another time, I should advise you young ladies not to talk so loud when I am taking my siesta in the bay window.

THORA.

Oh ! so you were behind the curtains ?

FIELDBO.

Now I understand !

THE CHAMBERLAIN.

Yes, you are the one to keep your own counsel——

FIELDBO.

Would it have been of any use for me to speak earlier ?

THE CHAMBERLAIN

You are right, Fieldbo. These days have taught me a lesson.

THORA.

[*Aside to* FIELDBO.] Yes, you can keep your own counsel. All this about Mr. Stensgård—why did you tell me nothing ?

FIELDBO.

When a hawk is hovering over the dove-cote, one watches and shields his little dove—one does not alarm her.

[*They are interrupted by* MADAM RUNDHOL-MEN.

HEIRE.

[*To the* CHAMBERLAIN.] I'm sorry to tell you, Chamberlain, that the settlement of our little legal differences will have to be adjourned indefinitely.

THE CHAMBERLAIN.

Indeed ! Why so ?

HEIRE.

You must know I've accepted a post as society reporter on Aslaksen's paper.

THE CHAMBERLAIN.
I am glad to hear it.

HEIRE.
And of course you'll understand—with so much business on hand——

THE CHAMBERLAIN.
Very well, my old friend; I can wait.

MADAM RUNDHOLMEN.
[*To* THORA.] Yes, I can tell you he's cost me many a tear, that bad man. But now I thank the Lord for Bastian. The other was false as the sea-foam; and then he's a terrible smoker, Miss Bratsberg, and frightfully particular about his meals. I found him a regular gourmand.

A SERVANT.
[*Enters from the left.*] Dinner is on the table.

THE CHAMBERLAIN.
Come along, then, all of you. Mr. Lundestad, you shall sit beside me; and you too, Mr. Aslaksen.

RINGDAL.
We shall have a lot of toasts to drink after dinner!

HEIRE.
Yes; and perhaps an old man may be allowed to put in a claim for the toast of "Absent Friends."

LUNDESTAD.
One absent friend will return, Mr. Heire.

HEIRE.
Stensgård?

LUNDESTAD.

Yes; you'll see, gentlemen! In ten or fifteen years, Stensgård will either be in Parliament or in the Ministry—perhaps in both at once.[1]

FIELDBO.

In ten or fifteen years? Perhaps; but then he can scarcely stand at the head of the League of Youth.

HEIRE.

Why not?

FIELDBO.

Why, because by that time his youth will be—questionable.

HEIRE.

Then he can stand at the head of the Questionable League, sir. That's what Lundestad means. He says like Napoleon—"It's the questionable people that make politicians"; hee-hee!

FIELDBO.

Well, after all is said and done, our League shall last through young days and questionable days as well; and it shall continue to be the League of Youth. When Stensgård founded his League, and was carried shoulder-high amid all the enthusiasm of Independence Day, he said—"Providence is on the side of the League of Youth." I think even Mr. Helle, theologian as he is, will let us apply that saying to ourselves.

[1] When this play was written, Ministers did not sit in the Storthing, and were not responsible to it. This state of things was altered—as Ibsen here predicts—in the great constitutional struggle of 1872–84, which ended in the victory of the Liberal party, their leader, Johan Sverdrup, becoming Prime Minister.

THE CHAMBERLAIN.

I think so too, my friends; for truly we have
been groping and stumbling in darkness; but
good angels guided us.

LUNDESTAD.

Oh, for that matter, I think the angels were
only middling.

ASLAKSEN.

Yes; that comes of the local situation, Mr.
Lundestad.

THE END.

PILLARS OF SOCIETY
(1877)

CHARACTERS.

CONSUL BERNICK.

MRS. BERNICK, *his wife.*

OLAF, *their son, a boy of thirteen.*

MISS BERNICK [MARTHA], *the Consul's sister.*

JOHAN TÖNNESEN, *Mrs. Bernick's younger brother.*

MISS HESSEL [LONA], *her elder step-sister.*

HILMAR TÖNNESEN, *Mrs. Bernick's cousin.*

DOCTOR RÖRLUND, *a schoolmaster.*

RUMMEL,
VIGELAND, } *Merchants.*
SANDSTAD,

DINA DORF, *a young girl living in the Consul's house.*

KRAP, *the Consul's chief clerk.*

AUNE, *a foreman shipbuilder.*

MRS. RUMMEL.

MRS. POSTMASTER HOLT.

MRS. DOCTOR LYNGE.

MISS RUMMEL.

MISS HOLT.

Townspeople and others, foreign sailors, steamboat passengers, etc.

The action takes place in Consul Bernick's house, in a small Norwegian seaport.

Pronunciation of Names: Rörlund = Rörloond ; Dina = Deena ; Rummel=Roomel ; Vigeland=Veeghёland ; Aune= Ownё ; Lynge=Lynghё. The modified " ö " is pronounced much as in German.

PILLARS OF SOCIETY.

ACT FIRST.

A spacious garden-room in CONSUL BERNICK'S *house.
In front, to the left, a door leads into the Consul's
office ; farther back, in the same wall, a similar
door. In the middle of the opposite wall is a
large entrance door. The back wall is almost
entirely composed of plate-glass, with an open
doorway leading to a broad flight of steps,[1] over
which a sun-shade is let down. Beyond the
steps a part of the garden can be seen, enclosed
by a railing with a little gate. Beyond the
railing, and running parallel with it, is a street
of small, brightly painted wooden houses. It is
summer, and the sun shines warmly. Now and
then people pass along the street : they stop and
speak to each other : customers come and go at
the little corner shop, and so forth.*
*In the garden-room a number of ladies are gathered
round a table. At the head of the table sits*
MRS. BERNICK. *On her left sit* MRS. HOLT
and her daughter ; next to them, MRS. *and* MISS
RUMMEL. *On* MRS. BERNICK'S *right sit* MRS.

---

[1] "Havetrappe" here seems to imply a flight of steps with
so wide a landing at the top as practically to form a verandah,
under the sun-shade. In subsequent stage directions, the word
is rendered by "verandah."

LYNGE, MISS BERNICK (MARTHA), *and* DINA DORF. *All the ladies are busy sewing. On the table lie large heaps of half-finished and cut-out linen, and other articles of clothing. Farther back, at a little table on which are two flower-pots and a glass of* eau sucré, *sits* DOCTOR RÖRLUND, *reading from a book with gilt edges, a word here and there being heard by the audience. Out in the garden* OLAF BERNICK *is running about, shooting at marks with a crossbow.*

Presently AUNE, *the foreman shipbuilder, enters quietly by the door on the right. The reading ceases for a moment ;* MRS. BERNICK *nods to him and points to the left-hand door.* AUNE *goes quietly to the Consul's door, knocks softly, pauses a moment, then knocks again.* KRAP, *the Consul's clerk, opens the door and comes out with his hat in his hand and papers under his arm.*

KRAP.

Oh, it's you knocking?

AUNE.

The Consul sent for me.

KRAP.

Yes; but he can't see you just now ; he has commissioned me——

AUNE.

You ? I'd a deal sooner——

KRAP.

——commissioned me to tell you this : You must stop these Saturday lectures to the workmen.

AUNE.

Indeed? I sort of thought my free time was my own to——

KRAP.

Not to make the men useless in work-time. Last Saturday you must needs hold forth about the harm that will be done to the workmen by our machines and new method of work. What makes you do that?

AUNE.

I do it to support society.

KRAP.

That's an odd notion! The Consul says you are undermining society.

AUNE.

My "society" is not the Consul's "society," Mr. Krap! Seeing as I'm the foreman of the Industrial Society, I have to——

KRAP.

Your first duty is as foreman of Consul Bernick's shipyard. Your first duty is to the society called Bernick & Co., for by it we all live.—Well, now you know what the Consul wanted to say to you.

AUNE.

The Consul wouldn't have said it like that, Mr. Krap! But I know well enough what I've got to thank for this. It's that cursèd American that has put in for repairs. These people think work can be done here as they do it over there, and that——

KRAP.

Well, well—I have no time to go into generalities. I have told you the Consul's wishes, and

that is enough.   Now you had better go down to
the yard again ; you re sure to be wanted ; I shall
be down myself presently.—I beg your pardon,
ladies !

> [*He bows, and goes out through the garden
> and down the street.   AUNE goes quietly
> out to the right.   DOCTOR RÖRLUND, who
> during the whole of the foregoing conver-
> sation has continued reading, presently
> closes the book with a bang.*

RÖRLUND.

There, my dear ladies, that is the end.

MRS. RUMMEL.

Oh, what an instructive tale!

MRS. HOLT.

And so moral!

MRS. BERNICK.

Such a book really gives one a great deal to
think over.

RÖRLUND.

Yes ; it forms a refreshing contrast to what we
unhappily see every day, both in newspapers and
magazines.   The rouged and gilded exterior
flaunted by the great communities—what does it
really conceal ?   Hollowness and rottenness, if I
may say so.   They have no moral foundation
under their feet.   In one word—they are whited
sepulchres, these great communities of the modern
world.

MRS. HOLT.

Too true ! too true !

MRS. RUMMEL.

We have only to look at the crew of the American ship that's lying here.

RÖRLUND.

Oh, I won't speak of such scum of humanity. But even in the higher classes—how do matters stand?   Doubt and fermenting unrest on every side; the soul at war with itself; insecurity in every relation of life.   See how the family is undermined!—how a brazen spirit of subversion is assailing the most vital truths!

DINA.

[*Without looking up.*]   But many great things are done there too, are they not?

RÖRLUND.

Great things—— ?   I don't understand——

MRS. HOLT.

[*Astonished.*]   Good heavens, Dina——!

MRS. RUMMEL.

[*At the same time.*]   Oh, Dina, how can you?

RÖRLUND.

It would scarcely be for our good if such "great things" came into fashion among us.   No; we ought to thank God that our lot is ordered as it is. A tare, alas! will now and then spring up among the wheat; but we honestly do our best to weed it out. The great point, ladies, is to keep society pure—to exclude from it all the questionable elements which an impatient age would force upon us.

MRS. HOLT.

Ah, there's more than enough of that sort of thing, unfortunately.

MRS. RUMMEL.

Yes; last year we only escaped the railway by a hair's-breadth.

MRS. BERNICK.

Karsten managed to put a stop to that.

RÖRLUND.

Providentially, Mrs. Bernick! You may be sure your husband was an instrument in a higher hand when he refused to support that scheme.

MRS. BERNICK.

And yet the papers said such horrid things about him! But we are quite forgetting to thank you, my dear Doctor. It is really more than kind of you to sacrifice so much of your time to us.

RÖRLUND.

Oh, not at all; in holiday-time, you know——

MRS. BERNICK.

Yes, yes; but it's a sacrifice, nevertheless.

RÖRLUND.

[*Drawing his chair nearer.*] Pray don't speak of it, dear lady. Do not all of you make sacrifices for a good cause? And do you not make them willingly and gladly? The Lapsed and Lost, for whom we are working, are like wounded soldiers on a battlefield; you, ladies, are the Red Cross Guild, the Sisters of Mercy, who pick lint for these unhappy sufferers, tie the bandages gently round the wounds, dress, and heal them——

MRS. BERNICK.

It must be a great blessing to see everything in so beautiful a light.

RÖRLUND.

The gift is largely inborn ; but it can in some measure be acquired. The great point is to see things in the light of a serious vocation. What do you say, Miss Bernick ? Do you not find that you have, as it were, firmer ground under your feet since you have devoted your life to your school-work ?

MARTHA.

I scarcely know what to say. Often, when I am pent up in the schoolroom, I wish I were far out upon the stormy sea.

RÖRLUND.

Yes, yes; that is temptation, my dear Miss Bernick. You must bar the door against such an unquiet guest. The stormy sea—of course you do not mean that literally ; you mean the great billowing world, where so many go to wreck. And do you really find so much to attract you in the life you hear rushing and surging outside ? Just look out into the street. Look at the people in the sweltering sunshine, toiling and moiling over their paltry affairs! Ours, surely, is the better part, sitting here in the pleasant shade, and turning our backs toward the quarter from which disturbance might arise.

MARTHA.

Yes, no doubt you are quite right——

RÖRLUND.

And in a house like this—in a good and pure home, where the Family is seen in its fairest shape—where peace and unity reign—— [*To* MRS. BERNICK.] What are you listening to, Mrs. Bernick?

MRS. BERNICK.

[*Who has turned towards the door of the Consul's room.*] How loudly they are talking in there!

RÖRLUND.

Is anything particular going on?

MRS. BERNICK.

I don't know. There is evidently some one with my husband.

HILMAR TÖNNESEN, *with a cigar in his mouth, comes in by the door on the right, but stops on seeing so many ladies.*

HILMAR.

Oh, I beg your pardon—— [*Turning to go.*

MRS. BERNICK.

Come in, Hilmar, come in; you are not disturbing us. Do you want anything?

HILMAR.

No, I just happened to be passing. Good-morning, ladies. [*To* MRS. BERNICK.] Well, what is going to come of it?

MRS. BERNICK.

Of what?

HILMAR.

You know Bernick has called a cabinet council.

MRS. BERNICK.

Indeed ! What is it about ?

HILMAR.

Oh, this railway nonsense again.

MRS. RUMMEL.

No ! Is it possible ?

MRS. BERNICK.

Poor Karsten—is he to have all that worry over again——?

RÖRLUND.

Why, what can be the meaning of this, Mr. Tönnesen ? Consul Bernick gave it plainly to be understood last year that he would have no railway here.

HILMAR.

Yes, I thought so too ; but I met Krap just now, and he told me the railway question was to the fore again, and that Bernick was holding a conference with three of our capitalists.

MRS. RUMMEL.

I was certain I heard Rummel's voice.

HILMAR.

Yes, Mr. Rummel is there, of course, and Sandstad and Michael Vigeland—" Holy Michael," as they call him.

RÖRLUND.

H'm——

HILMAR.

I beg your pardon, Doctor.

Mrs. Bernick.

Just when everything was so nice and quiet too !

Hilmar.

Well, for my part, I shouldn't mind their beginning their bickerings again. It would be a variety at least.

Rörlund.

I think we can dispense with that sort of variety.

Hilmar.

It depends upon one's constitution. Some natures crave for a Titanic struggle now and then. But there's no room for that sort of thing in our petty provincial life, and it's not every one that can—— [*Turning over the leaves of* Rörlund's *book.*] "Woman as the Servant of Society"—what rubbish is this !

Mrs. Bernick.

Oh, Hilmar, you mustn't say that. You have surely not read the book.

Hilmar.

No, and don't intend to.

Mrs. Bernick.

You seem out of sorts to-day.

Hilmar.

Yes, I am.

Mrs. Bernick.

Perhaps you didn't sleep well last night ?

Hilmar.

No, I slept very badly. I went a walk yesterday evening, by my doctor's orders. Then I looked in at the club, and read an account of a polar expedition. There is something bracing in watching men at war with the elements.

MRS. RUMMEL.

But it doesn't seem to have agreed with you, Mr. Tönnesen?

HILMAR.

No, it didn't agree with me at all. I lay tossing all night half asleep, and dreamt I was being chased by a horrible walrus.

OLAF.

[*Who has come up the garden steps.*] Have you been chased by a walrus, Uncle?

HILMAR.

I dreamt it, little stupid! Do you still go on playing with that ridiculous bow? Why don't you get hold of a proper gun?

OLAF.

Oh, I should love to, but——

HILMAR.

There would be some sense in a gun; the very act of pulling the trigger braces your nerves.

OLAF.

And then I could shoot bears, Uncle. But father won't let me.

MRS. BERNICK.

You really must not put such ideas into his head, Hilmar.

HILMAR.

Ha—there we have the rising generation nowadays! Goodness knows there's plenty of talk

about pluck and daring, but it all ends in play;
no one has any real craving for the discipline that
lies in looking danger manfully in the face. Don't
stand and point at me with your bow, stupid; it
might go off.

OLAF.

No, Uncle, there's no bolt in it.

HILMAR.

How do you know? There may very likely be
a bolt in it. Take it away, I tell you!—Why the
deuce have you never gone to America in one of
your father's ships? There you could go buffalo-
hunting or fighting the redskins.

MRS. BERNICK.

Oh, Hilmar——

OLAF.

I should like to very much, Uncle; and then
perhaps I might meet Uncle Johan and Aunt
Lona.

HILMAR.

H'm—don't talk nonsense.

MRS. BERNICK.

Now you can go down the garden again, Olaf.

OLAF.

Mayn't I go out into the street, mother?

MRS. BERNICK.

Yes; but take care not to go too far.
        [OLAF *runs out through the garden gate.*

RÖRLUND.

You ought not to put such notions into the
child's head, Mr. Tönnesen.

HILMAR.

No, of course, he's to be a mere stick-in-the-mud, like so many others.

RÖRLUND.

Why do you not go to America yourself?

HILMAR.

I? With my complaint? Of course no one here has any consideration for that. But besides —one has duties towards the society one belongs to. There must be some one to hold high the banner of the ideal. Ugh, there he is shouting again!

THE LADIES.

Who is shouting?

HILMAR.

Oh, I don't know. They are talking rather loud in there, and it makes me so nervous.

MRS. RUMMEL.

It is my husband you hear, Mr. Tönnesen; you must remember he is so accustomed to addressing great assemblies——

RÖRLUND.

The others are not whispering either, it seems to me.

HILMAR.

No, sure enough, when it's a question of keeping the purse-strings tight——; everything here ends in paltry material calculations. Ugh!

MRS. BERNICK.

At least that is better than it used to be, when everything ended in dissipation.

MRS. LYNGE.

Were things really so bad as all that?

MRS. RUMMEL.

They were as bad as bad could be, Mrs. Lynge. You may thank your stars that you didn't live here then.

MRS. HOLT.

Yes, there has certainly been a great change! When I think of the time when I was a girl——

MRS. RUMMEL.

Oh, you needn't go back more than fourteen or fifteen years—heaven help us, what a life people led! There was a dancing club and a music club——

MARTHA.

And the dramatic club—I remember it quite well.

MRS. RUMMEL.

Yes; it was there your play was acted, Mr. Tönnesen.

HILMAR.

[At the back.] Oh, nonsense——!

RÖRLUND.

Mr. Tönnesen's play?

MRS. RUMMEL.

Yes; that was long before you came here, Doctor. Besides, it only ran one night.

MRS. LYNGE.

Wasn't it in that play you told me you played the heroine, Mrs. Rummel?

MRS. RUMMEL.

[*Glancing at* RÖRLUND.] I? I really don't remember, Mrs. Lynge. But I remember too well all the noisy gaiety that went on among families.

MRS. HOLT.

Yes; I actually know houses where two great dinner-parties were given in one week.

MRS. LYNGE.

And then there was a company of strolling actors, they tell me.

MRS. RUMMEL.

Yes, that was the worst of all——!

MRS. HOLT.

[*Uneasily.*] H'm, h'm——

MRS. RUMMEL.

Oh, actors did you say? No, I remember nothing about them.

MRS. LYNGE.

Why, I was told they caused all sorts of trouble. What was it that really happened?

MRS. RUMMEL.

Oh, nothing at all, Mrs. Lynge.

MRS. HOLT.

Dina, dear, hand me that piece of linen, please.

MRS. BERNICK.

[*At the same time.*] Dina, my love, will you go and ask Katrina to bring in the coffee.

MARTHA.

I will go with you, Dina.

> [DINA *and* MARTHA *go out by the second door on the left.*

MRS. BERNICK.

[*Rising.*] And you must excuse me for a moment, ladies; I think we had better take our coffee outside.

> [*She goes out to the verandah and begins arranging a table;* RÖRLUND *stands in the doorway talking to her.* HILMAR *sits outside smoking.*

MRS. RUMMEL.

[*Softly.*] Oh dear, Mrs. Lynge, how you frightened me!

MRS. LYNGE.

I?

MRS. HOLT.

Ah, but you began it yourself, Mrs. Rummel.

MRS. RUMMEL.

I? Oh, how can you say so, Mrs. Holt? Not a single word passed my lips.

MRS. LYNGE.

But what is the matter?

MRS. RUMMEL.

How could you begin to talk about——! Only think—didn't you see that Dina was in the room?

MRS. LYNGE.

Dina? Why, bless me! what has she to do with——?

MRS. HOLT.

Here, in this house, too! Don't you know
that it was Mrs. Bernick's brother——?

MRS. LYNGE.

What about him? I know nothing at all;
remember I am quite new to the town——

MRS. RUMMEL.

Then you haven't heard that——? H'm——
[*To her daughter.*] You can go down the garden
for a little while, Hilda.

MRS. HOLT.

You too, Netta. And be sure you are very
kind to poor Dina when she comes.
            [MISS RUMMEL *and* MISS HOLT *go out into
                the garden.*

MRS. LYNGE.

Well, what about Mrs. Bernick's brother?

MRS. RUMMEL.

Don't you know, he was the hero of the scandal?

MRS. LYNGE.

Mr. Hilmar the hero of a scandal!

MRS. RUMMEL.

Good heavens, no; Hilmar is her cousin Mrs.
Lynge. I am speaking of her brother——

MRS. HOLT.

The Prodigal Tönnesen——

MRS. RUMMEL.

Johan was his name. He ran away to America.

MRS. HOLT.

Had to run away, you understand.

MRS. LYNGE.

Then the scandal was about him?

MRS. RUMMEL.

Yes, it was a sort of—what shall I call it?—a sort of a—with Dina's mother. Oh, I remember it as if it were yesterday. Johan Tönnesen was in old Mrs. Bernick's office; Karsten Bernick had just come home from Paris—it was before his engagement——

MRS. LYNGE.

Yes, but the scandal——?

MRS. RUMMEL.

Well, you see, that winter Möller's comedy company was in the town——

MRS. HOLT.

——and in the company were Dorf and his wife. All the young men were mad about her.

MRS. RUMMEL.

Yes, heaven knows what they could see in her. But one evening Dorf came home very late——

MRS. HOLT.

——and quite unexpectedly——

MRS. RUMMEL.

And there he found—no, really I don't think I can tell you.

MRS. HOLT.

Why, you know, Mrs. Rummel, he found nothing, for the door was locked on the inside.

Mrs. Rummel.

Yes; that's what I say—he found the door
locked.   And—only think!—some one inside had
to jump out of the window.

Mrs. Holt.

Right from the attic window!

Mrs Lynge.

And it was Mrs. Bernick's brother?

Mrs. Rummel.

Of course it was.

Mrs. Lynge.

And that was why he ran away to America?

Mrs. Holt.

He had to make himself scarce, I can assure you.

Mrs. Rummel.

For afterwards something else was found out,
almost as bad.   Only think, he had been making
free with the cash-box——

Mrs. Holt.

But, after all, no one knows exactly about that
Mrs. Rummel ; it may have been mere gossip.

Mrs. Rummel.

Well, I really must say——!   Wasn't it known
over the whole town?   For that matter, wasn't
old Mrs. Bernick on the point of going bankrupt?
Rummel himself has told me that.   But heaven
forbid *I* should say anything!

Mrs. Holt.

Well, the money didn't go to Madam Dorf, at
any rate, for she——

MRS. LYNGE.

Yes, what became of Dina's parents?

MRS. RUMMEL.

Oh, Dorf deserted both wife and child. But Madam was impudent enough to remain here a whole year. She didn't dare to show herself in the theatre again; but she made a living by washing and sewing——

MRS. HOLT.

And she tried to set up a dancing-school.

MRS. RUMMEL.

Of course it was a failure. What parents could trust their children with such a person? But she could not hold out long; the fine Madam wasn't accustomed to work, you see; some chest trouble set in, and carried her off.

MRS. LYNGE.

What a wretched story!

MRS. RUMMEL.

Yes, you may believe it has been a terrible thing for the Bernicks. It is the dark spot on the sun of their happiness, as Rummel once expressed it. So you must never talk of these things in this house again, Mrs. Lynge.

MRS. HOLT.

And, for heaven's sake, don't mention the step-sister either.

MRS. LYNGE.

Yes, by-the-bye, Mrs. Bernick has a step-sister too?

MRS. RUMMEL.

Used to have—fortunately ; for now they don't
recognise the relationship.   Yes, she was a strange
being ! Would you believe it, she cut her hair
short, and went about in rainy weather with men's
shoes on !

MRS. HOLT.

And when her step-brother—the ne'er-do-well
—had run away, and the whole town was of course
crying out against him—what do you think she
did ? Why, she followed him.

MRS. RUMMEL.

Yes, but think of the scandal before she left,
Mrs. Holt !

MRS. HOLT.

Hush—don't talk about it.

MRS. LYNGE.

What, was there a scandal about her too ?

MRS. RUMMEL.

Yes, I'll tell you all about it, Mrs. Lynge. Bernick
had just proposed to Betty Tönnesen ; and as he
was coming, with her on his arm, into her aunt's
room to announce the engagement to her——

MRS. HOLT.

The Tönnesens were orphans, you understand.

MRS. RUMMEL.

——Lona Hessel rose from her chair, and gave
the handsome, aristocratic Karsten Bernick a
ringing box on the ear !

MRS. LYNGE.

Well, I never—— !

MRS. HOLT.

Yes, every one knows it.

MRS. RUMMEL.

And then she packed up her traps and went off
to America.

MRS. LYNGE.

She must have had designs upon him herself.

MRS. RUMMEL.

Yes, that was just it. She imagined he was
going to propose to her as soon as he came home
from Paris.

MRS. HOLT.

Just fancy her dreaming of such a thing!
Bernick — a polished young man-of-the-world
—a perfect gentleman—the darling of all the
ladies——

MRS. RUMMEL.

——and so high-principled, too, Mrs. Holt—so
moral.

MRS. LYNGE.

Then what has become of this Miss Hessel in
America ?

MRS. RUMMEL.

Well—over that, as Rummel once expressed
it, there rests a veil which should scarcely be
lifted.

MRS. LYNGE.

What does that mean ?

MRS. RUMMEL.

Of course the family hears nothing from her
now ; but every one in town knows that she has
sung for money in taverns over there——

MRS. HOLT.

——and has given lectures——

MRS. RUMMEL.

——and has published an utterly crazy book.

MRS. LYNGE.

Is it possible——?

MRS. RUMMEL.

Yes, Lona Hessel, too, is certainly a sun-spot in the Bernicks' happiness.   But now you know the whole story, Mrs. Lynge.   Heaven knows, I have only told it to put you on your guard as to what you say.

MRS. LYNGE.

You may be quite easy on that point.   But poor Dina Dorf! I really feel very sorry for her.

MRS. RUMMEL.

Oh, for her it was an absolute stroke of luck. Only think, if she had remained in her parents' hands!   Of course we all took an interest in her, and tried to instil good principles into her mind. At last Miss Bernick arranged that she should come and live here.

MRS. HOLT.

But she has always been a difficult girl to deal with—the effect of bad example, you know.   Of course she is not like one of our own children— we have to make the best of her, Mrs. Lynge.

MRS. RUMMEL.

Hush, there she comes.   [*Loud.*]   Yes, as you say, Dina is really quite a clever girl—— What, are you there, Dina? We are just finishing our work here.

MRS. HOLT.

Ah, how nice your coffee smells, my dear Dina.
Such a cup of coffee in the forenoon——

MRS. BERNICK.

[*In the verandah.*]   The coffee is ready, ladies.
> [MARTHA *and* DINA *have meanwhile helped
> the servant to bring in the coffee things.
> All the ladies go out and sit down ; they
> vie with each other in talking kindly to*
> DINA. *After a time she comes into the
> room and looks for her sewing.*

MRS. BERNICK.

[*Out at the coffee-table.*]   Dina, don't you
want—— ?

DINA.

No, thanks ; I don't care for any.
> [*She sits down to sew.* MRS. BERNICK
> *and* RÖRLUND *exchange a few words ; a
> moment after, he comes into the room.*

RÖRLUND.

[*Goes up to the table, as if looking for something,
and says in a low voice.*]   Dina.

DINA.

Yes.

RÖRLUND.

Why will you not come out ?

DINA.

When I came with the coffee I could see by
the strange lady's looks that they had been talking about me.

RÖRLUND.

And did you not notice, too, how kindly she
spoke to you ?

DINA.

But that is what I can't bear.

RÖRLUND.

Yours is a rebellious nature, Dina.

DINA.

Yes.

RÖRLUND.

What makes it so ?

DINA.

It has never been otherwise.

RÖRLUND.

But could you not try to change ?

DINA.

No.

RÖRLUND.

Why not ?

DINA.

[*Looks up at him.*] Because I belong to the
" Lapsed and Lost."

RÖRLUND.

Fie, Dina !

DINA.

And so did my mother before me.

RÖRLUND.

Who has spoken to you of such things ?

DINA.

No one ; they never speak.   Why don't they ?
They all handle me as gingerly as though I would

fall to pieces, if—— Oh, how I hate all this good-heartedness!

RÖRLUND.

My dear Dina, I can very well understand that you must feel oppressed here, but——

DINA.

Oh, if I could only go far away! I could get on well enough by myself, if only I lived among people that weren't so—so——

RÖRLUND.

So what?

DINA.

So proper and moral.

RÖRLUND.

Come, Dina, you do not mean that.

DINA.

Oh, you know very well how I mean it. Every day Hilda and Netta come here that I may take example by them. I can never be as well-behaved as they are, and I will not be. Oh, if only I were far away, I daresay I could be good.

RÖRLUND.

You are good, my dear Dina.

DINA.

What good does that do me, here?

RÖRLUND.

Then you are seriously thinking of going away?

DINA.

I would not remain here a day longer, if you were not here.

RÖRLUND.

Tell me, Dina—what is it that really makes you
like to be with me?

DINA.

You teach me so much that is beautiful.

RÖRLUND.

Beautiful? Do you call what I can teach you
beautiful?

DINA.

Yes; or rather—you teach me nothing; but
when I hear you speak, it makes me think of so
much that is beautiful.

RÖRLUND.

What do you understand, then, by a beautiful
thing?

DINA.

I have never thought of that.

RÖRLUND.

Then think of it now. What do you understand
by a beautiful thing?

DINA.

A beautiful thing is something great—and far
away.

RÖRLUND.

H'm.—My dear Dina—I sympathise with you
from the bottom of my heart.

DINA.

Is that all?

RÖRLUND.

You know very well how unspeakably dear you
are to me.

DINA.

If I were Hilda or Netta you would not be afraid to let any one see it.

RÖRLUND.

Oh, Dina, you cannot possibly realise the thousand considerations—— When a man is singled out as a moral pillar of the society he lives in, why—he cannot be too careful. If I were only sure that people would not misinterpret my motives—— But no matter; you must and shall be helped to rise. Dina, shall we make a bargain that when I come—when circumstances permit me to come—and say: Here is my hand—you will take it and be my wife ?—Do you promise me that, Dina ?

DINA.

Yes.

RÖRLUND.

Thank you, thank you!—Oh, Dina, I love you so—— Sh! some one is coming. Dina, for my sake—go out to the others.

[*She goes out to the coffee-table. At the same moment* RUMMEL, SANDSTAD, *and* VIGELAND *enter from the Consul's office, followed by* CONSUL BERNICK, *who has a bundle of papers in his hand.*

BERNICK.

Then that matter is settled.

VIGELAND.

Yes, with the blessing of God, so let it be.

RUMMEL.

It is settled, Bernick! A Norseman's word stands firm as the Dovrefjeld, you know¹

BERNICK.

And no one is to give in or fall away, whatever opposition we may meet with.

RUMMEL.

We stand or fall together, Bernick.

HILMAR.

[*Coming up from the garden.*] Excuse me, isn't it the railway that falls?

BERNICK.

On the contrary, it is to go ahead——

RUMMEL.

——full steam, Mr. Tönnesen.

HILMAR.

[*Coming forward.*] Indeed!

RÖRLUND.

What?

MRS. BERNICK.

[*At the door.*] My dear Karsten, what's the meaning——?

BERNICK.

Oh, my dear Betty, it can't possibly interest you. [*To the three men.*] Now we must get the prospectus ready; the sooner the better. Of course we four put our names down first. Our position in society renders it our duty to do as much as we can.

SANDSTAD.

No doubt, Consul.

RUMMEL.

We will make it go, Bernick; we are bound to.

BERNICK.

Oh, yes ; I have no fear as to the result. We must work hard, each in his own circle; and if we can once point to a really lively interest in the affair among all classes of society, it follows that the town, too, mnst contribute its share.

MRS. BERNICK.

Now, Karsten, you must really come and tell us——

BERNICK.

Oh, my dear Betty, ladies don't understand these things.

HILMAR.

Then you are actually going to back up the railway after all ?

BERNICK.

Yes, of course.

RÖRLUND.

But last year, Consul——?

BERNICK.

Last year it was a different matter altogether. Then it was a coast line that was proposed——

VIGELAND.

——which would have been entirely superfluous, Doctor ; for have we not steamboats ?

SANDSTAD.

——and would have been outrageously expensive——

RUMMEL.

——yes, and would actually have interfered with important vested interests here in the town.

BERNICK.

The chief objection was that it would have conferred no benefit on the great mass of the community. Therefore I opposed it; and then the inland line was adopted.

HILMAR.

Yes, but that won't touch the towns about here.

BERNICK.

It will touch our town, my dear Hilmar, for we are going to build a branch line.

HILMAR.

Aha; an entirely new idea, then?

RUMMEL.

Yes; a magnificent idea, isn't it?

RÖRLUND.

H'm——

VIGELAND.

It cannot be denied that Providence seems specially to have smoothed the way for a branch line.

RÖRLUND.

Do you really say so, Mr. Vigeland?

BERNICK.

Yes, for my part, I cannot but regard it as a special guidance that sent me up country on business this spring, and led me by chance into a valley where I had never been before. It struck me like a flash of lightning that here was the very track for a branch line. I at once sent an engineer to inspect it; I have here the provisional

calculations and estimates ; nothing now stands
in our way.

MRS. BERNICK.

[*Still standing, along with the other ladies, at the
garden door.*]   But, my dear Karsten, why have
you kept all this so secret ?

BERNICK.

Oh, my good Betty, you would not have seen
the situation in its true light.   Besides, I have
spoken of it to no living creature until to-day.
But now the decisive moment has come ; now we
must go to work openly, and with all our might.
Ay, if I have to risk all I possess in the affair, I am
determined to see it through.

RUMMEL.

So are we, Bernick ; you may rely on us.

RÖRLUND.

Do you really expect such great results from
this undertaking, gentlemen ?

BERNICK.

Yes, indeed we do.   What a stimulus it will
give to our whole community !   Think of the
great tracts of forest it will bring within reach ,
think of all the rich mineral-seams it will allow
us to work ; think of the river, with its one waterfall above the other !   What rare advantages for
manufactures of all kinds !

RÖRLUND.

And you have no fear that more frequent intercourse with a depraved outer world——

BERNICK.

No; make your mind easy, Doctor. Our busy little town now rests, heaven be thanked, on a sound moral foundation; we have all helped to drain it, if I may say so; and that we will continue to do, each in his own way. You, Doctor, will carry on your beneficent activity in the school and in the home. We, the practical men of business, will support society by furthering the welfare of as wide a circle as possible. And our women— yes, come nearer, ladies; I am glad that you should hear—our women, I say, our wives and daughters, will proceed unwearied in their charitable labours, and be a help and comfort to those nearest and dearest to them, as my dear Betty and Martha are to me and Olaf—— [*Looks around.*] Why, where is Olaf to-day?

MRS. BERNICK.

Oh, in the holidays it's impossible to keep him at home.

BERNICK.

Then he's certain to have gone down to the water again! You'll see, this will end in a misfortune.

HILMAR.

Bah—a little sport with the forces of nature——

MRS. RUMMEL.

How nice it is of you to be so domestic, Mr Bernick.

BERNICK.

Ah, the Family is the kernel of society. A good home, upright and trusty friends, a little close-drawn circle, where no disturbing elements cast their shadow——

KRAP *enters from the right with letters and papers.*

KRAP.

The foreign mail, Consul—and a telegram from New York.

BERNICK.

[*Taking it.*]   Ah, from the owners of the *Indian Girl.*

RUMMEL.

Oh, the mail is in? Then you must excuse me——

VIGELAND.

And me too.

SANDSTAD

Good-bye, Consul.

BERNICK.

Good-bye, good-bye, gentlemen.   And remember we have a meeting this afternoon at five o'clock.

THE THREE.

Yes—of course—all right.

[*They go out to the right.*

BERNICK.

[*Who has read the telegram.*]   Well, this is really too American!   Positively shocking——!

MRS. BERNICK.

Why, Karsten, what is it?

BERNICK.

Look here, Krap—read this!

KRAP.

[*Reads.*]   " Fewest possible repairs; despatch *Indian Girl* without delay ; good season : at worst, cargo will keep her afloat."   Well, I must say——

BERNICK.

The cargo keep her afloat! These gentlemen
know very well that, if anything should happen,
that cargo will send her to the bottom like a
stone.

RÖRLUND.

Ay, this shows the state of things in these
vaunted great nations.

BERNICK.

You are right there—even human life counts
for nothing when dollars are at stake. [*To* KRAP.]
Can the *Indian Girl* be ready for sea in four or five
days?

KRAP.

Yes, if Mr. Vigeland will agree to let the *Palm
Tree* stand over in the meantime.

BERNICK.

H'm—he will scarcely agree to that. Oh, just
look through the mail, please. By the way, did
you see Olaf down on the pier?

KRAP.

No, Consul.   [*He goes into Consul's office.*

BERNICK.

[*Looking again at the telegram.*] These gentlemen think nothing of risking the lives of eighteen
men——

HILMAR.

Well, it's a sailor's calling to brave the elements.
It must brace up your nerves to feel that you have
only a thin plank between you and eternity——

BERNICK.

I should like to see the shipowner among us that would have the conscience to do such a thing! There isn't one, not a single one. [*Catches sight of* OLAF.] Ah, thank goodness, nothing has happened to him.

> [OLAF, *with a fishing-line in his hand, comes running up the street and through the garden-gate.*

OLAF.

[*Still in the garden.*] Uncle Hilmar, I've been down seeing the steamboat.

BERNICK.

Have you been on the pier again?

OLAF.

No, I was only out in a boat. But just fancy, Uncle Hilmar, a whole circus company came ashore from the steamer, with horses and wild beasts; and there were a lot of passengers besides.

MRS. RUMMEL.

Oh, are we to have a circus?

RÖRLUND.

We? Really I should hope not.

MRS. RUMMEL.

No, of course not we, but——

DINA.

I should like to see a circus.

OLAF.

Oh, and me too!

HILMAR.

You're a little blockhead. What is there to see? Nothing but trickery and make-believe. Now it would be something worth while to see the gaucho sweeping over the Pampas on his snorting mustang. But, hang it all, here in these little towns——

OLAF.

[*Pulling* MARTHA's *dress.*] Aunt Martha, look, look—there they come !

MRS. HOLT.

Yes indeed, here we have them.

MRS. LYNGE.

Oh, what horrid people !
> [*Many travellers, and a whole crowd of townspeople, come up the street.*

MRS. RUMMEL.

Aren't they a regular set of mountebanks ! Just look at that one in the grey dress, Mrs. Holt ; the one with the knapsack on her back.

MRS. HOLT.

Yes, see, she has it slung on the handle of her parasol. Of course it's the manager's wife.

MRS. RUMMEL.

Oh, and there's the manager himself, the one with the beard. Well, he does look a regular pirate. Don't look at him, Hilda !

MRS. HOLT.

Nor you either, Netta !

OLAF.

Oh, mother, the manager is bowing to us.

BERNICK.

What?

MRS. BERNICK.

What do you say, child?

MRS. RUMMEL.

Yes, and I declare the woman is nodding too!

BERNICK.

Come, this is really too much!

MARTHA.

[*With an involuntary cry.*] Ah——!

MRS. BERNICK.

What is it, Martha?

MARTHA.

Oh, nothing—only I thought——

OLAF.

[*Shrieks with delight.*] Look, look, there come
the others, with the horses and wild beasts! And
there are the Americans too! All the sailors
from the *Indian Girl*——

> [*" Yankee Doodle " is heard, accompanied
> by a clarinet and drum.*

HILMAR.

[*Stopping his ears.*] Ugh, ugh, ugh!

RÖRLUND.

I think we should withdraw for a moment,
ladies. This is no scene for us. Let us resume
our work.

MRS. BERNICK.

Perhaps we ought to draw the curtains ?

RÖRLUND.

Yes, that is just what I was thinking.

> [*The ladies take their places at the table ;*
> RÖRLUND *shuts the garden door and
> draws the curtains over it and over the
> windows ; it becomes half dark in the
> room.*

OLAF.

[*Peeping out.*] Mother, the manager's wife
is standing at the fountain washing her face !

MRS. BERNICK.

What? In the middle of the market-place ?

MRS. RUMMEL.

And in broad daylight !

HILMAR.

Well, if I were travelling in the desert and
came upon a well, I should never hesitate to——
Ugh, that abominable clarinet !

RÖRLUND.

The police ought really to interfere.

BERNICK.

Oh, come ; one must not be too hard upon
foreigners ; these people are naturally devoid of
the deep-rooted sense of propriety that keeps us
within the right limits. Let them do as they
please ; it cannot affect us. All this unseemli-
ness, this rebellion against good taste and good
manners, fortunately finds no echo, if I may say
so, in our society.—What is this !

A STRANGE LADY *enters briskly by the door on the right.*

THE LADIES.

[*Frightened, and speaking low.*] The circus woman! The manager's wife!

MRS. BERNICK.

Why, what does this mean!

MARTHA.

[*Starts up.*] Ah——!

THE LADY.

Good-morning, my dear Betty! Good-morning, Martha! Good-morning, brother-in-law!

MRS. BERNICK.

[*With a shriek.*] Lona——!

BERNICK.

[*Staggers back a step.*] Merciful heavens——!

MRS. HOLT.

Why, goodness me——!

MRS. RUMMEL.

It can't be possible——!

HILMAR.

What? Ugh!

MRS. BERNICK.

Lona——! Is it really——?

LONA.

Really me? Yes, indeed it is. You may fall on my neck and embrace me, for that matter.

HILMAR.

Ugh! ugh .

MRS. BERNICK.

And you come here as—— ?

BERNICK.

You are actually going to appear—— ?

LONA.

Appear ?   How appear?

BERNICK.

I mean—in the circus—— ?

LONA.

Ha ha ha ! What nonsense, brother-in-law.
Do you think I belong to the circus?   No; it's
true I have turned my hand to all sorts of things,
and made a fool of myself in many ways——

MRS. RUMMEL.

H'm——

LONA.

——but I've never learnt to play tricks on
horseback.

BERNICK.

Then you are not—— ?

MRS. BERNICK.

Oh, thank God !

LONA.

No, no ; we came like other respectable people
—second class, it's true ; but we're used to that.

MRS. BERNICK.

We, you say ?

BERNICK.

[*Advancing a step.*]   What we?

LONA.

Why, my boy and I, of course.

THE LADIES.

[*With a cry.*]   Your boy!

HILMAR.

What?

RÖRLUND.

Well, I must say——

MRS. BERNICK.

Why, what do you mean, Lona?

LONA.

Of course I mean John; I have no other boy
but John, that I know of—or Johan, as you call
him.

MRS. BERNICK.

Johan——!

MRS. RUMMEL.

[*Aside to* MRS. LYNGE.]   The prodigal brother.

BERNICK.

[*Hesitatingly.*]   Is Johan with you?

LONA.

Of course, of course; I would never travel
without him.   But you're all looking so dismal
—and sitting here in this twilight, sewing at
something white.   There hasn't been a death
in the family?

RÖRLUND.

This is a meeting, Miss Hessel, of the Society for the Moral Regeneration of the Lapsed and Lost.

LONA.

[*Half to herself.*] What? These nice-looking, well-behaved ladies, can they be—— ?

MRS. RUMMEL.

Oh, this is too much—— !

LONA.

Ah, I see, I see! Why, good gracious, that's Mrs. Rummel! And there sits Mrs. Holt too! Well, we three haven't grown younger since last we met. But listen now, good people : let the Lapsed and Lost wait for one day; they'll be none the worse for it. On a joyful occasion like this——

RÖRLUND.

A return home is not always a joyful occasion.

LONA.

Indeed? Then how do you read your Bible, Pastor?

RÖRLUND.

I am not a clergyman.

LONA.

Oh ; then you will be one, for certain.—But, pah !—this moral linen here has a tainted smell— just like a shroud. I'm accustomed to the air of the prairies now, I can tell you.

BERNICK.

[*Wiping his forehead.*]   Yes; it really is rather oppressive in here.

LONA.

Wait a moment — we'll soon rise from the sepulchre.   [*Draws back the curtains.*]   We must have broad daylight here when my boy comes. Ah—then you shall see a boy that has washed himself——

HILMAR.

Ugh!

LONA.

[*Opens the door and the windows.*]   ——when he has washed himself, I mean—up at the hotel—for on board the steamer you get as dirty as a pig.

HILMAR.

Ugh, ugh!

LONA.

" Ugh " ?   Why if that isn't——!   [*Points to* HILMAR, *and asks the others.*]   Does he still loaf about here saying " ugh " to everything ?

HILMAR.

I do not loaf; I remain here by my doctor's orders.

RÖRLUND.

Ahem—ladies, I hardly think that——

LONA.

[*Catches sight of* OLAF.]   Is this your youngster, Betty ?   Give us your fist, my boy !   Or are you afraid of your ugly old aunt ?

RÖRLUND.

[*Putting his book under his arm.*]   I do not think, ladies, that we are quite in the mood for

doing more work to-day. But we shall meet
again to-morrow?

LONA.

[*As the visitors rise to go.*]   Yes, by all means—
I shall be here.

RÖRLUND.

You? Allow me to ask, Miss Hessel, what you
will do in our Society?

LONA.

I will let in fresh air, Pastor.

ACT SECOND.

The garden-room in CONSUL BERNICK'S *house.*

MRS. BERNICK *is sitting alone at the work-table, sewing. In a little while* CONSUL BERNICK *enters from the right, with his hat and gloves on, and a stick in his hand.*

MRS. BERNICK.

Are you home already, Karsten?

BERNICK.

Yes.   I have an appointment here.

MRS. BERNICK.

[*Sighing.*]   Oh, yes; I suppose Johan will be down here again.

BERNICK.

No; it's with one of my men.   [*Takes off his hat.*]   Where are all the ladies to-day?

MRS. BERNICK.

Mrs. Rummel and Hilda hadn't time to come.

BERNICK.

Indeed!   They have sent excuses?

MRS. BERNICK.

Yes; they had so much to do at home.

BERNICK.

Of course.   And the others are not coming either, I suppose ?

MRS. BERNICK.

No ; something has prevented them too.

BERNICK.

I was sure it would.   Where is Olaf ?

MRS. BERNICK.

I allowed him to go for a walk with Dina.

BERNICK.

H'm ; that scatter-brained hussy, Dina——! How could she go and forthwith strike up a friendship with Johan——!

MRS. BERNICK.

Why, my dear Karsten, Dina has no idea——

BERNICK.

Well, then, Johan at least should have had tact enough to take no notice of her.   I could see Vigeland's expressive glances.

MRS. BERNICK.

[*Dropping her work into her lap.*]   Karsten, can you understand what has brought them home ?

BERNICK.

Well, he has a farm over there, that doesn't seem to be very flourishing ; and she mentioned yesterday that they had to travel second-class——

MRS. BERNICK.

Yes, I was afraid it must be something of that sort.   But that she should have come with

him ! She ! After the terrible way she insulted
you——— !

MRS. BERNICK.

Oh, don't think of those old stories.

MRS. BERNICK.

How can I think of anything else ?   He is my
own brother——— ; and yet it is not of him that I
think, but of all the unpleasantness it will bring
upon you.   Karsten, I am so dreadfully afraid
that———

BERNICK.

What are you afraid of ?

MRS. BERNICK.

Might they not think of arresting him for that
money your mother lost ?

BERNICK.

What nonsense !   Who can prove that she lost
the money ?

MRS. BERNICK.

Why, the whole town knows it, unfortunately ;
and you said yourself———

BERNICK.

I said nothing. The town knows nothing whatever of the matter; it was all idle gossip.

MRS. BERNICK.

Oh, how noble you are, Karsten .

BERNICK.

Put all those old stories out of your head, I say !
You don't know how you torture me by raking
them up again.   [*He walks up and down the room ;*

then he throws his stick away from him.] To think of their coming home just at this time, when so much depends on unmixed good-feeling, both in the press and in the town! There will be paragraphs in the papers all over the country-side. Whether I receive them well or ill, my action will be discussed, my motives turned inside out. People will rip up all those old stories—just as you do. In a society like ours—— [*Tosses down his gloves upon the table.*] And there isn't a soul here that I can confide in, or that can give me any support.

MRS. BERNICK.

No one at all, Karsten?

BERNICK.

No; you know there is not.—That they should descend upon me just at this moment! They are certain to make a scandal in one way or another—especially she. It is nothing less than a calamity to have such people in one's family.

MRS. BERNICK.

Well, it's not my fault that——

BERNICK.

What is not your fault? That you are related to them? No; that's true enough.

MRS. BERNICK.

And it wasn't I that asked them to come home.

BERNICK.

Aha, there we have it! "*I* didn't ask them to come home; *I* didn't write for them; *I* didn't drag them home by the hair of their heads." Oh, I know the whole story off by heart.

Mrs. Bernick.

[*Bursting into tears.*] Oh, why are you so unkind ?

Bernick

Yes, that's right; set to crying, so that the town may have that to chatter about too. Stop this nonsense, Betty. You had better sit outside there; some one might come in. Perhaps you want people to see Madam with red eyes? It would be a nice thing indeed if it got abroad that—— Ah! I hear some one in the passage. [*A knock.*] Come in.

> [Mrs. Bernick *goes out to the verandah with her work.* Aune *comes in from the right.*

Aune.

Good-morning, Consul.

Bernick.

Good-morning. Well, I suppose you can guess what I want with you?

Aune.

Your clerk told me yesterday that you were not pleased with——

Bernick.

I am altogether displeased with the way things are going at the yard, Aune. You are not getting on at all with the repairs. The *Palm Tree* should have been at sea long ago. Mr. Vigeland comes worrying me about it every day. He is a troublesome partner.

Aune.

The *Palm Tree* can sail the day after to-morrow.

BERNICK.

At last! But the American, the *Indian Girl*, that has been lying here five weeks, and——

AUNE.

The American? I sort of understood that we was to do all we could to get your own ship out of hand first.

BERNICK.

I have given you no reason for such an idea. You should have made all possible progress with the American too; but you have done nothing.

AUNE.

The vessel's bottom is as rotten as matchwood, Consul; the more we patch at it the worse it gets.

BERNICK.

That is not the real reason. Krap has told me the whole truth. You don't understand how to work the new machines I have introduced—or rather, you won't work with them.

AUNE.

I'm getting on in years, Consul Bernick—nigh upon sixty. From a boy I've been used to the old ways——

BERNICK.

They are quite inadequate nowadays. You mustn't think, Aune, that it's a question of mere profit; luckily I could do without that; but I must consider the community I live in, and the business I have to manage. It is from me that progress must come, or it will never come at all.

AUNE.

I have nought to say against progress, Consu .

BERNICK.

No, for your own narrow circle, for the working class.   Oh, I know all about your agitations !
You make speeches; you stir people up ; but
when it comes to a tangible piece of progress, as
in the case of the machines, you will have nothing
to do with it ; you are afraid.

AUNE.

Yes, I'm afraid, Consul ; I'm afraid for the
hundreds of poor folks as the machines 'll take the
bread out of their mouths.   You talk a deal of
duty towards Society, Consul, but it seems to me
as Society has duties of its own as well.   What
business have science and capital to bring all
these new-fangled inventions into the field before
Society has turned out a breed of men that can
use them ?

BERNICK.

You read and think too much, Aune ; it does
you no good ; that is what makes you dissatisfied
with your position.

AUNE.

It's not that, Consul ; but I can't abear to see
one good workman after another packed off to
starve for the sake of these machines.

BERNICK.

H'm ; when printing was discovered, many
copyists had to starve.

AUNE.

Would you have thought printing such a fine
thing, Consul, if you'd have been a copyist ?

BERNICK.

I didn't get you here to argue with you. I sent for you to tell you that the *Indian Girl* must be ready to sail the day after to-morrow.

AUNE.

Why, Consul——

BERNICK.

The day after to-morrow, do you hear? At the same time as our own ship; not an hour later. I have my reasons for hurrying on the affair. Have you read this morning's paper? Ah!—then you know that the Americans have been making disturbances again. The ruffianly crew turn the whole town topsy-turvy. Not a night passes without fights in the taverns or on the street; not to speak of other abominations.

AUNE.

Yes, they're a bad lot, for certain.

BERNICK.

And who gets the blame of all this? It is I— yes, I—that suffer for it. These wretched newspaper-men are covertly carping at us for giving our whole attention to the *Palm Tree*. And I, whose mission it is to set an example to my fellow citizens, must have such things thrown in my teeth! I won't bear it. I cannot have my name bespattered in this way.

AUNE.

Oh, the name of Bernick is good enough to bear that, and more.

BERNICK.

Not just now; precisely at this moment I need all the respect and goodwill of my fellow citizens,

I have a great undertaking in hand, as you have
probably heard; and if evil-disposed persons
should succeed in shaking people's unqualified
confidence in me, it may involve me in the most
serious difficulties. I must silence these carping
and spiteful scribblers at any cost; and that is
why I give you till the day after to-morrow.

AUNE.

You might just as well give me till this afternoon, Consul Bernick.

BERNICK.

You mean that I am demanding impossibilities?

AUNE.

Yes, with the present working staff——

BERNICK.

Oh, very well;—then we must look about us
elsewhere.

AUNE.

Would you really turn off still more of the old
workmen?

BERNICK.

No, that is not what I am thinking of.

AUNE.

I'm certain sure, if you did, there would be a
fine to-do both in the town and in the newspapers.

BERNICK.

Very possibly; therefore I won't do it. But
if the *Indian Girl* is not cleared the day after
to-morrow, I shall dismiss you.

Aune.

[*With a start.*] Me! [*Laughing.*] Oh, that's only your joke, Consul.

Bernick.

I advise you not to trust to that.

Aune.

You can think of turning me away! Why, my father before me, and his father too, worked in the shipyard all their lives ; and I myself——

Bernick.

Who forces me to it ?

Aune.

You want me to do things as can't be done, Consul.

Bernick.

Oh, where there's a will there's a way. Yes or no ?   Answer me definitely, or I dismiss you on the spot.

Aune.

[*Coming nearer.*]   Consul Bernick, have you rightly bethought what it means to turn an old workman away ?   You say he can look about for another job.   Ay, ay, maybe he can—but is that everything ?   Ah, you should just see what it looks like in a turned-off workman's house, the night when he comes home and puts his tool-chest behind the door.

Bernick.

Do you think I part with you willingly ? Haven't I always been a good master to you ?

AUNE.

So much the worse, Consul; for that means as my folks at home won't put the blame on you. They won't say nothing to me, for they durstn't; but they'll look at me when I'm not noticing, as much as to say: Certain sure, it must 'a' been his fault. You see, it's that—it's that as I can't abear God knows, I'm a poor man, but I've always been used to be the first in my own house. My bit of a home is in a manner of speaking a little community, Consul Bernick. That little community I've been able to support and hold together because my wife believed in me, my children believed in me. And now the whole thing is to fall to pieces.

BERNICK.

Well, if it cannot be otherwise, the less must fall before the greater; the part must, in heaven's name, be sacrificed to the whole. I can give you no other answer; and you'll find it is the way of the world. But you are an obstinate fellow, Aune! You stand against me, not because you · can't help it, but because you will not prove the superiority of machinery to manual labour.

AUNE.

And you're so dead set on this, Consul, because you know that, if you send me about my business, leastways you'll have shown the papers your goodwill.

BERNICK.

What if it were so? I have told you how much. it means to me—I must either conciliate the papers, or have them all attacking me at the moment when I am working for a great and

beneficent cause.   What follows?   Can I possibly
act otherwise than I am doing?   Would you have
me, in order to hold your home together, as you
call it, sacrifice hundreds of other homes—homes
that will never be founded, will never have a
smoking hearthstone, if I do not succeed in my
present enterprise?   You must make your choice.

AUNE.

Well, if you put it that way, I've got no more
to say.

BERNICK.

H'm—; my dear Aune, I am truly sorry we
must part.

AUNE.

We will not part, Consul Bernick.

BERNICK.

What?

AUNE.

Even a common man has his rights to stand up
for here in the world.

BERNICK.

Of course, of course.   Then you can promise——?

AUNE.

The *Indian Girl* shall be ready for sea the day
after to-morrow. [*He bows and goes out to the right.*

BERNICK.

Aha, I've made that stiff neck bend.   I take
that as a good omen——

HILMAR TÖNNESEN, *with a cigar in his mouth,*
comes through the garden gate.

HILMAR.

[*On the verandah steps.*]   Good-morning, Betty!
Good-morning, Bernick!

MRS. BERNICK.

Good-morning.

HILMAR.

Oh, you've been crying, I see.   Then you've
heard?

MRS. BERNICK.

Heard what?

HILMAR.

That the scandal is in full swing!   Ugh!

BERNICK.

What do you mean?

HILMAR.

[*Coming into the room.*] Why, that the two
Americans are flaunting about the streets in
company with Dina Dorf.

MRS. BERNICK.

[*Also coming in.*] Oh, Hilmar, is it possible——?

HILMAR.

I can bear witness, worse luck! Lona had
even the want of tact to call out to me; but I
naturally pretended not to hear her.

BERNICK.

And of course all this has not passed unnoticed.

HILMAR.

No; you may be sure it hasn't. People turned
round and looked after them. It ran like wild-
fire over the town—like a fire on the Western

prairies. There were people at the windows of
all the houses, head to head behind the curtains,
waiting for the procession to pass. Ugh! You
must excuse me, Betty; I say ugh! for it makes
me so nervous. If this goes on I shall have to go
for a change of air somewhere, pretty far off.

Mrs. Bernick.

But you should have spoken to him, and pointed
out——

Hilmar.

In the public street? No; I beg to be ex-
cused. But how the deuce can the fellow dare
to show himself here! Well, we shall see if the
papers don't put a stopper on him. I beg your
pardon, Betty, but——

Bernick.

The papers, you say? Have you heard anything to make you think so?

Hilmar.

I should rather say I had! When I left here
last night, I took my constitutional up to the
club. I could tell from the sudden silence when
I came in that they had been discussing the two
Americans. And then in came that impertinent
editor-fellow, Hammer, or whatever they call
him, and congratulated me, before everybody,
upon my rich cousin's return.

Bernick.

Rich——?

Hilmar.

Yes; that was what he said. Of course I
measured him from top to toe with the contempt

he deserved, and gave him to understand that I
knew nothing of Johan Tönnesen being rich.
" Indeed ! " says he ; " that's strange. In America
people generally get on when they have something to start with, and we know your cousin
didn't go over empty-handed."

BERNICK.

H'm, be so good as to——

MRS. BERNICK.

[*Troubled.*]   There, you see, Karsten——

HILMAR.

Well, at any rate, not a wink have I slept for
thinking of the fellow.   And there he goes calmly
marching about the streets, as if he had nothing
to be ashamed of.   Why couldn't he have been
disposed of for good ?   Some people are intoler-
ably tough.

MRS. BERNICK.

Oh, Hilmar, what are you saying ?

HILMAR.

Oh, nothing, nothing.   Only here he escapes
safe and sound from railways accidents, and fights
with Californian bears and Blackfoot Indians ;
why, he's not even scalped——   Ugh ! here they
are.

BERNICK.

[*Looks down the street.*]   Olaf with them too.

HILMAR.

Yes, of course ; catch them letting people
forget that they belong to the first family in the
town.   Look, look, there come all the loafers out of

the drug-store to stare at them and make remarks
Really, this is too much for my nerves; how a
man under such circumstances is to hold high the
banner of the ideal——

BERNICK.

They are coming straight here.   Listen, Betty :
it is my decided wish that you should be as friendly
as possible to them.

MRS. BERNICK.

May I, Karsten ?

BERNICK.

Of course, of course ; and you too, Hilmar.   I
daresay they won't remain very long ; and when
we are alone with them—let us have no allusions
to the past—we must on no account hurt their
feelings.

MRS. BERNICK.

Oh, Karsten, how noble you are.

BERNICK.

No, no, nothing of the sort.

MRS. BERNICK.

Oh, but you must let me thank you ; and forgive me for being so hasty.   You had every reason
to——

BERNICK.

Don't talk of it, don't talk of it, I say.

HILMAR.

Ugh !

JOHAN TÖNNESEN *and* DINA, *followed by* LONA
and OLAF, *come through the garden.*

LONA.

Good-morning, good-morning, my dear people.

JOHAN.

We have been out looking all round the old place, Karsten.

BERNICK.

Yes, so I hear.   Greatly changed, is it not ?

LONA.

Consul Bernick's great and good works on every hand.   We've been up in the gardens you have presented to the town——

BERNICK.

Oh, there !

LONA.

" Karsten Bernick's Gift," as the inscription over the entrance says.   Yes ; everything here seems to be your work.

JOHAN.

And you have splendid ships too.   I met my old school-fellow, the captain of the *Palm Tree*——

LONA.

Yes, and you've built a new school-house ; and they owe both the gas- and the water-works to you, I hear.

BERNICK.

Oh, one must work for the community one lives in.

LONA.

Well, you've done your part finely, brother-in-law ; but it's a pleasure, too, to see how people appreciate you.   I don't think I'm vain, but I couldn't help reminding one or two of the people we talked to that we belong to the family.

HILMAR.

Ugh—— !

LONA.

Do you say " Ugh ! " to that ?

HILMAR.

No, I said " H'm "——

LONA.

Oh, was that all, poor fellow ? But you are quite alone here to-day !

MRS. BERNICK.

Yes, to-day we are quite alone.

LONA.

By-the-bye, we met one or two of the Moral Regenerators up in the market-place ; they seemed to be very busy. But we have never had a proper talk yet ; yesterday we had the three pioneers of progress here, and the Pastor too——

HILMAR.

The Doctor.

LONA.

I call him the Pastor. But now—what do you think of my work for these fifteen years ? Hasn't he grown a fine boy ? Who would recognise him now for the scapegrace that ran away from home ?

HILMAR.

H'm——

JOHAN.

Oh, Lona, don't boast too much.

LONA.

I don't care, I'm really proud of it. Well, well, it's the only thing I have done in the world, but it gives me a sort of right to exist. Yes, Johan, when I think how we two began life over there with only our four bare paws——

HILMAR.

Hands.

LONA.

I say paws, they were so dirty——

HILMAR.

Ugh !

LONA.

——and empty too.

HILMAR.

Empty ! Well, I must say '

LONA.

What must you say ?

BERNICK.

H'm !

HILMAR.

I must say—ugh ! [*Goes out upon the verandah.*

LONA.

Why, what's wrong with the man ?

BERNICK.

Oh, never mind him; he's rather nervous just now. Should you like to take a look round the garden ? You haven't been down there yet, and I happen to have an hour to spare.

Lona.

Yes, I should like it very much; you may be sure my thoughts have often been with you all, here in the garden.

Mrs. Bernick.

There have been great changes there too, as you'll see.

> [Consul Bernick, Mrs. Bernick, *and* Lona *go down the garden, where they are now and then visible during the following scene.*

Olaf.

[*At the garden door.*] Uncle Hilmar, do you know what Uncle Johan asked me? He asked if I'd like to go with him to America.

Hilmar.

You, you little muff, that go about tied to your mother's apron-strings——

Olaf.

Yes, but I won't be so any more. You shall see when I'm big——

Hilmar.

Oh, rubbish; you have no real craving for the discipline of danger——

> [*They go down the garden together.*

Johan.

[*To* Dina, *who has taken off her hat, and stands at the door to the right, shaking the dust from her dress.*] The walk has made you very warm.

Dina.

Yes; it was splendid. I have never had such a nice walk before.

JOHAN.

Perhaps you don't often go for a walk in the morning ?

DINA.

Oh, yes; but only with Olaf.

JOHAN.

Ah!—Should you like to go down the garden, or to stay here ?

DINA.

I would rather stay here.

JOHAN.

And I too. Then it's settled that we go for a walk together every morning ?

DINA.

No, Mr. Tönnesen, you mustn't do that.

JOHAN.

Why not ? You know you promised.

DINA.

Yes, but on thinking it over, I—— You mustn't go about with me.

JOHAN.

Why on earth should I not ?

DINA.

Ah, you are a stranger here; you don't understand; but I must tell you——

JOHAN.

Well ?

DINA.

No, I would rather not speak about it.

JOHAN.

Oh, yes—surely you can speak to me about anything you wish to.

DINA.

Then I must tell you that I am not like the other girls here ; there is something—something about me. That is why you mustn't walk with me.

JOHAN.

But I don't understand a word of this. You haven't done anything wrong ?

DINA.

No, not I, but——; no, I won't say anything more about it. You are sure to hear it from the others.

JOHAN.

H'm——

DINA.

But there was something else I wanted to ask you about.

JOHAN.

And what was that ?

DINA.

Is it really so easy to lead a life that is worth living over in America ?

JOHAN.

Well it isn't always easy ; you have generally to rough it a good deal, and work hard, to begin with.

DINA.

I would willingly do that.

JOHAN.

You?

DINA.

I can work well enough; I am strong and healthy, and Aunt Martha has taught me a great deal.

JOHAN.

Then, hang it all, why not come with us?

DINA.

Oh, now you are only joking; you said the same to Olaf. But I wanted to know, too, if people over there are very—very moral, you know?

JOHAN.

Moral?

DINA.

Yes, I mean, are they as—as proper and well-behaved as they are here?

JOHAN.

Well, at any rate, they are not so bad as people here think. Don't be at all afraid of that.

DINA.

You don't understand. What I want is just that they should not be so very proper and moral.

JOHAN.

Indeed? What would you have them then?

DINA.

I would have them natural.

JOHAN.

Well, that is perhaps just what they are.

DINA.

Then that would be the place for me.

JOHAN.

Yes, I am sure it would ; so you must come with us.

DINA.

No, I wouldn't go with you; I should have to go alone. Oh, I should get on; I should soon be fit for something——

BERNICK.

[*At the foot of the verandah steps with the two ladies.*] Stay here, stay here; I'll fetch it, my dear Betty. You might easily catch cold.

[*Comes into the room and looks for his wife's shawl.*

MRS. BERNICK.

[*From the garden.*] You must come too, Johan ; we are going down to the grotto.

BERNICK.

No, Johan must stay here just now. Here, Dina ; take my wife's shawl and go with them. Johan will stay here with me, my dear Betty. I want him to tell me a little about things in America.

MRS. BERNICK.

Very well ; then come after us ; you know where to find us.

[MRS. BERNICK, LONA, *and* DINA *go down through the garden to the left.*

BERNICK.

[*Looks out after them for a moment, goes and shuts the second door on the left, then goes up to* JOHAN, *seizes both his hands, shakes them, and presses them warmly.*] Johan, now we are alone ; now you must give me leave to thank you.

JOHAN.

Oh, nonsense !

BERNICK.

My house and home, my domestic happiness, my whole position in society—all these I owe to you.

JOHAN.

Well, I am glad of it, my dear Karsten ; so some good came of that foolish story after all.

BERNICK.

[*Shaking his hands again.*] Thanks, thanks, all the same ! Not one in ten thousand would have done what you did for me then.

JOHAN.

Oh, nonsense ! Were we not both of us young and a bit reckless ? One of us had to take the blame upon him——

BERNICK.

Yes, and the guilty one was the obvious person.

JOHAN.

Stop ! Then the obvious person was the innocent one. I was alone, free, an orphan ; it was a positive blessing to me to escape from the grind of the office. You, on the other hand, had your mother still living ; and, besides, you had just got secretly engaged to Betty, and she was devoted to you. What would have become of her if she had learnt—— ?

BERNICK

True, true, true; but——

JOHAN.

And was it not just for Betty's sake that you broke off the entanglement with Madam Dorf? It was for the very purpose of putting an end to it that you were up at her house that night——

BERNICK.

Yes, the fatal night when that drunken brute came home—— ! Yes, Johan, it was for Betty's sake; but yet — that you should have the generosity to turn appearances against yourself and go away——

JOHAN.

You need have no qualms, my dear Karsten. We agreed that it should be so; you had to be saved, and you were my friend. I can tell you I was proud of that friendship! Here was I, poor stay-at-home, plodding along, when you came back like a very prince from your great foreign tour—from London and Paris, no less! Then what should you do but choose me for your bosom friend, though I was four years younger than you. Well, that was because you were making love to Betty ; now I understand it well enough. But how proud I was of it then! And who would not have been proud! Who would not gladly have served as your scapegoat, especially when it only meant a month's town-talk, and an excuse for making a dash into the wide world.

BERNICK.

H'm—my dear Johan, I must tell you frankly that the story is not so entirely forgotten yet.

JOHAN.

Isn't it ? Well, what does it matter to me when once I am back again at my farm ?

BERNICK.

Then you are going back ?

JOHAN.

Of course.

BERNICK.

But not so very soon, I hope ?

JOHAN.

As soon as possible. It was only to please Lona that I came over at all.

BERNICK.

Indeed ! How so ?

JOHAN.

Well, you see, Lona is not so young as she once was, and for some time past a sort of home-sick-ness has come over her, though she would never admit it. [*Smiling.*] She dared not leave behind her a scapegrace like me, who, before I was out of my teens, had been mixed up in——

BERNICK.

And then ?

JOHAN.

Well, Karsten, now I must make a confession I am really ashamed of.

BERNICK.

You haven't told her the whole story ?

JOHAN.

Yes, I have. It was wrong of me, but I couldn't help it. You have no conception what Lona has been to me. You could never endure her; but to me she has been a mother. The first few years over there, when we were desperately poor—oh, how she worked! And when I had a long illness, and could earn nothing, and couldn't keep her from doing it, she took to singing songs in the cafés; gave lectures that people laughed at; wrote a book she has both laughed and cried over since—and all to keep my soul and body together. Last winter, when I saw her pining for home, and thought how she had toiled and slaved for me, could I sit still and look on? No, Karsten, I couldn't. I said, "Go, go, Lona; don't be anxious on my account. I'm not such a ne'er-do-well as you think." And then—then I told her everything.

BERNICK.

And how did she take it?

JOHAN.

Oh, she said what was quite true—that as I was innocent I could have no objection to taking a trip over here myself. But you needn't be afraid; Lona will say nothing, and I shall take better care of my own tongue another time.

BERNICK.

Yes, yes; I am sure you will.

JOHAN.

Here is my hand upon it. And now don't let us talk any more of that old story; fortunately it is the only escapade either you or I have been

mixed up in, I hope. And now I mean thoroughly
to enjoy the few days I shall have here. You
can't think what a splendid walk we have had this
forenoon. Who could have imagined that the
little baggage that used to trot about and play
angels in the theatre——! But tell me—what
became of her parents afterwards ?

BERNICK.

Oh, there's nothing to tell except what I wrote
you immediately after you left. You got my two
letters, of course ?

JOHAN.

Of course, of course ; I have them both. The
drunken scoundrel deserted her ?

BERNICK.

And was afterwards killed in a drinking-bout.

JOHAN.

And she herself died soon after ? I suppose
you did all you could for her without exciting
attention ?

BERNICK.

She was proud ; she betrayed nothing, but she
would accept nothing.

JOHAN.

Well, at any rate, you did right in taking Dina
into your house.

BERNICK.

Oh, yes—— However, it was really Martha
that arranged that.

JOHAN.

Ah, it was Martha ? By-the-bye, where is
Martha to-day?

BERNICK.

Oh, she is always busy either at the school, or among her sick people.

JOHAN.

Then it was Martha that took charge of Dina?

BERNICK.

Yes; education has always been Martha's hobby. That is why she accepted a place in the national school. It was a piece of folly on her part.

JOHAN.

She certainly looked very much done up yesterday. I should scarcely think her health would stand it.

BERNICK.

Oh, I don't think there's much amiss with her health. But it's unpleasant for me. It looks as if I, her brother, were not willing to maintain her.

JOHAN.

Maintain her? I thought she had enough of her own to——

BERNICK.

Not a halfpenny. I daresay you remember what difficulties my mother was in when you left. She got on for some time with my help; but of course that arrangement could not permanently satisfy me. So I determined to go into partnership with her; but even then things were far from going well. At last I had to take over the whole affair; and when we came to make up accounts, there was scarcely anything left to my mother's share. Then, shortly afterwards, she died; and Martha, of course, was left with nothing.

JOHAN.

Poor Martha!

BERNICK.

Poor! Why so? You don't suppose I let her want for anything? Oh no; I think I may say I am a good brother to her. Of course she lives here and has her meals with us; her salary as a teacher is quite enough for her dress, and—what can a single woman want more?

JOHAN.

H'm; that's not the way we think in America.

BERNICK.

No, I daresay not; there are too many agitators at work over there. But here, in our little circle, where, thank heaven, corruption has not as yet managed to creep in—here women are content with a modest and unobtrusive position. For the rest, it is Martha's own fault; she could have been provided for long ago if she had cared to.

JOHAN.

You mean she could have married?

BERNICK.

Yes, and married very well too; she has had several good offers. Strangely enough!—a woman without money, no longer young, and quite insignificant.

JOHAN.

Insignificant?

BERNICK.

Oh, I am not blaming her at all. Indeed, I would not have her otherwise. In a large house like ours, you know, it is always convenient to

have some steady-going person like her, whom one
can put to anything that may turn up.

JOHAN.

Yes, but she herself—— ?

BERNICK.

She herself? What do you mean? Oh, of
course she has plenty to interest herself in—
Betty, and Olaf, and me, you know. People ought
not to think of themselves first; women least of
all. We have each our community, great or small,
to support and work for. I do so, at any rate.
[*Pointing to* KRAP, *who enters from the right.*] See,
here you have an instance. Do you think it is
my own business I am occupied with? By no
means. [*Quickly to* KRAP.] Well?

KRAP.

[*Whispers, showing him a bundle of papers.*] All
the arrangements for the purchase are complete.

BERNICK.

Capital! excellent!—Oh, Johan, you must
excuse me for a moment. [*Low, and with a pressure
of the hand.*] Thanks, thanks, Johan; and be sure
that anything I can do to serve you—you understand—— Come, Mr. Krap!
    [*They go into the Consul's office.*

JOHAN.

[*Looks after him for some time.*] H'm——!
    [*He turns to go down the garden. At the
    same moment* MARTHA *enters from the
    right with a little basket on her arm.*

JOHAN.

Ah, Martha!

MARTHA.

Oh—Johan—is that you?

JOHAN.

Have you been out so early too?

MARTHA.

Yes.   Wait a little; the others will be here
soon.   [*Turns to go out to the left.*

JOHAN.

Tell me, Martha—why are you always in such
a hurry?

MARTHA.

I?

JOHAN.

Yesterday you seemed to keep out of my way,
so that I could not get a word with you; and
to-day——

MARTHA.

Yes, but——

JOHAN.

Before, we were always together—we two old
playfellows.

MARTHA.

Ah, Johan, that is many, many years ago.

JOHAN.

Why, bless me, it's fifteen years ago, neither
more nor less.   Perhaps you think I have changed
a great deal?

MARTHA.

You?   Oh yes, you too, although——

JOHAN.

What do you mean?

MARTHA.

Oh, nothing.

JOHAN.

You don't seem overjoyed to see me again.

MARTHA.

I have waited so long, Johan—too long.

JOHAN.

Waited?   For me to come?

MARTHA.

Yes.

JOHAN.

And why did you think I would come?

MARTHA.

To expiate where you had sinned.

JOHAN.

I?

MARTHA.

Have you forgotten that a woman died in shame and need for your sake?   Have you forgotten that by your fault a young girl's best years have been embittered?

JOHAN.

And you say this to me?   Martha, has your brother never——?

MARTHA.

What of him?

JOHAN.

Has he never——? Oh, I mean has he never said so much as a word in my defence?

MARTHA.

Ah, Johan, you know Karsten's strict principles.

JOHAN.

H'm—of course, of course—yes, I know my
old friend Karsten's strict principles.—But this
is——! Well, well—I have just been talking to
him. It seems to me he has changed a good
deal.

MARTHA.

How can you say so? Karsten has always
been an excellent man.

JOHAN.

That was not exactly what I meant; but let
that pass.—H'm; now I understand the light you
have seen me in; it is the prodigal's return that
you have been waiting for.

MARTHA.

Listen, Johan, and I will tell you in what light
I have seen you. [*Points down to the garden.*] Do
you see that girl playing on the lawn with Olaf?
That is Dina. Do you remember that confused
letter you wrote me when you went away? You
asked me to believe in you. I have believed
in you, Johan. All the bad things that there
were rumours of afterwards must have been
done in desperation, without thought, without
purpose——

JOHAN.

What do you mean?

MARTHA.

Oh, you understand me well enough; no more
of that. But you had to go away—to begin afresh

—a new life. See, Johan, I have stood in your place here, I, your old playfellow. The duties you forgot, or could not fulfil, I have fulfilled for you. I tell you this, that you may have the less to reproach yourself with. I have been a mother to that much-wronged child ; I have brought her up as well as I could——

JOHAN.

And thrown away your whole life in doing so !

MARTHA.

It has not been thrown away. But you have been long of coming, Johan.

JOHAN.

Martha—if I could say to you—— Well, at all events let me thank you for your faithful friendship.

MARTHA.

[*Smiling sadly.*] Ah——! Well now we have made a clean breast of things, Johan. Hush, here comes some one. Good-bye ; I don't want them to——

[*She goes out through the second door on the left. LONA HESSEL comes from the garden, followed by MRS. BERNICK.*

MRS. BERNICK.

[*Still in the garden.*] Good heavens, Lona, what can you be thinking of ?

LONA.

Let me alone, I tell you ; I must and will talk to him.

MRS. BERNICK.

Think what a frightful scandal it would be! Ah, Johan, are you still here?

LONA.

Out with you, boy; don't hang about indoors in the stuffy rooms; go down the garden and talk to Dina.

JOHAN.

Just what I was thinking of doing.

MRS. BERNICK.

But——

LONA.

Listen, Johan; have you ever really looked at Dina?

JOHAN.

Yes; I should think I had.

LONA.

Well, you should look at her to some purpose. She's the very thing for you.

MRS. BERNICK.

But, Lona——!

JOHAN.

The thing for me?

LONA.

Yes, to look at, I mean.   Now go!

JOHAN.

Yes, yes; I don't need any driving.

[*He goes down the garden.*

MRS. BERNICK.

Lona, you amaze me.   You cannot possibly be in earnest.

LONA.

Yes, indeed I am. Isn't she fresh, and sound,
and true? She's just the wife for John. She's
the sort of companion he needs over there; a
different thing from an old step-sister.

MRS. BERNICK.

Dina! Dina Dorf! Just think——!

LONA.

I think first and foremost of the boy's happiness. Help him I must and will; he needs a
little help in such matters; he has never had
much of an eye for women.

MRS. BERNICK.

He? Johan! Surely we have sad cause to
know that——

LONA.

Oh, deuce take that foolish old story? Where
is Bernick? I want to speak to him.

MRS. BERNICK.

Lona, you shall not do it, I tell you!

LONA.

I shall do it. If the boy likes her, and she
him, why then they shall make a match of it.
Bernick is such a clever man; he must manage
the thing——

MRS. BERNICK.

And you think that these American infamies
will be tolerated here——

LONA.

Nonsense, Betty——

MRS. BERNICK.

——that a man like Karsten, with his strict moral ideas——

LONA.

Oh, come now, surely they're not so tremendously strict as all that.

MRS. BERNICK.

What do you dare to say?

LONA.

I dare to say that I don't believe Karsten Bernick is so very much more moral than other men.

MRS. BERNICK.

Do you still hate him, then, so bitterly? What can you want here, since you have never been able to forget that——? I can't understand how you dare look him in the face, after the shameful way you insulted him.

LONA.

Yes, Betty, I forgot myself terribly that time.

MRS. BERNICK.

And how nobly he has forgiven you—he, who had done no wrong? For he couldn't help your foolish fancies. But since that time you have hated me too. [*Bursts into tears.*] You have always envied me my happiness. And now you come here to heap this trouble upon me—to show the town what sort of a family I have brought Karsten into. Yes; it is I that have to suffer for it all; and that's just what you want. Oh, it's hateful of you!

> [*She goes out crying, by the second door on the left.*

LONA.

[*Looking after her.*]   Poor Betty !
                [CONSUL BERNICK *comes out of his office.*

BERNICK.

[*Still at the door.*]   Yes, yes ; that's all right,
Krap—that's excellent.   Send four hundred
crowns for a dinner to the poor.   [*Turns.*]   Lona ?
[*Advancing.*]   You are alone ?   Is not Betty here ?

LONA.

No.   Shall I call her ?

BERNICK.

No, no ; please don't !   Oh, Lona, you don't
know how I have been burning to talk openly
with you—to beg for your forgiveness.

LONA.

Now listen, Karsten : don't let us get senti-
mental.   It doesn't suit us.

BERNICK.

You must hear me, Lona.   I know very well
how much appearances are against me, since you
have heard all about Dina's mother.   But I swear
to you it was only a momentary aberration ; at
one time I really, truly, and honestly loved you.

LONA.

What do you think has brought me home just
now ?

BERNICK.

Whatever you have in mind, I implore you to
do nothing before I have justified myself.   I can
do it, Lona ; at least I can show that I was not
altogether to blame.

LONA.

Now you are frightened.—You once loved me, you say? Yes, you assured me so, often enough, in your letters; and perhaps it was true, too—after a fashion—so long as you were living out there in a great, free world, that gave you courage to think freely and greatly yourself. Perhaps you found in me a little more character, and will, and independence than in most people at home here. And then it was a secret between us two; no one could make fun of your bad taste.

BERNICK.

Lona, how can you think—— ?

LONA.

But when you came home; when you saw the ridicule that poured down upon me; when you heard the laughter at what were called my eccentricities——

BERNICK.

You were inconsiderate in those days.

LONA.

Mainly for the sake of annoying the prudes, both in trousers and petticoats, that infested the town. And then you fell in with that fascinating young actress——

BERNICK.

The whole thing was a piece of folly—nothing more. I swear to you, not a tithe of the scandal and tittletattle was true.

LONA.

Perhaps not; but then Betty came home—young, beautiful, idolised by every one—and when

it became known that she was to have all our
aunt's money, and I nothing——

BERNICK.

Yes, here we are at the root of the matter,
Lona; and now you shall hear the plain truth. I
did not love Betty then; it was for no new fancy
that I broke with you. It was entirely for the
sake of the money; I was forced to do it; I had
to make sure of the money.

LONA.

And you tell me this to my face!

BERNICK.

Yes, I do. Hear me, Lona——

LONA.

And yet you wrote me that an irresistible
passion for Betty had seized you, appealed to my
magnanimity, conjured me for Betty's sake to say
nothing of what had passed between us——

BERNICK.

I had to, I tell you.

LONA.

Now, by all that's holy, I am not sorry I forgot
myself as I did that day.

BERNICK.

Let me tell you, calmly and deliberately, what
my position was at that time. My mother, you
know, stood at the head of the business; but
she had no business capacity. I was hurriedly
called home from Paris; the times were critical ;
I was to retrieve the situation. What did I find ?
I found—and this, remember, had to be kept

strictly secret—a house as good as ruined.   Yes,
it was as good as ruined, the old, respected house,
that had stood through three generations.   What
could I, the son, the only son, do, but cast about
me for a means of saving it ?

LONA.

So you saved the house of Bernick at the
expense of a woman.

BERNICK.

You know very well that Betty loved me.

LONA.

But I ?

BERNICK.

Believe me, Lona, you would never have been
happy with me.

LONA.

Was it your care for my happiness that made
you play me false ?

BERNICK.

Do you think it was from selfish motives that I
acted as I did ?   If I had stood alone then, I
would have begun the world again, bravely and
cheerfully.   But you don't understand how the
head of a great house becomes a living part of the
business he inherits, with its enormous responsibility.   Do you know that the welfare of hundreds,
ay of thousands, depends upon him ?   Can you
not consider that it would have been nothing short
of a disaster to the whole community, which both
you and I call our home, if the house of Bernick
had fallen ?

LONA.

Is it for the sake of the community, then, that
for these fifteen years you have stood upon a lie ?

BERNICK.

A lie?

LONA.

How much does Betty know of all that lay beneath and before her marriage with you?

BERNICK.

Can you think that I would wound her to no purpose by telling her these things?

LONA.

To no purpose, you say? Well well, you are a business man ; you should understand what is to the purpose.—But listen, Karsten : I, too, will speak calmly and deliberately. Tell me—after all, are you really happy?

BERNICK.

In my family, do you mean?

LONA.

Of course.

BERNICK.

I am indeed, Lona. Oh, you have not sacrificed yourself in vain. I can say truly that I have grown happier year by year. Betty is so good and docile. In the course of years she has learnt to mould her character to what is peculiar in mine——

LONA.

H'm.

BERNICK.

At first, it is true, she had some high-flown notions about love ; she could not reconcile herself to the thought that, little by little, it must pass over into a placid friendship.

LONA.

But she is quite reconciled to that now ?

BERNICK.

Entirely.   You may guess that daily intercourse
with me has not been without a ripening influence
upon her.   People must learn to moderate their
mutual claims if they are to fulfil their duties in
the community in which they are placed.   Betty
has by degrees come to understand this, so that
our house is now a model for our fellow citizens.

LONA.

But these fellow citizens know nothing of the
lie ?

BERNICK.

Of the lie ?

LONA.

Yes, of the lie upon which you have stood for
these fifteen years.

BERNICK.

You call that—— ?

LONA.

I call it the lie—the threefold lie.   First the
lie towards me ; then the lie towards Betty ; then
the lie towards Johan.

BERNICK.

Betty has never asked me to speak.

LONA.

Because she has known nothing.

BERNICK.

And you will not ask me to ;—out of consideration for her, you will not.

LONA.

Oh, no ; I daresay I shall manage to bear all the ridicule ; I have a broad back.

BERNICK.

And Johan will not ask me either—he has promised me that.

LONA.

But you yourself, Karsten ? Is there not something within you that longs to get clear of the lie ?

BERNICK.

You would have me voluntarily sacrifice my domestic happiness and my position in society !

LONA.

What right have you to stand where you are standing ?

BERNICK.

For fifteen years I have every day earned a clearer right—by my whole life, by all I have laboured for, by all I have achieved.

LONA.

Yes, you have laboured for much and achieved much, both for yourself and others. You are the richest and most influential man in the town ; they have to bow before your will, all of them, because you are held to be a man without stain or flaw— your home is a model, your life is a model. But all this magnificence, and you yourself along with it, stand on a trembling quicksand. A moment may come, a word may be spoken—and, if you do not save yourself in time, you and all your grandeur go to the bottom.

BERNICK.

Lona—what did you come here to do ?

LONA.

To help you to get firm ground under your feet,
Karsten.

BERNICK.

Revenge ! You want to revenge yourself. I
thought as much ! But you will not succeed !
There is only one who has a right to speak, and
he is silent.

LONA.

Johan ?

BERNICK.

Yes, Johan. If any one else accuses me, I shall
deny everything. If you try to crush me, I shall
fight for my life. You will never succeed, I tell
you ! He who could destroy me will not speak—
and he is going away again.

RUMMEL *and* VIGELAND *enter from the right.*

RUMMEL.

Good-morning, good-morning, my dear Bernick.
You are coming with us to the Trade Council ?
We have a meeting on the railway business, you
know.

BERNICK.

I cannot. It's impossible just now.

VIGELAND.

You really must, Consul——

RUMMEL.

You must, Bernick. There are people working
against us. Hammer and the other men who
were in favour of the coast line, declare that there
are private interests lurking behind the new proposal.

BERNICK

Why, then, explain to them——

VIGELAND.

It's no good our explaining to them, Consul——

RUMMEL.

No, no, you must come yourself. Of course no one will dare to suspect you of anything of that sort.

LONA.

No, I should think not.

BERNICK.

I cannot, I tell you ; I am unwell ;—at any rate wait—let me collect myself.

DOCTOR RÖRLUND *enters from the right.*

RÖRLUND.

Excuse me, Consul ; you see me most painfully agitated——

BERNICK.

Well, well, what is the matter with you ?

RÖRLUND.

I must ask you a question, Consul Bernick.   Is it with your consent that the young girl who has found an asylum under your roof shows herself in the public streets in company with a person whom——

LONA.

What person, Pastor ?

RÖRLUND.

With the person from whom, of all others in the world, she should be kept furthest apart.

LONA.

Ho-ho!

RÖRLUND.

Is it with your consent, Consul?

BERNICK.

I know nothing about it. [*Looking for his hat and gloves.*] Excuse me; I am in a hurry; I am going up to the Trade Council.

HILMAR.

[*Enters from the garden and goes over to the second door to the left.*] Betty, Betty, come here!

MRS. BERNICK.

[*In the doorway.*] What is it?

HILMAR.

You must go down the garden and put a stop to the flirtation a certain person is carrying on with Miss Dina Dorf. It has made me quite nervous to listen to it.

LONA.

Indeed? What did the person say?

HILMAR.

Oh, only that he wants her to go with him to America. Ugh!

RÖRLUND.

Can such things be possible!

MRS. BERNICK.

What do you say?

LONA.

Why, that would be capital.

BERNICK.

Impossible! You must have misunderstood him.

HILMAR.

Then ask him himself. Here come the couple. Only don't drag me into the business.

BERNICK.

[*To* RUMMEL *and* VIGELAND.] I shall follow you —in a moment——

> [RUMMEL *and* VIGELAND *go out to the right.*
> JOHAN TÖNNESEN *and* DINA *come in from the garden.*

JOHAN.

Hurrah, Lona, she's coming with us!

MRS. BERNICK.

Oh, Johan—how can you!

RÖRLUND.

Can this be true? Such a crying scandal? By what vile arts have you——?

JOHAN.

What, what, man? What are you saying?

RÖRLUND.

Answer me, Dina: is this your intention?—deliberately formed, and of your own free will?

DINA.

I must get away from here.

RÖRLUND.

But with him—with him!

DINA.

Tell me of any one else that has courage to set
me free?

RÖRLUND.

Then you shall know who he is.

JOHAN.

Be silent!

BERNICK.

Not a word more!

RÖRLUND.

Then I should ill serve the community over
whose manners and morals it is my duty to keep
watch ; and I should act most indefensibly towards
this young girl, in whose training I have borne an
important share, and who is to me——

JOHAN.

Take care what you are doing!

RÖRLUND.

She shall know it! Dina, it was this man who
caused all your mother's misfortune and shame.

BERNICK.

Rector—— !

DINA.

He! [*To* JOHAN.] Is this true?

JOHAN.

Karsten, do you answer!

BERNICK.

Not a word more! Not a word more to-day.

DINA.

Then it is true.

RÖRLUND.

True, true! And more than that. This person,
in whom you were about to placé your trust, did
not run away empty-handed—Mrs. Bernick's
strong-box—the Consul can bear witness!

LONA.

Liar!

BERNICK.

Ah——!

MRS. BERNICK.

Oh God! oh God!

JOHAN.

[*Goes towards him with uplifted arm.*]   You dare
to——!

LONA.

[*Keeping him back.*]   Don't strike him, Johan.

RÖRLUND.

Yes, yes; assault me if you like. But the truth
shall out; and this is the truth. Consul Bernick
has said so himself; it is notorious to the whole
town.—Now, Dina, now you know him.

[*A short pause.*

JOHAN.

[*Softly seizing* BERNICK's *arm.*]   Karsten, Karsten,
what have you done?

MRS. BERNICK.

[*Softly, in tears.*]   Oh, Karsten, that I should
bring all this shame upon you!

SANDSTAD.

[*Enters hastily from the right, and says, with his
hand still on the door-handle.*]   You must really come

now, Consul! The whole railway is hanging by a thread.

BERNICK.

[*Absently.*] What is it? What am I to——?

LONA.

[*Earnestly and with emphasis.*] You are to rise and support society, brother-in-law :

SANDSTAD.

Yes, come, come; we need all your moral predominance.

JOHAN.

[*Close to him.*] Bernick, we two will talk of this to-morrow.

> [*He goes out through the garden ;* BERNICK *goes out to the right with* SANDSTAD, *as if his will were paralysed.*

ACT THIRD.

The garden-room in CONSUL BERNICK'S *house.*

BERNICK, *with a cane in his hand, enters, in a violent passion, from the second room on the left, leaving the door half open.*

BERNICK.

There, now! At last I've done it in earnest; I don't think he'll forget that thrashing. [*To some one in the other room.*] What do you say?—*I* say you are a foolish mother! You make excuses for him, and encourage him in all his naughtiness—— Not naughtiness? What do you call it then? To steal out of the house at night and go to sea in a fishing-boat; to remain out till late in the day, and put me in mortal terror, as if I hadn't enough anxiety without that. And the young rascal dares to threaten me with running away! Just let him try it!—You? No, I daresay not; you don't seem to care much what becomes of him. I believe if he were to break his neck——! Oh, indeed? But it happens that *I* need some one to carry on my work in the world; it would not suit me to be left childless. Don't argue, Betty; I have said it, once for all; he is not to leave the house. [*Listens.*] Hush, don't let people notice anything.

KRAP *comes in from the right.*

KRAP.

Can you spare me a moment, Consul.

BERNICK.

[*Throws away the cane.*]   Of course, of course
Have you come from the shipyard ?

KRAP.

Just this moment.   H'm——

BERNICK.

Well ?   Nothing wrong with the *Palm Tree*, I
hope ?

KRAP.

The *Palm Tree* can sail to-morrow, but——

BERNICK.

The *Indian Girl*, then ?   I might have guessed
that that stiff-necked——

KRAP.

The *Indian Girl* can sail to-morrow, too ; but—
I don't think she will get very far.

BERNICK.

What do you mean ?

KRAP.

Excuse me, Consul, that door is ajar, and I
think there is some one in the room——

BERNICK.

[*Shuts the door.*]   There then.   But what is the
meaning of all this secrecy ?

KRAP.

It means this : I believe Aune intends to send
the *Indian Girl* to the bottom, with every soul on
board.

BERNICK.

Good heavens ! how can you think—— ?

KRAP.

I can explain it in no other way, Consul.

BERNICK.

Well then, tell me as shortly as you can——

KRAP.

I will. You know how things have been dragging in the yard since we got the new machines and the new inexperienced workmen ?

BERNICK.

Yes, yes.

KRAP.

But this morning, when I went down there, I noticed that the repairs on the American had been going at a great rate. The big patch in her bottom—the rotten place, you know——

BERNICK.

Yes, yes ; what about it ?

KRAP.

It was completly repaired—to all appearance ; plastered up ; looked as good as new. I heard that Aune himself had been working at it by lantern-light the whole night through.

BERNICK.

Yes, yes, and then—— ?

KRAP.

I was a good deal puzzled. It happened that the workmen were at breakfast, so I could ferret about as I pleased, both outside and inside. It was difficult to get down into the hold, among the cargo ; but I saw enough to convince me. There is rascality at work, Consul.

BERNICK.

I can't believe it, Mr. Krap.   I cannot· and will
not believe such a thing of Aune.

KRAP.

I'm sorry for it, but it's the simple truth.
There is rascality at work, I say.   Not a stick of
new timber had been put in, so far as I could see.
It was only plugged and puttied up, and covered
with plates and tarpaulins, and so forth.   All
bogus !   The *Indian Girl* will never get to New
York.   She'll go to the bottom like a cracked
pot.

BERNICK.

Why, this is hcrrible !   What do you think can
be his motive ?

KRAP.

He probably wants to bring the machines into
discredit ; wants to revenge himself ; wants to
have the old workmen taken on again.

BERNICK.

And for that he would send all these men to
their death ?

KRAP.

He has been heard to say that the crew of the
Indian Girl are brute beasts, not men.

BERNICK.

Yes, yes, that may be ; but does he not think of
the great loss of capital ?

KRAP.

Aune is not over-fond of capital, Consul.

BERNICK.

True enough ; he is an agitator and mischief-
maker; but such a piece of villainy as this——!

I'll tell you what, Mr. Krap : this affair must be looked into again. Not a word of it to any one. Our yard would lose its reputation if this came to people's ears.

KRAP.

Of course, but——

BERNICK.

During the dinner-hour you must go down there again ; I must have absolute certainty.

KRAP.

You shall, Consul. But, excuse me, what will you do then ?

BERNICK.

Why, report the case of course. We cannot be accessories to a crime. I must keep my conscience clear. Besides, it will make a good impression on both the press and the public, to see me disregard all personal interests, and let justice take its course.

KRAP.

Very true, Consul.

BERNICK.

But, first of all, absolute certainty—and, until then, silence.

KRAP.

Not a word, Consul ; and you shall have absolute certainty.

[*He goes out through the garden and down the street.*

BERNICK.

[*Half aloud.*] Horrible ! But no, it's impossible —inconceivable !

[*As he turns to go to his own room* HILMAR TÖNNESEN *enters from the right.*

HILMAR.

Good-day, Bernick! Well, I congratulate you
on your field-day in the Trade Council yesterday.

BERNICK.

Oh, thank you.

HILMAR.

It was a brilliant victory, I hear; the victory of
intelligent public spirit over self-interest and
prejudice—like a French razzia upon the Kabyles.
Strange, that after the unpleasant scene here,
you——

BERNICK.

Yes, yes, don't speak of it.

HILMAR.

But the tug-of-war is yet to come.

BERNICK.

In the matter of the railway, you mean?

HILMAR.

Yes. I suppose you have heard of the egg that
our editor-friend is hatching?

BERNICK.

[*Anxiously.*] No! What is it?

HILMAR.

Oh, he has got hold of the rumour that's floating about, and is coming out with an article on
the subject.

BERNICK.

What rumour?

HILMAR.

Why, about the great buying-up of property
along the branch line, of course.

BERNICK.

What do you mean ?   Is there any such rumour
about ?

HILMAR.

Yes, over the whole town.   I heard it at the
club.   They say that one of our lawyers has been
secretly commissioned to buy up all the forests,
all the mining rights, all the water-power——

BERNICK.

And is it known for whom ?

HILMAR.

They thought at the club that it must be for a
syndicate from some other town that had got wind
of your scheme, and had rushed in before the
prices rose.   Isn't it disgraceful ?   Ugh !

BERNICK.

Disgraceful ?

HILMAR.

Yes, that outsiders should trespass on our pre-
serves in that way.   And that one of our own
lawyers could lend himself to such a transaction !
Now all the profit will go to strangers.

BERNICK.

But this is only a vague rumour.

HILMAR.

People believe it, at any rate ; and to-morrow
or next day you may look for some editorial com-
ments on the fact.   Every one is indignant about
it already.   I heard several people say that if this
rumour is confirmed they will strike their names
off the lists.

BERNICK.

Impossible !

HILMAR.

Indeed ? Why do you think these peddling creatures were so ready to join you in your undertaking? Do you think they weren't themselves hankering after——?

BERNICK.

Impossible, I say ; there is at least so much public spirit in our little community——

HILMAR.

Here ? Oh yes, you are an optimist, and judge others by yourself. But I am a pretty keen observer, and I tell you there is not a person here —except ourselves, of course—not one, I say, that holds high the banner of the ideal. [*Up towards the back.*] Ugh, there they are !

BERNICK.

Who ?

HILMAR.

The two Americans. [*Looks out to the right.*] And who is that with them ? Why, it's the captain of the *Indian Girl.* Ugh !

BERNICK.

What can they want with him ?

HILMAR.

Oh, it's very appropriate company. They say he has been a slave-dealer or a pirate ; and who knows what that couple have turned their hands to in all these years.

BERNICK.

I tell you, such innuendoes are utterly unjust.

HILMAR.

Yes, you are an optimist.   But here we have them upon us again of course ; so I shall get away in time.   [*Goes towards the door on the left.*

LONA HESSEL *enters from the right.*

LONA.

What, Hilmar, am I driving you away ?

HILMAR.

Not at all, not at all.   I really oughtn't to have been wasting time here ; I have something to say to Betty.   [*Goes out by the second door on the left.*

BERNICK.

[*After a short pause.*]   Well, Lona ?

LONA.

Well ?

BERNICK.

What do you think of me to-day ?

LONA.

The same as yesterday ; a lie more or less——'

BERNICK.

I must clear all this up.   Where has Johan gone to ?

LONA.

He will be here directly ; he is talking to a man outside there.

BERNICK.

After what you heard yesterday, you can understand that my whole position is ruined if the truth comes to light.

LONA.

I understand.

BERNICK.

Of course I need not tell you that *I* was not guilty of the supposed crime.

LONA.

Of course not.   But who was the thief?

BERNICK.

There was no thief.   There was no money stolen; not a halfpenny was missing.

LONA.

What?

BERNICK.

Not a halfpenny, I say.

LONA.

But the rumour?   How did that shameful rumour get abroad, that Johan——?

BERNICK.

Lona, I find I can talk to you as I can to no one else; I shall conceal nothing from vou.   *I* had my share in spreading the rumour.

LONA.

You!   And you could do this wrong to the man who, for your sake——?

BERNICK.

You must not condemn me without remember-ing how matters stood at the time.   As I told you yesterday, I came home to find my mother involved in a whole series of foolish undertakings. Disasters of various kinds followed; all possible ill-luck seemed to crowd in upon us; our house was on the verge of ruin.   I was half reckless

and half in despair. Lona, I believe it was
principally to deaden thought that I got into
that entanglement which ended in Johan's
going away.

LONA.

H'm——

BERNICK.

You can easily imagine that there were all sorts
of rumours in the air after you two had left. It
was said that this was not his first misdemeanour.
Some said Dorf had received a large sum of money
from him to hold his tongue and keep out of the
way; others declared she had got the money.
At the same time it got abroad that our house
had difficulty in meeting its engagements. What
more natural than that the scandal-mongers should
put these two rumours together? Then, as Madam
Dorf remained here in unmistakable poverty,
people began to say that he had taken the money
with him to America; and rumour made the sum
larger and larger every day.

LONA.

And you, Karsten——?

BERNICK.

I clutched at the rumour as a drowning man
clutches at a straw.

LONA.

You helped to spread it?

BERNICK.

I did not contradict it. Our creditors were
beginning to press upon us; I had to quiet them
—to prevent them from doubting the solidity of
the firm. I let it be thought that a momentary

misfortune had befallen us, but that if people only refrained from pressing us—if they would only give us time—every one should be paid in full.

LONA.

And every one was paid in full?

BERNICK.

Yes, Lona; that rumour saved our house and made me the man I am.

LONA.

A lie, then, has made you the man you are.

BERNICK.

Whom did it hurt, then? Johan intended never to return.

LONA.

You ask whom it hurt? Look into yourself and see if it has not hurt you.

BERNICK.

Look into any man you please, and you will find at least one dark spot that must be kept out of sight.

LONA.

And you call yourselves pillars of society '

BERNICK.

Society has none better.

LONA.

Then what does it matter whether such a society is supported or not? What is it that passes current here? Lies and shams—nothing else. Here are you, the first man in the town,

prosperous, powerful, looked up to by every one
—you, who have set the brand of crime upon an
innocent man.

BERNICK.

Do you think I do not feel deeply the wrong I
have done him? Do you think I am not prepared
to atone for it?

LONA.

How? By speaking out?

BERNICK.

Can you ask me to do that?

LONA.

How else can you atone for such a wrong?

BERNICK.

I am rich, Lona; Johan may ask for what he
pleases——

LONA.

Yes, offer him money, and you'll see what he
will answer.

BERNICK.

Do you know what he intends to do?

LONA.

No. Since yesterday he has said nothing to
me. It seems as if all this had suddenly made a
full-grown man of him.

BERNICK.

I must speak to him.

LONA.

Then here he is.

JOHAN TÖNNESEN *enters from the right.*

BERNICK.

[*Going towards him.*]   Johan——!

JOHAN.

[*Waving him off.*]   Let me speak first.   Yesterday morning I gave you my word to be silent.

BERNICK.

You did.

JOHAN.

But I did not know then——

BERNICK.

Johan, let me in two words explain the circumstances——

JOHAN.

There is no necessity; I understand the circumstances very well.   Your house was in a difficult
position; and I was far away, and you had my
unprotected name and fame to do what you liked
with——   Well, I don't blame you so much for it;
we were young and thoughtless in those days.   But
now I need the truth, and now you must speak out.

BERNICK.

And just at this moment I require all my moral
authority, and therefore I cannot speak out.

JOHAN.

I don't care so much about the falsehoods you
have trumped up at my expense; it is the other
thing that you must take upon your own shoulders.
Dina shall be my wife, and I will live here, here
in this town, along with her.

LONA.

You will?

BERNICK.

With Dina ! As your wife ? Here, in this town '

JOHAN.

Yes, just here; I will stay here to outface all
these liars and backbiters. And that I may win
her, you must set me free.

BERNICK.

Have you considered that, if I plead guilty to
the one thing, I plead guilty to the other as well ?
I can prove by our books, you say, that there was
no embezzlement at all ? But I cannot ; our books
were not so accurately kept in those days. And
even if I could, what would be gained by it ?
Should I not figure, at best, as the man who,
having once saved himself by falsehood, had let
that falsehood, and all its consequences, run on for
fifteen years, without taking a single step to retract
it ? You have forgotten what our society is, or you
would know that that would crush me to the very
dust.

JOHAN.

I can only repeat that I shall make Madam
Dorf's daughter my wife, and live with her here,
in this town.

BERNICK.

[*Wipes the perspiration from his forehead.*] Hear
me, Johan—and you, too, Lona. My position at
this moment is not an ordinary one. I am so
situated, that if you strike this blow you destroy
me utterly, and not only me, but also a great and
golden future for the community which was, after
all, the home of your childhood.

JOHAN.

And if I do not strike the blow, I destroy all
that makes my own future of value to me.

LONA.

Go on, Karsten.

BERNICK.

Then listen. Everything turns upon this question
of the railway, and that is not so simple as you
think. Of course you have heard that last year
there was some talk of a coast-line? It had many
powerful advocates in the district, and especially in
the press; but I succeeded in blocking it, because
it would have injured our steamboat trade along
the coast.

LONA.

Have you an interest in this steamboat trade?

BERNICK.

Yes; but no one dared to impugn my motives
on that account. My spotless name was an ample
safeguard. For that matter, I could have borne
the loss; but the town could not. Then the inland
line was determined on. As soon as the route was
fixed, I assured myself secretly that a branch con-
.   nection between it and the town was practicable.

LONA.

Why secretly, Karsten?

BERNICK.

Have you heard any talk of the great buying-up
of forests, mines, and water-power?

JOHAN.

Yes, for a company in some other town——

BERNICK.

As these properties now lie, they are as good as worthless to their scattered owners ; so they have sold comparatively cheap. If the purchaser had waited until the branch line was known to be in contemplation, the vendors would have demanded fancy prices.

LONA.

Very likely ; but what then ?

BERNICK.

Now comes the point which may or may not be interpreted favourably—a risk which no man in our community could afford to incur, unless he had a spotless and honoured name to rely upon.

LONA.

Well ?

BERNICK.

It is I who have bought up the whole.

LONA.

You ?

JOHAN.

On your own account ?

BERNICK.

On my own account. If the branch line is made, I am a millionaire ; if not, I am ruined.

LONA.

This is a great risk, Karsten.

BERNICK.

I have staked all I possess upon the throw.

LONA.

I was not thinking of the money; but when it comes out that——

BERNICK.

Yes, that is the great point. With the unblemished reputation I have hitherto borne, I can take the whole affair upon my shoulders and carry it through, saying to my fellow citizens, "See, this I have ventured for the good of the community!"

LONA.

Of the community?

BERNICK.

Yes; and not a soul will question my motives.

LONA.

Then there are some people, it seems, who have acted more openly than you, with no private interests, no ulterior designs.

BERNICK.

Who?

LONA.

Why, Rummel and Sandstad and Vigeland, of course.

BERNICK.

To make sure of their support, I had to let them into the secret.

LONA.

And they?

BERNICK.

They have stipulated for a fifth of the profits.

LONA

Oh, these pillars of society!

BERNICK.

Can you not see that it is society itself that compels us to adopt these indirect courses? What would have happened if I had not acted secretly? Why, every one would have thrown himself into the undertaking, and the whole thing would have been broken up, frittered away, bungled, and ruined. There is not a single man here, except myself, that knows how to organise an enormous concern such as this will become ; in this country the men of real business ability are almost all of foreign descent. That is why my conscience acquits me in this matter. Only in my hands can all this property be of permanent benefit to the many whose subsistence will depend upon it.

LONA.

I believe you are right there, Karsten.

JOHAN.

But I know nothing of " the many," and my life's happiness is at stake.

BERNICK.

The welfare of your native place is no less at stake. If things come to the surface which cast a slur upon my past life, all my opponents will join forces and overwhelm me. In our society a boyish error is never effaced. People will scrutinise my whole career, will rake up a thousand trifling incidents, and interpret and comment upon them in the light of these disclosures. They will crush me beneath the weight of rumours and slanders. I shall have to retire from the railway board ; and if I take my hand away, the whole thing will fall to pieces, and I shall have to face not only ruin but social extinction.

LONA.

Johan, after what you have heard, you must go away, and say nothing.

BERNICK.

Yes, yes, Johan, you must!

JOHAN.

Yes, I will go away, and say nothing; but I will come back again, and then I will speak.

BERNICK.

Remain over there, Johan; be silent, and I am ready to share with you——

JOHAN.

Keep your money, and give me back my good name.

BERNICK.

And sacrifice my own!

JOHAN.

You and your "community" must settle that between you. I must and will make Dina my wife. So I shall sail to-morrow in the *Indian Girl*——

BERNICK.

In the *Indian Girl?*

JOHAN.

Yes; the captain has promised to take me. I shall go across, I tell you, sell my farm, and settle up my affairs. In two months I shall be back again.

BERNICK.

And then you will tell all?

JOHAN.

Then the wrong-doer must take up his own
burden.

BERNICK.

Do you forget that I must also take upon me
wrong-doing of which I was not guilty?

JOHAN.

Who was it that, fifteen years ago, reaped the
benefit of that shameful rumour?

BERNICK.

You drive me to desperation!   But if you speak,
I will deny everything!   I will say it is all a
conspiracy against me; a piece of revenge; that
you have come here to blackmail me!

LONA.

Shame on you, Karsten!

BERNICK.

I am desperate, I tell you; I am fighting for my
life.   I will deny everything, everything!

JOHAN.

I have your two letters.   I found them in my
box among my other papers.   I read them through
this morning; they are plain enough.

BERNICK.

And you will produce them?

JOHAN.

If you force me to.

BERNICK.

And in two months you will be here again?

JOHAN.

I hope so. The wind is fair. In three weeks I shall be in New York—if the *Indian Girl* doesn't go to the bottom.

BERNICK.

[*Starting.*] Go to the bottom? Why should the *Indian Girl* go to the bottom?

JOHAN.

That's just what I say.

BERNICK.

[*Almost inaudibly.*] Go to the bottom?

JOHAN.

Well, Bernick, now you know what you have to expect; you must do what you can in the meantime. Good-bye! Give my love to Betty, though she certainly has not received me in a very sisterly fashion. But Martha I must see. She must tell Dina—she must promise me——
[*He goes out by the second door on the left.*

BERNICK.

[*To himself.*] The *Indian Girl*——? [*Quickly.*] Lona, you must prevent this!

LONA.

You see yourself, Karsten—I have lost all power over him.
[*She follows* JOHAN *into the room on the left.*

BERNICK.

[*In unquiet thought.*] Go to the bottom——?

AUNE *enters from the right.*

AUNE.

Asking your pardon, Consul, might I speak to you—— ?

BERNICK.

[*Turns angrily.*]   What do you want?

AUNE.

I wanted, if I might, to ask you a question, Consul Bernick.

BERNICK.

Well, well; be quick.   What is it about?

AUNE.

I wanted to know if you're still determined—firmly determined—to turn me adrift if the *Indian Girl* should not be ready for sea to-morrow?

BERNICK.

What now?   The ship will be ready for sea.

AUNE.

Yes—she will.   But supposing as she wasn't—should I have to go?

BERNICK.

Why ask such useless questions?

AUNE.

I want to make quite sure, Consul.   Just answer me: should I have to go?

BERNICK.

Am I in the habit of changing my mind?

AUNE.

Then to-morrow I should have lost the place that rightly belongs to me in my home and family —lost my influence among the workmen—lost all my chances of helping them as are lowly and down-trodden ?

BERNICK.

We have discussed that point long ago, Aune.

AUNE.

Then the *Indian Girl* must sail.   [*A short pause.*

BERNICK.

Listen : I cannot look after everything myself, and be responsible for everything. I suppose you are prepared to assure me that the repairs are thoroughly carried out?

AUNE.

It was very short time you gave me, Consul.

BERNICK.

But the repairs are all right, you say ?

AUNE.

The weather is fine, and it is midsummer.
    [*Another silence.*

BERNICK.

Have you anything more to say to me ?

AUNE.

I don't know as there's aught else, Consul.

BERNICK.

Then—the *Indian Girl* sails——

AUNE.

To-morrow ?

BERNICK.

Yes.

AUNE.

Very well.   [*He bows and goes out.*
    [BERNICK *stands for a moment irresolute;
    then he goes quickly towards the door as
    if to call* AUNE *back, but stops and stands
    hesitating with his hand on the knob. At
    that moment the door is opened from out-
    side, and* KRAP *enters.*

KRAP.

[*Speaking low.*]   Aha, he has been here   Has
he confessed ?

BERNICK.

H'm——; have you discovered anything ?

KRAP.

What need was there ? Did you not see the
evil conscience looking out of his very eyes ?

BERNICK.

Oh, nonsense ;—no one can see such things. I
asked if you had discovered anything ?

KRAP.

I couldn't get at it ; I was too late ; they were
busy hauling the ship out of dock. But this very
haste proves plainly that——

BERNICK.

It proves nothing. The inspection has taken
place, then ?

KRAP.

Of course ; but——

BERNICK.

There you see! And they have, of course, found nothing to complain of?

KRAP.

Consul, you know very well how such inspections are conducted, especially in a yard that has such a name as ours.

BERNICK.

No matter; it relieves us of all reproach.

KRAP.

Could you really not read in Aune's face, Consul—— ?

BERNICK.

Aune has entirely satisfied me, I tell you.

KRAP.

And I tell you I am morally convinced——

BERNICK.

What does this mean, Mr. Krap? I know very well that you have a grudge against the man; but if you want to attack him, you should choose some other opportunity. You know how essential it is for me—or rather for the owners—that the *Indian Girl* should sail to-morrow.

KRAP.

Very well; so be it; but if ever we hear of that ship again—h'm!

VIGELAND *enters from the right.*

VIGELAND.

How do you do, Consul? Have you a moment to spare?

BERNICK.

At your service, Mr. Vigeland.

VIGELAND.

I only want to know if you agree with me that the *Palm Tree* ought to sail to-morrow?

BERNICK.

Yes—I thought that was settled.

VIGELAND.

But the captain has just come to tell me that the storm-signals have been hoisted.

KRAP.

The barometer has fallen rapidly since this morning.

BERNICK.

Indeed? Is a storm threatening?

VIGELAND.

A stiff breeze at any rate; but not a contrary wind; quite the reverse——

BERNICK.

H'm; what do you say, then?

VIGELAND.

I say, as I said to the captain, that the *Palm Tree* is in the hands of Providence. And besides, she is only going over the North Sea to begin with; and freights are pretty high in England just now, so that——

BERNICK.

Yes, it would probably mean a loss if we delayed.

VIGELAND.

The vessel is soundly built, you know, and fully insured too. I can tell you it's another matter with the *Indian Girl*——

BERNICK.

What do you mean?

VIGELAND.

Why, she is to sail to-morrow too.

BERNICK.

Yes, the owners hurried us on, and besides——

VIGELAND.

Well, if that old hulk can venture out—and with such a crew into the bargain—it would be a shame if we couldn't——

BERNICK.

Well well; I suppose you have the ship's papers with you.

VIGELAND.

Yes, here they are.

BERNICK.

Good; then perhaps you will go with Mr. Krap——

KRAP.

This way, please; we shall soon put them in order.

VIGELAND

Thanks.—And the result we will leave in the hands of Omnipotence, Consul.

[*He goes with* KRAP *into the foremost room on the left.* DOCTOR RÖRLUND *comes through the garden.*

RÖRLUND.

What ' You at home at this time of the day,
Consul !

BERNICK.

[*Absently.*]   As you see !

RÖRLUND.

I looked in to see your wife. I thought she
might need a word of consolation.

BERNICK.

I daresay she does.   But I, too, should be glad
of a word with you.

RÖRLUND.

With pleasure, Consul.   But what is the matter
with you ?   You look quite pale and upset.

BERNICK.

Indeed ?   Do I ?   Well, can you wonder at it,
with such a host of things crowding upon me all
at once.   Besides all my usual business, I have
this affair of the railway——   Give me your
attention for a moment, Doctor ; let me ask you
a question.

RÖRLUND.

By all means, Consul.

BERNICK.

A thought has occurred to me lately : When
one stands on the threshold of a great undertaking, that is to promote the welfare of thousands,
—if a single sacrifice should be demanded—— ?

RÖRLUND.

How do you mean ?

BERNICK.

Take, for example, a man who is starting a large manufactory. He knows very well—for all experience has taught him—that sooner or later, in the working of that manufactory, human life will be lost.

RÖRLUND.

Yes, it is only too probable.

BERNICK.

Or suppose he is about to open a mine. He takes into his service both fathers of families and young men in the heyday of life. May it not be predicted with certainty that some will perish in the undertaking?

RÖRLUND.

Unhappily there can be little doubt of that.

BERNICK.

Well; such a man, then, knows beforehand that his enterprise will undoubtedly, some time or other, lead to the loss of life. But the undertaking is for the greater good of the greater number; for every life it costs, it will, with equal certainty, promote the welfare of many hundreds.

RÖRLUND.

Ah, you are thinking of the railway—of all the dangerous tunnellings, and blastings, and that sort of thing——

BERNICK.

Yes—yes, of course—I am thinking of the railway. And, besides, the railway will bring with it both manufactories and mines. But don't you think that——

RÖRLUND.

My dear Consul, you are almost too scrupulous.
If you place the affair in the hands of Providence——

BERNICK.

Yes; yes, of course; Providence——

RÖRLUND.

——you can have nothing to reproach yourself
with. Go on and prosper with the railway

BERNICK.

Yes, but let us take a peculiar case. Let us
suppose a blasting has to be made at a dangerous
place; and unless it is carried out, the railway
will come to a standstill. Suppose the engineer
knows that it will cost the life of the workman
who fires the fuse; but fired it must be, and it is
the engineer's duty to send a workman to do it.

RÖRLUND.

H'm——

BERNICK.

I know what you will say: It would be heroic
if the engineer himself took the match and went
and fired the fuse. But no one does such things.
So he must sacrifice a workman.

RÖRLUND.

No engineer among us would ever do that.

BERNICK

No engineer in the great nations would think
twice about doing it.

RÖRLUND.

In the great nations? No, I daresay not.   In
those corrupt and unscrupulous communities——

BERNICK.

Oh, those communities have their good points
too.

RÖRLUND.

Can you say that—you, who yourself——?

BERNICK.

In the great nations one has at least elbow-
room for useful enterprise.   There, men have the
courage to sacrifice something for a great cause.
But here, one is hampered by all sorts of petty
considerations.

RÖRLUND.

Is a human life a petty consideration?

BERNICK.

When that human life is a menace to the welfare
of thousands.

RÖRLUND.

But you are putting quite inconceivable cases,
Consul!   I don't understand you to-day.   And
then you refer me to the great communities.
Yes, there—what does a human life count for
there?   They think no more of staking life than
of staking capital.   But we, I hope, look at things
from an entirely different moral standpoint.   Think
of our exemplary shipowners!   Name me a single
merchant here among us who, for the sake of
paltry profit, would sacrifice one human life!   And
then think of those scoundrels in the great communities who enrich themselves by sending out
one unseaworthy ship after another——

BERNICK.

I am not speaking of unseaworthy ships !

RÖRLUND.

But I am, Consul.

BERNICK.

Yes, but to what purpose ? It has nothing to do with the question.—Oh, these little craven qualms of conscience ! If a general among us were to lead his troops under fire, and get some of them shot, he would never sleep o' nights after it. Elsewhere it is very different. You should hear what he says——

[*Pointing to the door on the left.*

RÖRLUND.

He ? Who ? The American—— ?

BERNICK.

Of course. You should hear how people in America——

RÖRLUND.

Is he in there ? Why did you not tell me ? I shall go at once——

BERNICK.

It's of no use. You will make no impression on him.

RÖRLUND.

That we shall see. Ah, here he is.

JOHAN TÖNNESEN *comes from the room on the left*

JOHAN.

[*Speaking through the open doorway.*] Yes, yes, Dina, so be it ; but don't think that I shall give you up. I shall return, and things will come all right between us.

RÖRLUND.

May I ask what you mean by these words?
What is it you want?

JOHAN.

I want the girl to whom you yesterday traduced
me, to be my wife.

RÖRLUND.

Your——? Can you imagine that——?

JOHAN.

She shall be my wife.

RÖRLUND.

Well, then, you shall hear—— [*Goes to the
half-open door.*] Mrs. Bernick, will you be kind
enough to be a witness—— And you too, Miss
Martha. And bring Dina with you. [*Sees* LONA.]
Ah, are you here, too?

LONA.

[*In the doorway.*] Shall I come?

RÖRLUND.

As many as will—the more the better.

BERNICK.

What are you going to do?

LONA, MRS. BERNICK, MARTHA, DINA, *and* HILMAR
TÖNNESEN *come out of the room on the left.*

MRS. BERNICK.

Doctor, nothing I can say will stop him from——

RÖRLUND.

I shall stop him, Mrs. Bernick.—Dina, you are
a thoughtless girl. But I do not blame you very

much.   You have stood here too long without the moral support that should have sustained you.   I blame myself for not having given you that support sooner.

DINA.

You must not speak now !

MRS. BERNICK.

What is all this ?

RÖRLUND.

It is now that I must speak, Dina, though your conduct yesterday and to-day has made it ten times more difficult for me.   But all other considerations must give place to your rescue.   You remember the promise I gave you.   You remember what you promised to answer, when I found that the time had come.   Now I can hesitate no longer, and therefore—[To JOHAN TÖNNESEN]—I tell you that this girl, whom you are pursuing, is betrothed to me.

MRS. BERNICK.

What do you say ?

BERNICK.

Dina !

JOHAN.

She !   Betrothed to——?

MARTHA.

No, no, Dina !

LONA.

A lie !

JOHAN.

Dina—does that man speak the truth ?

DINA.

[*After a short pause.*]   Yes.

RÖRLUND.

This, I trust, will paralyse all your arts of
seduction. The step I have determined to take
for Dina's welfare may now be made known to our
whole community. I hope—nay, I am sure—that
it will not be misinterpreted. And now, Mrs.
Bernick, I think we had better take her away
from here, and try to restore her mind to peace
and equilibrium.

MRS. BERNICK.

Yes, come. Oh, Dina, what happiness for you !
[*She leads* DINA *out to the left ;* DOCTOR
RÖRLUND *goes along with them.*

MARTHA.

Good-bye, Johan !   [*She goes out.*

HILMAR.

[*At the garden door.*] H'm—well, I really must
say——

LONA.

[*Who has been following* DINA *with her eyes.*]
Don't be cast down, boy ! I shall stay here and
look after the Pastor.   [*She goes out to the right.*

BERNICK.

Johan, you won't sail now with the *Indian Girl.*

JOHAN.

Now more than ever.

BERNICK.

Then you will not come back again ?

JOHAN.

I shall come back.

BERNICK.

After this? What would you do after this?

JOHAN.

Revenge myself on the whole band of you ; crush as many of you as I can.

[*He goes out to the right.* VIGELAND *an .* KRAP *come from the Consul's office.*

VIGELAND.

Well, the papers are in order now, Consul.

BERNICK.

Good, good——

KRAP.

[*In a low voice.*] Then it is settled that the *Indian Girl* is to sail to-morrow.

BERNICK.

She is to sail.

[*He goes into his room.* VIGELAND *and* KRAP *go out to the right.* HILMAR TÖNNESEN *is following them, when* OLAF *peeps cautiously out at the door on the left.*

OLAF.

Uncle ! Uncle Hilmar !

HILMAR.

Ugh, is that you ? Why don't you stay upstairs ? You know you are under arrest.

OLAF.

[*Comes a few steps forward.*] Sh ! Uncle Hilmar, do you know the news ?

HILMAR.

I know that you got a thrashing to-day.

OLAF.

[*Looks threateningly towards his father's room.*]
He sha'n't thrash me again. But do you know
that Uncle Johan is to sail to-morrow with the
Americans ?

HILMAR.

What's that to you ?   You get upstairs again !

OLAF.

Perhaps I may go buffalo-hunting yet, uncle.

HILMAR.

Rubbish ! such a young milksop as you——

OLAF.

Just wait a little; you shall hear something
to-morrow !

HILMAR.

Little blockhead !
        [*He goes out through the garden.* OLAF,
           catching sight of KRAP, *who comes from
           the right, runs in again and shuts the door.*

KRAP.

[*Goes up to the Consul's door and opens it a little.*]
Excuse my coming again, Consul, but it's blow-
ing up to a hurricane. [*He waits a moment ; there
is no answer.*]   Is the *Indian Girl* to sail in spite
of it ?   [*After a short pause.*

BERNICK.

[*Answers from the office.*]   The *Indian Girl* is to
sail in spite of it.
        [KRAP *shuts the door and goes out again to
           the right.*

ACT FOURTH.

The garden-room in CONSUL BERNICK'S *house. The table has been removed. It is a stormy afternoon, already half dark, and growing darker.*

A man-servant lights the chandelier; two maid-servants bring in flower-pots, lamps, and candles, which are placed on tables and brackets along the wall. RUMMEL, *wearing a dress-coat, white gloves, and a white necktie, stands in the room giving directions.*

RUMMEL.

[*To the servant.*] Only every second candle, Jacob. The place mustn't look too brilliant; it's supposed to be a surprise, you know. And all these flowers—— ? Oh, yes, let them stand; it will look as if they were always there——

CONSUL BERNICK *comes out of his room.*

BERNICK.

[*At the door.*] What is the meaning of all this?

RUMMEL.

Tut, tut, are you there? [*To the servants.*] Yes, you can go now.

[*The servants go out by the second door on the left.*

BERNICK.

[*Coming into the room.*] Why, Rummel, what the meaning of all this?

RUMMEL.

It means that the proudest moment of your life
has arrived. The whole town is coming in procession to do homage to its leading citizen.

BERNICK.

What do you mean?

RUMMEL.

With banners and music, sir! We should have
had torches too; but it was thought dangerous in
this stormy weather. However, there's to be an
illumination; and that will have an excellent
effect in the newspapers.

BERNICK.

Listen, Rummel—I will have nothing to do with
all this.

RUMMEL.

Oh, it's too late now; they'll be here in half
an hour.

BERNICK.

Why did you not tell me of this before?

RUMMEL.

Just because I was afraid you would make
objections. But I arranged it all with your wife;
she allowed me to put things in order a little, and
she is going to look to the refreshments herself.

BERNICK.

[*Listening.*] What's that? Are they coming
already? I thought I heard singing.

RUMMEL.

[*At the garden-door.*] Singing ? Oh, it's only the Americans. They are hauling the *Indian Girl* out to the buoy.

BERNICK.

Hauling her out! Yes——! I really cannot this evening, Rummel ; I am not well.

RUMMEL.

You're certainly not looking well. But you must pull yourself together. Come, come, man, pull yourself together! I and Sandstad and Vigeland attach the greatest importance to this affair. Our opponents must be crushed by an overwhelming utterance of public opinion. The rumours are spreading over the town ; the announcement as to the purchase of the property cannot be kept back any longer. This very evening, amid songs and speeches and the ring of brimming goblets—in short, amid all the effervescent enthusiasm of the occasion—you must announce what you have ventured to do for the good of the community. With the aid of effervescent enthusiasm, as I said just now, it is astonishing what one can effect in this town. But we must have the effervescence, or it won't do.

BERNICK.

Yes, yes, yes——

RUMMEL.

And especially when such a ticklish point is to be dealt with. Thank heaven, you have a name that will carry us through, Bernick. But listen now : we must arrange a little programme. Hilmar Tönnesen has written a song in your honour. It begins charmingly with the line, "Wave th' Ideal's banner high." And Doctor Rörlund has been commissioned to make the speech of the evening. Of course, you must reply to it.

BERNICK.

I cannot, I cannot this evening, Rummel. Couldn't you—— ?

RUMMEL.

Impossible, much as I should like to. The Doctor's speech will, of course, be mainly addressed to you. Perhaps a few words will be devoted to the rest of us. I have spoken to Vigeland and Sandstad about it. We had arranged that your reply should take the form of a toast to the general welfare of the community. Sandstad will say a few words on the harmony between the different classes of the community; Vigeland will express the fervent hope that our new undertaking may not disturb the moral basis upon which we stand; and I will call attention, in a few well-chosen words, to the claims of Woman, whose more modest exertions are not without their use in the community. But you are not listening——

BERNICK.

Yes—yes, I am. Tell me, do you think the sea is running very high outside?

RUMMEL.

Oh, you are anxious on account of the *Palm Tree?* She's well insured, isn't she?

BERNICK.

Yes, insured; but——

RUMMEL.

And in good repair ; that's the main thing.

BERNICK.

H'm.—And even if anything happens to a vessel, it does not follow that lives will be lost. The ship and cargo may go down—people may lose chests and papers——

RUMMEL.

Good gracious, chests and papers don't matter much——

BERNICK.

Not matter ! No, no, I only meant—— Hark—that singing again !

RUMMEL.

It's on board the *Palm Tree.*

VIGELAND *enters from the right.*

VIGELAND.

Yes, they are hauling out the *Palm Tree.* Good-evening, Consul.

BERNICK.

And you, who know the sea so well, don't hesitate to—— ?

VIGELAND.

I don't hesitate to trust in Providence, Consul ! Besides, I have been on board and distributed a few leaflets, which I hope will act with a blessing.

SANDSTAD *and* KRAP *enter from the right.*

SANDSTAD.

[*At the door.*] It's a miracle if they manage to pull through. Ah, here we are—good-evening, good-evening.

BERNICK.

Is anything the matter, Mr. Krap?

KRAP.

I have nothing to say, Consul.

SANDSTAD.

Every man on board the *Indian Girl* is drunk. If those animals ever get over alive, I'm no prophet.

LONA *enters from the right.*

LONA.

[*To* BERNICK.]   Johan told me to say good-bye for him.

BERNICK.

Is he on board already?

LONA.

He will be soon, at any rate.   We parted outside the hotel.

BERNICK.

And he holds to his purpose?

LONA.

Firm as a rock.

RUMMEL.

[*At one of the windows.*]   Deuce take these new-fangled arrangements.   I can't get these curtains drawn.

LONA.

Are they to be drawn?   I thought, on the contrary——

RUMMEL.

They are to be drawn at first, Miss Hessel.   Of course you know what is going on?

Lona.

Oh, of course. Let me help you. [*Takes one of the cords.*] I shall let the curtain fall upon my brother-in-law—though I would rather raise it.

Rummel.

That you can do later. When the garden is filled with a surging multitude, then the curtains are drawn back, and reveal an astonished and delighted family. A citizen's home should be transparent to all the world.

> [Bernick *seems about to say something, but turns quickly and goes into his office.*

Rummel.

Well, let us hold our last council of war. Come, Mr. Krap ; we want you to supply us with a few facts.

> [*All the men go into the Consul's office.* Lona *has drawn all the curtains over the windows, and is just going to draw the curtain over the open glass door, when* Olaf *drops down from above, alighting at the top of the garden stair ; he has a plaid over his shoulder and a bundle in his hand.*

Lona.

Good heavens, child, how you startled me !

Olaf.

[*Hiding the bundle.*] Sh, auntie !

Lona.

Why did you jump out at the window ?—Where are you going ?

OLAF.

Sh, don't tell, auntie. I'm going to Uncle Johan ; only down to the pier, you know ;—just to say good-bye to him. Good-night, auntie !

[*He runs out through the garden.*

LONA.

No ! stop ! Olaf !—Olaf !

JOHAN TÖNNESEN, *in travelling dress, with a bag over his shoulder, steals in by the door on the right.*

JOHAN.

Lona !

LONA.

[*Turning.*] What ! You here again ?

JOHAN.

There are still a few minutes to spare. I must see her once more. We cannot part so.

MARTHA *and* DINA, *both wearing cloaks, and the latter with a small travelling-bag in her hand, enter by the second door on the left.*

DINA.

I must see him ! I must see him !

MARTHA.

Yes, you shall go to him, Dina !

DINA.

There he is !

JOHAN.

Dina !

DINA.

Take me with you !

JOHAN.

What——!

LONA.

You will go?

DINA.

Yes, take me with you. The other has written to me, saying that this evening it is to be announced to every one——

JOHAN.

Dina—you do not love him?

DINA.

I have never loved that man. I would rather be at the bottom of the fjord than be engaged to him! Oh, how he seemed to make me grovel before him yesterday with his patronising phrases! How he made me feel that he was stooping to an abject creature! I will not be looked down upon any more. I will go away. May I come with you?

JOHAN.

Yes, yes—a thousand times yes!

DINA.

I shall not be a burden on you long. Only help me to get over there; help me to make a start——

JOHAN.

Hurrah! We shall manage all that, Dina!

LONA.

[*Pointing to the Consul's door.*] Hush! not so loud!

JOHAN.

Dina, I will take such care of you

DINA.

No, no, I won't have that. I will make my
own way; I shall manage well enough over there.
Only let me get away from here. Oh, those
women—you don't know—they have actually
written to me to-day, exhorting me to appreciate
my good fortune, impressing upon me what
magnanimity he has shown. To-morrow, and
every day of my life, they would be watching me
to see whether I showed myself worthy of it all.
I have a horror of all this propriety !

JOHAN.

Tell me, Dina, is that your only reason for
coming ? Am I nothing to you ?

DINA.

Yes, Johan, you are more to me than any one
else in the world.

JOHAN.

Oh, Dina—— !

DINA.

They all tell me that I must hate and detest
you ; that it is my duty. But I don't understand
all this about duty ; I never could understand it.

LONA.

And you never shall, my child !

MARTHA.

No, you shall not ; and that is why you must
go with him, as his wife.

JOHAN.

Yes, yes '

LONA.

What? I must kiss you for that, Martha! I didn't expect this of you.

MARTHA.

No, I daresay not; I didn't expect it myself. But sooner or later the crisis was bound to come. Oh, how we suffer here, under this tyranny of custom and convention! Rebel against it, Dina! Marry him. Show that it is possible to set this use-and-wont at defiance!

JOHAN.

What is your answer, Dina?

DINA.

Yes, I will be your wife.

JOHAN.

Dina!

DINA.

But first I will work, and become something for myself, just as you are. I will give myself; I will not be simply taken.

LONA.

Right, right! So it should be.

JOHAN.

Good; I shall wait and hope——

LONA.

——and win too, boy. But now, on board.

JOHAN.

Yes, on board! Ah, Lona, my dear, a word with you; come here——

[*He leads her up towards the back and talks rapidly to her.*

MARTHA.

Dina—happy girl! Let me look at you and
kiss you once more—for the last time.

DINA.

Not the last time ; no, my dear, dear aunt—
we shall meet again.

MARTHA.

Never! Promise me, Dina, never to come back
again. [*Seizes both her hands and looks into her face.*]
Now go to your happiness, my dear child—over
the sea. Oh, how often have I sat in the schoolroom and longed to be over there ! It must be
beautiful there ; the heaven is wider ; the clouds
sail higher than here ; a larger, freer air sweeps
over the heads of the people——

DINA.

Oh, Aunt Martha, you will follow us some day.

MARTHA.

I ? Never, never. My little life-work lies here ;
and now I think I can give myself to it wholly
and unreservedly.

DINA.

I cannot imagine being parted from you.

MARTHA.

Ah, one can part from so much, Dina. [*Kisses
her.*] But you will not have to learn that lesson,
my dear child. Promise me to make him happy.

DINA.

I will not promise anything. I hate this
promising. Things must come as they can.

MARTHA.

Yes, yes, you are right. You have only to remain as you are—true and faithful to yourself.

DINA.

That I will, Aunt Martha.

LONA.

[*Puts in her pocket some papers which Johan has given her.*] Good, good, my dear boy. But now, away.

JOHAN.

Yes, now there's no time to be lost. Good-bye, Lona; thanks, thanks for all you have been to me. Good-bye, Martha, and thanks to you too for your faithful friendship.

MARTHA.

Good-bye, Johan ! Good-bye, Dina ! And happiness be over all your days !

> [*She and* LONA *hurry them towards the door in the background.* JOHAN TÖNNESEN *and* DINA *go quickly out through the garden.* LONA *shuts the door and draws the curtain.*

LONA.

Now we are alone, Martha. You have lost her, and I him.

MARTHA.

You—him ?

LONA.

Oh, I had half lost him already over there. The boy longed to stand on his own feet; so I made him imagine that *I* was suffering from homesickness.

MARTHA.

That was it ? Now I understand why you came.
But he will want you back again, Lona.

LONA.

An old step-sister—what can he want with her
now ? Men break many a tie when happiness
beckons to them.

MARTHA.

That is true, sometimes.

LONA.

Now we two must hold together, Martha.

MARTHA.

Can I be anything to you ?

LONA.

Who more ? We two foster-mothers—have we
not both lost our children ? Now we are alone.

MARTHA.

Yes, alone. So now I will tell you this—I
have loved him more than all the world.

LONA.

Martha ? [*Seizes her arm.*]   Is this the truth ?

MARTHA.

My whole life lies in the words. I have loved
him, and waited for him. From summer to
summer I have looked for his coming. And then
he came—but he did not see me.

LONA.

Loved him ! And it was you that gave his
happiness into his hands.

MARTHA.

What else should I do, since I love him ? Yes
I have loved him. I have lived my whole life for
him, ever since he went away. What reason had
I to hope, you ask ? Oh, I think I had some
reason. But then, when he came again—it seemed
as if everything were wiped out of his memory.
He did not see me.

LONA.

It was Dina that overshadowed you, Martha.

MARTHA.

It is well that she did. When he went away
we were of the same age; when I saw him again
—oh, that horrible moment—I realised that I was
ten years older than he. He had lived out there
in the bright, quivering sunshine, and drunk in
youth and health at every breath ; and here sat I
the while, spinning and spinning——

LONA.

——the thread of his happiness, Martha.

MARTHA.

Yes, it was gold I spun. No bitterness ! We
have been two good sisters to him, Lona, have we
not ?

LONA.

[*Embraces her.*] Martha !

CONSUL BERNICK *comes out of his room.*

BERNICK.

[*To the men inside.*] Yes, yes, settle it as you
please. When the time comes, I shall be ready——
[*Shuts the door.*] Ah, are you there ? By-the-bye,
Martha, you had better look to your dress a little.

And tell Betty to do the same. I don't want anything out of the way, of course; just homely neatness. But you must be quick.

LONA.

And you must look bright and happy, Martha; remember this is a joyful surprise to you.

BERNICK.

Olaf must come down too. I will have him at my side.

LONA.

H'm, Olaf——

MARTHA.

I will tell Betty.
[*She goes out by the second door on the left.*

LONA.

Well, so the great and solemn hour has come.

BERNICK.

[*Walks restlessly up and down.*] Yes, it has come.

LONA.

At such a time, no doubt, a man must feel proud and happy.

BERNICK.

[*Looks at her.*] H'm——

LONA.

The whole town is to be illuminated, I hear.

BERNICK.

Yes, I believe there is some such idea.

LONA.

All the clubs will turn out with their banners. Your name will shine in letters of fire. To-night it will be telegraphed to every corner of the country—" Surrounded by his happy family, Consul Bernick received the homage of his fellow citizens as one of the pillars of society."

BERNICK.

So it will; and the crowd in the street will shout and hurrah, and insist on my coming forward into the doorway there, and I shall have to bow and thank them.

LONA.

Have to——?

BERNICK.

Do you think I feel happy at this moment?

LONA.

No, *I* do not think that you can feel altogether happy.

BERNICK.

Lona, you despise me.

LONA.

Not yet.

BERNICK.

And you have no right to. Not to despise me !—Lona, you cannot conceive how unspeakably alone I stand, here in this narrow, stunted society —how, year by year, I have had to put a tighter curb on my ambition for a full and satisfying life-work.   What have I accomplished, for all the show it makes ?   Scrap-work — odds and ends. There is no room here for other and larger work. If I tried to go a step in advance of the views and ideas of the day, all my power was gone.   Do you know what we are, we, who are reckoned the pillars

of society ?   We are the tools of society, neither
more nor less.

LONA.

Why do you only see this now ?

BERNICK.

Because I have been thinking much of late—
since you came home—and most of all this evening.—Oh, Lona, why did I not know you through
and through, then—in the old days ?

LONA.

What then ?

BERNICK.

I should never have given you up ; and, with
you by my side, I should not have stood where I
stand now.

LONA.

And do you never think what s h e might have
been to you—she, whom you chose in my stead ?

BERNICK.

I know, at any rate, that she has not been
anything that I required.

LONA.

Because you have never shared your life-work
with her.   Because you have never placed her in a
free and true relation to you.   Because you have
allowed her to go on pining under the weight of
shame you had cast upon those nearest her.

BERNICK.

Yes, yes, yes ; falsehood and hollowness are at
the bottom of it all.

LONA.

Then why not break with all this falsehood and hollowness?

BERNICK.

Now? It is too late now, Lona.

LONA.

Karsten, tell me—what satisfaction does this show and imposture give you?

BERNICK.

It gives me none. I must go under, along with the whole of this bungled social system. But a new generation will grow up after us ; it is my son that I am working for ; it is his life-work that I am laying out for him. There will come a time when truth will find its way into our social order, and upon it he shall found a happier life than his father's.

LONA.

With a lie for its groundwork? Think what it is you are giving your son for an inheritance.

BERNICK.

[*With suppressed despair.*] I am giving him an inheritance a thousand times worse than you know of. But, sooner or later, the curse must pass away. And yet—and yet—— [*Vehemently.*] How could you bring all this upon my head! But it is done now. I must go on now. You shall not succeed in crushing me !

HILMAR TÖNNESEN, *with an open note in his hand, and much discomposed, enters quickly from the right.*

HILMAR.

Why, this is—— Betty, Betty !

BERNICK.

What now?   Are they coming already?

HILMAR.

No, no; but I must speak to some one at once——

[*He goes out by the second door on the left.*

LONA.

Karsten, you say we came to crush you.   Then let me tell you what stuff he is made of, this prodigal whom your moral society shrinks from as if he were plague-stricken.   He can do without you all, for he has gone away.

BERNICK.

But he is coming back——

LONA.

Johan will never come back.   He has gone for ever, and Dina has gone with him.

BERNICK.

Gone for ever?   And Dina with him?

LONA.

Yes, to be his wife.   That is how these two strike your seraphic society in the face, as I once—— No matter!

BERNICK.

Gone!—she too !   In the *Indian Girl?*

LONA.

No; he dared not entrust such a precious freight to a ship with so ruffianly a crew.   Johan and Dina have sailed in the *Palm Tree.*

BERNICK.

Ah ! Then it was—to no purpose—— [*Rushes to the door of his office, tears it open, and calls in.*] Krap, stop the *Indian Girl !* She mustn't sail to-night !

KRAP.

[*Inside.*] The *Indian Girl* is already standing out to sea, Consul.

BERNICK.

[*Shuts the door and says feebly.*] Too late—and all for nothing.

LONA.

What do you mean ?

BERNICK

Nothing, nothing. Leave me alone—— !

LONA.

H'm. Listen, Karsten. Johan told me to tell you that he leaves in my keeping the good name he once lent you, and also that which you stole from him while he was far away. Johan will be silent ; and I can do or let alone in this matter as I will. See, I hold in my hand your two letters.

BERNICK.

You have them ! And now—now you will— this very night perhaps—when the procession——

LONA.

I did not come here to unmask you, but to try if I could not move you to throw off the mask of your own accord. I have failed. Remain standing in the lie. See ; I tear your two letters to shreds. Take the pieces ; here they are. Now, there is nothing to bear witness against you, Karsten. Now you are safe ; be happy too—if you can.

BERNICK.

[*Profoundly moved.*] Lona, why did you not do this before ! It is too late now ; my whole life is ruined now ; I cannot live after to-day.

LONA.

What has happened ?

BERNICK.

Don't ask me. And yet I must live ! I will live—for Olaf's sake. He shall restore all and atone for all——

LONA.

Karsten—— !

HILMAR TÖNNESEN *again enters hurriedly.*

HILMAR.

No one to be found ; all away ; not even Betty !

BERNICK.

What is the matter with you ?

HILMAR.

I daren't tell you.

BERNICK.

What is it ? You must and shall tell me.

HILMAR.

Well then—— Olaf has run away in the *Indian Girl.*

BERNICK.

[*Staggering backwards.*] Olaf—in the *Indian Girl* ! No, no

LONA.

Yes, it is true! Now I understand—— I saw him jump out of the window.

BERNICK.

[*At the door of his room, calls out in despair.*] Krap, stop the *Indian Girl* at any cost '

KRAP.

[*Comes into the room.*] Impossible, Consul. How should we be able to——

BERNICK.

We must stop her! Olaf is on board '

KRAP.

What!

RUMMEL.

[*Enters from the office.*] Olaf run away? Impossible !

SANDSTAD.

[*Enters from the office.*] They'll send him back with the pilot, Consul.

HILMAR.

No, no; he has written to me. [*Showing the letter.*] He says he's going to hide among the cargo until they are fairly out to sea.

BERNICK.

I shall never see him again !

RUMMEL.

Oh, nonsense; a good stout ship, newly repaired——

VIGELAND.

[*Who has also come in.*] ——and in your own yard, too, Consul.

BERNICK.

I shall never see him again, I tell you. I have lost him, Lona; and—I see it now—he has never been really mine. [*Listens.*] What is that?

RUMMEL.

Music. The procession is coming.

BERNICK.

I cannot, I will not see any one!

RUMMEL.

What are you thinking of? It's impossible——

SANDSTAD.

Impossible, Consul; think how much you have at stake.

BERNICK.

What does it all matter to me now? Whom have I now to work for?

RUMMEL.

Can you ask? You have us and society.

VIGELAND.

Yes, very true.

SANDSTAD.

And surely, Consul, you don't forget that we——

MARTHA *enters by the second door on the left.*
Music is heard, from far down the street.

MARTHA.

Here comes the procession; but Betty is not at home; I can't think where she——

BERNICK.

Not at home! There, you see, Lona; no
support either in joy or sorrow.

RUMMEL.

Back with the curtains! Come and help me,
Mr. Krap! You too, Sandstad! What a terrible
pity that the family should be scattered just at
this moment! Quite against the programme.

[*The curtains over the door and windows
are drawn back. The whole street is
seen to be illuminated. On the house
opposite is a large transparency with the
inscription,* " Long live Karsten Bernick, the Pillar of our Society!*"*

BERNICK.

[*Shrinking back.*] Away with all this! I will
not look at it! Out with it, out with it!

RUMMEL.

Are you in your senses, may I ask?

MARTHA.

What is the matter with him, Lona?

LONA.

Hush!   [*Whispers to her.*

BERNICK.

Away with the mocking words, I say! Can you
not see, all these lights are gibing at us?

RUMMEL.

Well, I must say——

BERNICK.

Oh, you know nothing——! But I, I—— '
They are the lights in a dead-room!

KRAP.

H'm—— !

RUMMEL.

Come now, really—you make far too much of it.

SANDSTAD.

The boy will have a trip over the Atlantic, and
then you'll have him back again.

VIGELAND.

Only put your trust in the Almighty, Consul.

RUMMEL.

And in the ship, Bernick; she's seaworthy
enough, I'm sure.

KRAP.

H'm——

RUMMEL.

Now, if it were one of those floating coffins we
hear of in the great nations——

BERNICK.

I can feel my very hair growing grey.

MRS. BERNICK, *with a large shawl over her head,
comes through the garden door.*

MRS. BERNICK.

Karsten, Karsten, do you know—— ?

BERNICK.

Yes, I know——; but you—you who can see
nothing—you who have not a mother's care for
him—— !

MRS. BERNICK.

Oh, listen to me—— !

BERNICK.

Why did you not watch over him? Now I
have lost him.   Give him back to me, if you can!

MRS. BERNICK.

I can, I can ; I have him !

BERNICK.

You have him !

THE MEN.

Ah !

HILMAR.

Ah, I thought so.

MARTHA.

Now you have him again, Karsten .

LONA.

Yes ; now win him as well.

BERNICK.

You have him !   Can this be true?   Where is
he ?

MRS. BERNICK.

I shall not tell you until you have forgiven him.

BERNICK.

Oh, forgiven, forgiven—— !   But how did you
come to know—— ?

MRS. BERNICK.

Do you think a mother has no eyes?   I was in
mortal terror lest you should hear of it.   A few
words he let fall yesterday—— ; and his room

being empty, and his knapsack and clothes gone——

BERNICK.

Yes, yes——?

MRS. BERNICK.

I ran ; I got hold of Aune ; we went out in his sailing-boat ; the American ship was on the point of sailing. Thank Heaven, we arrived in time—we got on board—we searched in the hold—and we found him. Oh, Karsten, you mustn't punish him !

BERNICK.

Betty !

MRS. BERNICK.

Nor Aune either !

BERNICK.

Aune? What of him? Is the *Indian Girl* under sail again ?

MRS. BERNICK.

No, that is just the thing——

BERNICK.

Speak, speak !

MRS. BERNICK.

Aune was as terrified as I was ; the search took some time ; darkness came on, and the pilot made objections : so Aune ventured—in your name——

BERNICK.

Well ?

MRS. BERNICK.

To stop the ship till to-morrow.

KRAP.

H'm——

BERNICK.

Oh, what unspeakable happiness !

MRS. BERNICK.

You are not angry ?

BERNICK.

Oh, what surpassing happiness, Betty !

RUMMEL.

Why, you're absurdly nervous.

HILMAR.

Yes ; the moment it comes to a little struggle
with the elements—ugh !

KRAP.

[*At the window.*]   The procession is coming
through the garden gate, Consul.

BERNICK.

Yes, now let them come !

RUMMEL.

The whole garden is full of people.

SANDSTAD.

The very street is packed.

RUMMEL.

The whole town has turned out, Bernick.   This
is really an inspiring moment.

VIGELAND.

Let us take it in a humble spirit, Mr. Rummel.

RUMMEL.

All the banners are out.   What a procession !
Ah, here's the Committee, with Doctor Rörlund
at its head.

BERNICK.

Let them come, I say !

RUMMEL.

But look here: in your agitated state of
mind——

BERNICK.

What then ?

RUMMEL.

Why, I should have no objection to speaking
for you.

BERNICK.

No, thank you ; to-night I shall speak myself.

RUMMEL.

But do you know what you have got to say ?

BERNICK.

Yes, don't be alarmed, Rummel—now I know
what I have to say.

> [*The music has meanwhile ceased.   The*
> *garden door is thrown open.*   DOCTOR
> RÖRLUND *enters at the head of the Com-*
> *mittee, accompanied by two porters carry-*
> *ing a covered basket.   After them come*
> *townspeople of all classes, as many as the*
> *room will hold.   An immense crowd,*
> *with banners and flags, can be seen in the*
> *garden and in the street.*

RÖRLUND.

Consul Bernick! I see from the surprise
depicted in your countenance, that it is as un-
expected guests that we intrude upon you in your
happy family circle, at your peaceful hearth,
surrounded by upright and public-spirited friends
and fellow citizens. Our excuse is that we obey
a heartfelt impulse in bringing you our homage.
It is not, indeed, the first time we have done so,
but the first time on so comprehensive a scale.
We have often expressed to you our gratitude for
the broad moral basis upon which you have, so to
speak, built up our society. This time we chiefly
hail in you the clear-sighted, indefatigable, un-
selfish, nay, self-sacrificing citizen, who has taken
the initiative in an undertaking which, we are
credibly assured, will give a powerful impetus to
the temporal prosperity and wellbeing of this
community.

VOICES.

Among the crowd.] Bravo, bravo!

RÖRLUND.

Consul Bernick, you have for many years stood
before our town as a shining example. I do not
here speak of your exemplary domestic life, your
spotless moral record. To such virtues we pay
tribute in the secret chamber of the heart ; we do
not proclaim them from the house-tops. I speak
rather of your activity as a citizen, as it lies open
to all men's view. Well-appointed ships sail from
your wharves, and fly our flag on the furthest seas.
A large and prosperous body of workmen looks up
to you as to a father. By calling into existence new
branches of industry, you have brought comfort

into hundreds of homes. In other words—you
are in an eminent sense the pillar and corner-
stone of this community.

VOICES.

Hear, hear ! Bravo !

RÖRLUND.

And it is the halo of disinterestedness resting
upon all your actions that is so unspeakably beneficent, especially in these times. You are now on
the point of procuring for us—I do not hesitate to
say the word plainly and prosaically—a railway.

MANY VOICES.

Bravo, bravo !

RÖRLUND.

But this undertaking seems destined to meet
with difficulties, principally arising from narrow
and selfish interests.

VOICES.

Hear, hear ! Hear, hear !

RÖRLUND.

It is no longer unknown that certain indi-
viduals, not belonging to our community, have
stolen a march upon the energetic citizens of this
place, and have secured certain advantages, which
should by rights have fallen to the share of our
own town.

VOICES.

Yes, yes ! Hear, hear !

RÖRLUND.

You are of course not unaware of this deplorable circumstance, Consul Bernick. But, never-

theless, you steadily pursue your undertaking, well knowing that a patriotic citizen must not be exclusively concerned with the interests of his own parish.

DIFFERENT VOICES.

H'm! No, no! Yes, yes!

RÖRLUND.

We have assembled, then, this evening to do homage, in your person, to the ideal citizen—the model of all the civic virtues. May your enterprise contribute to the true and lasting welfare of this community! The railway is, no doubt, an institution by means of which elements of evil may be imported from without, but it is also an institution that enables us to get quickly rid of them. From elements of evil from without we cannot even now keep ourselves quite free. But if, as I hear, we have, just on this auspicious evening, been unexpectedly relieved of certain elements of this nature——

VOICES.

Sh, sh!

RÖRLUND.

——I accept the fact as a good omen for the undertaking. If I touch upon this point here, it is because we know ourselves to be in a house where family ties are subordinated to the ethical ideal.

VOICES.

Hear, hear! Bravo!

BERNICK.

[At the same time.] Permit me——

Rörlund.

Only a few words more, Consul Bernick. Your
labours on behalf of this community have certainly
not been undertaken in the hope of any tangible
reward.   But you cannot reject a slight token of
your grateful fellow citizens' appreciation, least of
all on this momentous occasion, when, as practical
men assure us, we are standing on the threshold
of a new era.

Many Voices.

Bravo !   Hear, hear !   Hear, hear !
> [*He gives the porters a sign; they bring
> forward the basket; members of the
> Committee take out and present, during
> the following speech, the articles men-
> tioned.*

Rörlund.

Therefore, I have now, Consul Bernick, to hand
you a silver coffee service.   Let it grace your
board when we in future, as so often in the past,
have the pleasure of meeting under this hospitable
roof.

And you, too, gentlemen, who have so zealously
co-operated with the first man of our community,
we would beg to accept some trifling mementos.
This silver goblet we tender to you, Mr. Rummel.
You have many a time, amid the ring of wine-
cups, done battle in eloquent words for the civic
interests of our community; may you often find
worthy opportunities to lift and drain this goblet.
—To you, Mr. Sandstad, I hand this album, with
photographs of your fellow citizens.   Your well-
known and much-appreciated philanthropy has
placed you in the happy position of counting
among your friends members of all sections of the

community.—And to you, Mr. Vigeland, I have to
offer, for the decoration of your domestic sanctum,
this book of family devotion, on vellum, and
luxuriously bound.   Under the ripening influence
of years, you have come to view life from a serious
standpoint ; your activity in the daily affairs of
this world has long been purified and ennobled by
thoughts of things higher and holier.   [*Turns
towards the Crowd.*]   And now, my friends, long
live Consul Bernick and his fellow workers!
Hurrah for the Pillars of Society !

THE WHOLE CROWD.

Long live Consul Bernick !   Long live the
Pillars of Society !   Hurrah ! hurrah ! hurrah !

LONA.

I congratulate you, brother-in-law !
[*An expectant silence intervenes.*

BERNICK.

[*Begins earnestly and slowly.*]   My fellow citizens,
—your spokesman has said that we stand this
evening on the threshold of a new era ; and there,
I hope, he was right.   But in order that it may
be so, we must bring home to ourselves the truth
—the truth which has, until this evening, been
utterly and in all things banished from our community.   [*Astonishment among the audience.*

BERNICK.

I must begin by repudiating the panegyric with
which you, Dr. Rörlund, according to use and
wont on such occasions, have overwhelmed me.
I do not deserve it ; for until to-day I have not
been disinterested in my dealings.   If I have not
always striven for pecuniary profit, at least I am

now conscious that a desire, a craving, for power, influence, and respect has been the motive of most of my actions.

RUMMEL.

[*Half aloud.*]   What next?

BERNICK.

Before my fellow citizens I do not reproach myself for this; for I still believe that I may claim a place among the foremost of our men of practical usefulness.

MANY VOICES.

Yes, yes, yes!

BERNICK.

What I do blame myself for is my weakness in constantly adopting indirect courses, because I knew and feared the tendency of our society to suspect impure motives behind everything a man undertakes.   And now I come to a case in point.

RUMMEL.

[*Anxiously.*]   H'm—h'm!

BERNICK.

There are rumours abroad of great purchases of property along the projected line.   This property I have bought—all of it—I alone.

SUPPRESSED VOICES.

What does he say?   The Consul?   Consul Bernick?

BERNICK.

It is for the present in my hands.   Of course, I have confided in my fellow workers, Messrs. Rummel, Vigeland, and Sandstad, and we have agreed to——

RUMMEL.

It's not true ! Prove !—prove——— !

VIGELAND.

We have not agreed to anything !

SANDSTAD.

Well, I must say———

BERNICK.

Quite right ; we have not yet agreed on what I
was about to mention. But I am confident that
these three gentlemen will acquiesce when I say
that I have this evening determined to form a
joint-stock company for the exploitation of these
properties ; whoever will can have shares in it.

MANY VOICES.

Hurrah ! Long live Consul Bernick !

RUMMEL.

[*Aside to* BERNICK.] Such base treachery——— !

SANDSTAD.

[*Likewise.*] Then you've been fooling us——— !

VIGELAND.

Why then, devil take——— ! Oh, Lord, what am
I saying !

THE CROWD.

[*Outside.*] Hurrah, hurrah, hurrah !

BERNICK.

Silence, gentlemen. I have no right to this
homage ; for what I have now determined was not
my original intention. My intention was to retain
the whole myself; and I am still of opinion that
the property can be most profitably worked if it

remains in the control of one man.   But it is for
the shareholders to choose.   If they wish it, I am
willing to manage it for them to the best of my
ability.

VOICES.

Yes, yes, yes !

BERNICK.

But, first, my fellow citizens must know me to
the core.   Then let every one look into his own
heart, and let us realise the prediction that from
this evening we begin a new era.   The old, with
its tinsel, its hypocrisy and hollowness, its sham
propriety, and its despicable cowardice, shall lie
behind us like a museum, open for instruction ;
and to this museum we will present—will we not,
gentlemen ?—the coffee service, and the goblet,
and the album, and the family devotions on vellum
and luxuriously bound.

RUMMEL.

Yes, of course.

VIGELAND.

[*Mutters.*] When you've taken all the rest,
why——

SANDSTAD.

As you please.

BERNICK.

And now to come to the chief point in my settlement with society.   It has been said that elements
of evil have left us this evening.   I can add what
you do not know : the man thus alluded to did not
go alone ; with him went, to become his wife——

LONA.

[*Loudly.*]   Dina Dorf '

RÖRLUND.

What ?

MRS. BERNICK.

What do you say ?   [*Great sensation.*

RÖRLUND.

Fled ? Run away—with him ! Impossible !

BERNICK.

To become his wife, Doctor Rörlund. And I have more to add. [*Aside.*] Betty, collect yourself to bear what is coming. [*Aloud.*] I say : Honour to that man, for he has nobly taken upon himself another's sin. My fellow citizens, I will get clear of the lie; it has gone near to poisoning every fibre in my being. You shall know all. Fifteen years ago, it was *I* who sinned.

MRS. BERNICK.

[*In a low and trembling voice.*] Karsten .

MARTHA.

[*Likewise.*] Ah, Johan—— !

LONA.

At last you have found your true self !
[*Speechless astonishment among the listeners.*

BERNICK.

Yes, my fellow citizens, I was guilty, and he fled. The false and vile rumours which were afterwards current, it is now in no human power to disprove. But of this I cannot complain. Fifteen years ago I swung myself aloft by aid of these rumours; whether I am now to fall with them is for you to decide.

RÖRLUND.

What a thunderbolt! The first man in the town——! [*Softly to* MRS. BERNICK.] Oh, how I pity you, Mrs. Bernick!

HILMAR.

Such a confession! Well, I must say——

BERNICK.

But do not decide this eveming. I ask every one of you to go home—to collect himself—to look into himself. When your minds are calm again, it will be seen whether I have lost or gained by speaking out. Good-night! I have still much, very much, to repent of, but that concerns only my own conscience. Good-night! Away with all this show! We all feel that it is out of place here.

RÖRLUND.

Assuredly it is. [*Softly to* MRS. BERNICK.] Run away! So, after all, she was quite unworthy of me. [*Half aloud, to the Committee.*] Yes, gentlemen, after this, I think we had better withdraw as quickly as possible.

HILMAR.

How, after this, one is to hold high the banner of the ideal, I for one—— Ugh!

> [*The announcement has meanwhile been whispered from mouth to mouth. All the members of the procession retire through the garden.* RUMMEL, SANDSTAD, *and* VIGELAND *go off disputing earnestly but softly.* HILMAR TÖNNESEN *slips out to the right.* CONSUL BERNICK, MRS.

BERNICK, MARTHA, LONA, *and* KRAP
*alone remain in the room. There is a
short silence.*

BERNICK.

Betty, can you forgive me?

MRS. BERNICK.

[*Looks smilingly at him.*] Do you know, Karsten,
you have made me feel happier and more hopeful
than I have felt for many years?

BERNICK.

How so?

MRS. BERNICK.

For many years I have thought that you had
once been mine, and I had lost you. Now I know
that you never were mine; but I shall win you.

BERNICK.

[*Embracing her.*] Oh, Betty, you have won me!
Through Lona I have at last learnt really to know
you. But now let Olaf come.

MRS. BERNICK.

Yes, now you shall have him. Mr. Krap——!
[*She whispers to him in the background. He
goes out by the garden door. During the
following all the transparencies and lights
in the houses are gradually extinguished.*

BERNICK.

[*Softly.*] Thanks, Lona; you have saved what
is best in me—and for me.

LONA.

What else did I intend?

BERNICK.

Yes, what—what did you intend? I cannot fathom you.

LONA.

H'm——

BERNICK.

It was not hatred then? Not revenge? Why did you come over?

LONA.

Old friendship does not rust.

BERNICK.

Lona!

LONA.

When Johan told me all that about the lie, I swore to myself: The hero of my youth shall stand free and true.

BERNICK.

Oh, how little has a pitiful creature like me deserved this of you!

LONA.

Yes, if we women always asked for deserts, Karsten—— !

AUNE *and* OLAF *enter from the garden.*

BERNICK.

[*Rushing to him.*]   Olaf!

OLAF.

Father, I promise never to do it again.

BERNICK.

To run away?

OLAF.

Yes, yes, I promise, father.

BERNICK.

And I promise that you shall never have reason to.   In future you shall be allowed to grow up, not as the heir to my life-work, but as one who has a life-work of his own to look forward to.

OLAF.

And will you let me be whatever I want to?

BERNICK.

Whatever you like.

OLAF.

Thank you, father.   Then I won't be a pillar of society.

BERNICK.

Ah !   Why not?

OLAF.

Oh, I think it must be so tiresome.

BERNICK.

You shall be yourself, Olaf; and we won't trouble about anything else.   And you, Aune——

AUNE.

I know it, Consul : I am dismissed.

BERNICK.

We will not part company, Aune ; and forgive me——

AUNE.

What?   The ship can't get away to-night.

BERNICK.

Nor yet to-morrow.   I gave you too little time. She must be overhauled more thoroughly.

AUNE.

She shall be, Consul—and with the new machines !

BERNICK.

So be it—but thoroughly and honestly, mind. There are a good many things here that need thorough and honest overhauling. So good-night, Aune.

AUNE.

Good-night, Consul — and thank you heartily.

[*He goes out to the right.*

MRS. BERNICK.

Now they are all gone.

BERNICK.

And we are alone. My name no longer shines in the transparencies ; all the lights are out in the windows.

LONA.

Would you have them lighted again ?

BERNICK.

Not for all the world. Where have I been ? You will be horrified when you know. I am feeling now as if I had just come to my senses again after being poisoned. But I feel—I feel that I can be young and strong again. Oh, come nearer—closer around me. Come, Betty ! Come, Olaf ! Come, Martha ! Oh, Martha, it seems as though I had never seen you during all these years.

LONA.

No, I daresay not ; your society is a society of bachelor-souls ; you have no eyes for womanhood.

BERNICK.

True, true. And for that very reason—it is settled, Lona, is it not?—you won't leave Betty and me?

MRS. BERNICK.

No, Lona; you must not!

LONA.

No; how could I think of going away and leaving you young people, just beginning life? Am I not your foster-mother? You and I, Martha, we are the two old aunts—— What are you looking at?

MARTHA.

How the sky is clearing; how it grows light over the sea. The *Palm Tree* has fortune with it——

LONA.

And happiness on board.

BERNICK.

And we—we have a long, earnest day of work before us; I most of all. But let it come! Gather close around me, you true and faithful women. I have learnt this, in these days: it is you women who are the pillars of society.

LONA.

Then you have learnt a poor wisdom, brother-in-law. [*Lays her hand firmly upon his shoulder.*] No, no; the spirits of Truth and Freedom—these are the Pillars of Society.

THE END.

0 1341 1463928 6

DATE DUE	RETURNED

CPSIA information can be obtained at www.ICGtesting.com
Printed in the USA
LVOW131536210613

339728LV00001B/133/A

9 781434 493545